Pamper Yourself

or

Someone you Love

- Lola B.

PETTY CRIMES &HEAD CASES

A Citrus Salon Mystery

Lola Beatlebrox

ISBN (Print): 978-1-73341-340-4
ISBN (eBook): 978-1-73341-341-1

Acknowledgements

The author wishes to thank Tracy Lemon, owner of On the Fringe Salon in Heber, Utah, for fixing my head and my hair lo these many years. I watched Tracy's salon grow from a one-woman business to the thriving stylist spa she runs today. She has reviewed this manuscript and any errors in hairstyling technique are solely mine. All opinions of the characters in this book do not reflect the opinions of the real Tracy. Thank you, Tracy, for the fictitious use of your name. May you prosper forever.

Thank you also to my friend Patti Larrabee for arranging the review of an early manuscript by her book club including Sharon Bauman, Holly Carrier, Jan Coen, Kathy Heffron, Margo Shirley, and Samantha Walters. And, yes, the wine was lovely.

Brooke McIntyre, founder and concierge extraordinaire of inkedvoices. com deserves a huge shout-out. Her unique virtual writing workshop groups provide invaluable feedback. These wonderful writers have waded through my manuscript over the past four years: "Fast Track," Scott Alumbaugh, Aiko Elizabeth, Sheryl Tara Saunders McLean-Houle. "Historical Fiction Writers," Sondra Bateman, Blue, Gloria Bond, Maureen, Bess Trout, Amanda Witow. "Novel Review," Kelly Horn, Mike Marks, Stu Newman, Elizabeth Rourke, and Rose Wachowski.

I am grateful to my professional editor Linda Cashdan of the Word Process for her thoughtful suggestions for strengthening the story and plot line.

Thank you to the Park City Police Department for offering Citizen's Police Academy. Officer Terry Knechtel brought me up to speed in the many concerns of law enforcement.

My deepest appreciation goes to Sheriff Justin Martinez of the Summit County Sheriff's Department and Deputies Wilkinson, Daley and Bates for their review of the manuscript for technical accuracy. Any errors or omissions are mine and mine alone.

Finally, thank you to the fine police officers and deputies everywhere who keep us safe and respond to crises everyday with courage, courtesy, and community policing.

Contents

Case 1

When Spiderman Goes to Maverik®

● ● ● ● ● ● ● ● ●

I always knew I'd do anything to help my husband through life, but I never thought I'd solve crimes for him. My name is Tracy Lemon and I'm married to a policeman. The morning after Carl applied for a promotion to detective, we woke at dawn and snuggled as usual.

I love the moments when it's just the two of us. The house is quiet—our son, Jamie, isn't up yet. We talk and cuddle and talk some more.

"I think I know how to get you the detective job," I said.

"How?"

"People tell me things. If you solve more crimes than the competition, of course the chief will give you the job."

Carl burst out laughing. "Hairdressers don't solve crimes, Tracy."

"Why not?" I said.

"It's about good police work—following leads and using resources."

I pulled away from him. "And I'm not a good resource?"

"Of course you are, but—"

"Oh, I see. You think I listen to gossip all day."

"I didn't say that—"

"Listen, smarty pants. I'll bet I can solve the next crime in town before you do."

"Not likely."

"You'll see."

"All right, you're on."

I jumped on top of him and his eyes lit up.

"I think you're on, too," I said.

"Better turn the lock."

Twenty minutes later, there was a pounding on our bedroom door. "Mommy! Why won't this door open?"

Why indeed?

Carl slipped out from under me and grabbed a robe. "Hey, sport," he said, disappearing down the hall.

"Look!" our eight-year-old announced. "Spiderman has a cape. Now he can fly!"

The world's most famous arachnoid zoomed onto my bedspread. His new red cape was made from my Holiday Napkin Set for Six.

"Jamie!" My voice was sharp. "Why didn't you ask Mommy if you could use her napkins?"

"I tried to." His lower lip quivered. "But the door was locked."

Of course. I took a deep breath. "Okay, sweetheart. Get ready for school."

Jamie ran out just as Carl returned, dressed in his uniform. The phone dinged and Carl picked up his cell. "The chief wants a hair appointment right away," Carl said, looking up from the screen. "He's going on TV."

"What for?"

"He doesn't say."

"Mrs. Oscar is my eight-thirty," I said. "He can come at nine."

Texts dinged for a few more seconds.

"The chief wants Mrs. Oscar's spot," Carl said, "but nine'll do."

Two hours later I drove to work. The Citrus Salon is well-known in my town. Everybody comes to see me. People in our little western city have hair problems, money problems, and family problems. They drive pickup trucks and SUVs. There are as many cows as birds, and our Main Street is always clogged with tankers coming from the oil fields to the east.

I turned onto the road leading to the wealthier side of town, parked under my "Walk-Ins Welcome" sign, and unlocked the front door. Breezing past the front desk where the screen saver pulsed, I headed for the workroom to consult my client notebook.

This is my Bible, so to speak, my Life, my Guide. It contains every notation on all the customers I've ever had—their personal data, their cuts, their color formulas, their hopes, their fears. I also keep data on birthdays, marital status, and children. I jot down notes after every appointment so I can remember their last vacation or when their daughter got married or why their son got in trouble in school.

I flipped to the page on Mrs. Oscar. Age: 85. 7 children; 15 grandchildren. Owns 5 gas stations. Hairstyle: Marceled - a tight wavy style, popular in the 1930s. Or was it the 20s? I turned on the curling iron and readied the deep conditioning spray.

Mrs. Oscar arrived at the stroke of half past eight. "The weather is too cruel," she said.

Temperature that month was in the sixties. Fair skies. No wind. "What's the matter?" I asked.

"We have a tank leak," she said, handing me her coat. "One of our underground gas tanks. Buried below the frost line, but still sprang a leak. Those frigid temperatures this winter did the thing in."

I suspected poor welds and corrosion, but who was I to tell her so?

"The gas station must close for two days while we replace it," she said. "We'll lose thousands of dollars."

I wished my business had thousands to lose in just two days, but heads are worth less than cars.

"We'll get you all fixed up," I said, as I seated her in my stylist's chair and swathed her in pink crepe. She looked dainty in that cape; it matched her complexion, the white of her hair, and her buffed nails.

She peered up at me and smiled. "Oh, Tracy, you do take care of me."

I marcel her hair. No one marcels anymore but I do.

She smiled with her crinkly eyes and waved her hand at me. I gave her a magazine. *Modern Trends.* She looked at me as if I'd lost my mind. I laughed and reached for the book she always reads—*Solitary Séance: How You Can Talk with Spirits on Your Own.* I ordered it from Amazon. She nestled into it and I went to work.

The chief arrived.

I could hear him in my salon living room, barreling into the sofa, then crashing into my table of Pretty Perky Pamper lotions. They clattered to the floor. I heard him open the closet door where he always hangs his suit coat and button-down.

He appeared in my workroom wearing a T-shirt and brandishing his sidearm. He laid the pistol on the counter. I checked that the safety was on. He opened a drawer, put his service weapon next to my combs and brushes, and shut it with a slam.

"Chief Fortdoux," said Mrs. Oscar. She pronounced the name as everyone does—Fort Dukes. It gives him a cowboy air.

The Chief nodded. "Mrs. Oscar." He might begrudge her the first appointment, but he was polite all the same. "How are the children?"

"Just fine."

The Chief grasped my second stylist's chair as if it were a petty thief trying to spin away and lowered his body onto the Naugahyde. "And your grandkids?"

"Getting good grades."

As Mrs. Oscar's waves re-emerged, her eyes twinkled at me in the mirror. Then she pinned her vision onto Chief Fort Dukes whose reflection stared back at her. He looked a little alarmed, but then the chief always looks that way.

"What in heaven's name went on at the Maverik gas station last night?" she said, her voice shrill but commanding. She was a *citizen* with an *interest*.

"We're investigating—"

"Don't give me the Channel Five speech, give me the facts."

"Male in a Spiderman mask pointed a handgun at the cashier and forced her to open the cash register. He gave the cashier a backpack and told her to drop in the cash. Cigarettes too. Then he pulled the phone cord from the wall, knocked the girl out, and dragged her into the beer cooler. He put as many beers in the backpack as he could and left her inside."

"And what are you doing about it?"

"I'm—"

"How are you going to protect us and our gas stations?"

I'll never understand how Mrs. Oscar, who looks like a kind and innocent grandmother, could make our big police chief tremble. But she did.

"There's an all-points bulletin out. We have the security camera video on the internet. The TV stations are showing it."

"I've seen that video," Mrs. Oscar said. "Quite a costume. Spiderman! All covered up. Boots, gloves, mask, hoodie. It could be anyone in there." She fixed her cold stare on him. "And no fingerprints?"

"No."

"So?"

The chief looked miserable.

I finished Mrs. Oscar's tight waves with a cloud of hairspray, whisked off the pink cape, and gave her the hand mirror. She admired the back. Then I led her to the front desk and tapped my computer keys. Without lowering her voice, she said, "You know that chief of police is a buffoon."

"Everyone knows that." I whispered, even though the chief was hard of hearing.

"But he's your husband's boss," she said.

"Yes," I said, "and I can't forget it."

"So give him a haircut on the house." She handed me an extra twenty.

I laughed and took the bill.

She put *Solitary Séance* on the counter.

"The only way to solve this case is for you to go home and consult the spirits," I said.

"I have a better solution," she said, pretending to shoot me with her forefinger. "I've bought each of our cashiers a Colt .45."

I clutched my heart as she sailed out the door. I wouldn't want to be a robber in *her* convenience store.

Back in the salon chair, the chief looked grumpy.

"Nothing like a sweet old lady to put you in a good mood," I said.

"Humph."

"She's paid for your haircut." I put the twenty on the counter.

"Now I'll owe her at Rotary," he said. "She'll tell this story and I'll owe some Happy Bucks."

"How close are you to finding the guy?"

"It's a needle in a haystack."

I spun his chair around and draped him in a black cape with a yellow towel at the collar. He looked like the Caped Crusader.

"The same cut as last time?"

"Yes."

I set to work, snipping his short hair much shorter. "The guy was wearing a Spiderman mask. Surely that's unique."

"Do you know how many Spiderman masks have been sold at Walmart?"

I didn't answer. Obviously a lot. I snipped some more.

He looked at me, then at his reflection in the mirror. "Maverik's a big chain. They can handle the loss."

"Probably."

"They get hit all the time. Do you know how many robberies they've had in big cities alone? Go on the web sometime and see."

"The guys are never caught?"

"Rarely."

I squinted at the back of his neck. Things were looking good. I held the hand mirror up so he could see the back. He pointed at the sideburns. "Clean 'em up."

I got out my electric barber's shaver and used the sideburn trimmer. All military. Spit spot. I was glad he didn't ask me to do a Flat Top.

"Now do the makeup," he said.

I applied some concealer around his raccoon eyes, then a ruddy foundation. "How's that?"

He got up before I could take off the cape and towered over me looking like Batman without a mask. He pulled at the towel around his collar and dumped the whole covering on the floor.

"The TV reporter's going to be in my office in six minutes." He plucked his gun out of the drawer, went to the closet, put everything he took off back on, and stomped out the door.

I watched his retreating back from the front door window. Then I went into the rear of the salon and swept up his hair. The twenty I left on the counter was gone. In its place was a five dollar bill.

My tip.

My 11:30 appointment was a guy named Harry. He was nice-looking in a gangly kind of way. Non-descript features. No beard. Brown hair. Adam's apple sticking out over the hand towel I wrapped around his neck, his lean body hidden by the sable-brown nylon cape that reached down toward the floor.

"Did you hear about the robbery at the Maverik gas station?" he asked.

"The chief was just here." I chipped away at his layers.

"The cashier's a friend of mine. I just came from the hospital. Her name's April."

"From the sound of it, she was nearly frozen."

"She had hypothermia."

"I'll bet." I turned his chair and went for the right side of his head. I use the feathering technique. I hold a section of hair up between the second and third fingers of my left hand and chip into the hair as if I'm cutting out snowflakes in construction paper.

"April says the gunman had paint spatters on the toes of his shoes," he said.

"The chief didn't tell me that."

"I don't think April told him," he said. "The chief talks a lot."

"But April told you."

"I listen."

I turned the chair again and snipped away at his left side.

"April said she was mopping up some mess by the all-night coffee stand," he said. "The guy grabbed her and put the gun muzzle right up to her chin."

"She must have been scared."

"She was petrified." He paused and his voice lowered in that way a client's voice does when revealing a confidence. "She was crying in my arms. It felt good to be needed. I'd like to say we're together, but I'm afraid April has other ideas."

"Sounds like you're sad about that."

"A little."

I fluffed up his hair. Tiny chipped hair pieces rained down. I gave him a final comb-through. "Blow dry today?"

"Naw. I gotta get back to work."

I picked up the hand mirror. "Take a look at the back?"

He raised his arm out from under the cape and waved the mirror away. "I trust you."

I removed the towel and pulled the cape off.

He rose from the chair and reached into his pocket. His hand re-emerged with a roll of bills. "Twenty-five?"

"Yes."

He peeled off a twenty and a ten. "See you next month."

"So long, Harry."

"Bye, Tracy."

I only had a few minutes before my next appointment. No time for a cup of tea. Just a quick pee.

I came out of my powder room as Mrs. Alcott entered the salon. My powder room is designed for people like her. My hand towels are plush cotton terries. She can use a new one each time she goes in and drop it in a laundry basket afterwards. I have scent sticks in there so the air is "Clean Linen." There's a porcelain sink with a faucet that looks like an old-fashioned English farm spout. And there's a gilt mirror so Mrs. Alcott can check to see if she still looks fifty going on thirty-five.

If I could guarantee all customers her age look thirty-five, I would have a salon in a fancy metropolis instead of this little old western city.

"Mrs. Alcott," I said. "May I take your coat?"

She shrugged it off and I hung it in the closet. She wouldn't want to see it on a coat rack; that would be low-class.

"May I get you some organic tea? Water? A probiotic drink?"

"Tea, Tracy dear. With honey."

I handed her some magazines and fixed the tea with two teaspoons of honey just the way she liked it. When I brought it back, she was reading an article in *Architectural Digest*.

I subscribe to that and *Interiors* for customers like Mrs. Alcott. They wouldn't be caught dead reading *People* or *Cosmopolitan* or even *House Beautiful*. Those are for ordinary people.

I put her china cup and saucer on the table in front of the sofa and picked up my Client Notebook. On Mrs. Alcott's page, it said: Natural level: 6 Highlight: Naturlite White Powder (1 scoop) mixed with 10 vol developer (2 scoops). These were the notes from the month before: House renovation. Looking for contractor.

"How's the house renovation going?" I asked.

Mrs. Alcott's eyes shot heavenward. "Terrible."

"What's the matter?"

"The contractor we found has taken our money and hasn't shown up."

This was not surprising to me. This was the way all contractors worked. They take on jobs when they have other jobs going and then can't juggle them all.

"A delay then?" I said.

"Why can't these people start when they say they're going to?"

"You must be so frustrated."

"We've paid them enough."

"Of course."

"If only it weren't Henrietta's house, we would fix his wagon."

"Who?"

"Henrietta Sanborn. Our dear friend. That's where we got his name."

"I see."

"He's finishing up there. I suppose we'll just have to wait."

"Will they be done soon?"

"They're in the last stages of painting."

I put my Client Notebook down and examined Mrs. Alcott's hair. "Your highlights are a little bit thin on the left side and we need to take care of your roots."

"Could you make it a bit more honey-colored?"

I pulled out my color book and showed her the swatches. "Like this one or that?"

She stroked the hair samples surrounded by pictures of beautiful girls all thirty years younger than she. "Like this." She picked the hair sample she always picked and I knew that the color formula would be the same that time as it was the last time and the time before that.

I mixed the color formula as she sipped her tea and finished the article she was reading in *Architectural Digest.* She turned the pages just as fast as anyone ordinary browsing through *People* or *House Beautiful.*

I ushered her into the back workroom where the kind, warm lighting is designed to make fifty-somethings look thirty-five, even when wrinkles are involved. I draped her and she admired the soft gold cape which enhanced her honey-colored, highlighted hair.

Of course, when I was done brushing on the dye and weaving in the bleach she looked hideous. Everyone looks awful with tinfoil sprouting from their heads. I escorted her back to my "comfort area" where she could choose to relax with her feet in a pool of warm lavender water or lie on a heated massage table with cucumbers on her eyelids.

She chose the latter and I patted the cucumbers gently, massaged a bit of spearmint into her wrists for aromatherapy, and wished her a nice rest.

I went to the sofa where my Notebook lay on the low table with the magazines and the used tea cup and the centerpiece which was a bowl of fake fruit from Bali.

I don't know why people like fake fruit from Bali, although it's colorful and happy. I always thought that real fruit would be better. But customers wouldn't eat the real fruit I put there, even when I placed a discreet card offering apples, pears, bananas and peaches up for their enjoyment. It seems they prefer bags of chips and bars of chocolate. So I discontinued the fruit and now I offer tea, water, chips and chocolate.

And fake fruit from Bali.

My pen was waiting for me. I opened my Client Notebook and wrote down all the clues I had learned from Mrs. Alcott, Mrs. Oscar, Harry and the chief.

After thirty-five minutes, I re-visited Mrs. Alcott who was dozing under the cucumbers. I gently woke her, took her to the sink and rinsed off the chemicals. Miracle of miracles, she was transformed, once again, into a honey blonde with tasteful highlights. I styled and blow dried her hair. She presented her credit card and made an appointment for next month. I got her coat from the closet, helped her into it, and she left. Just like every other time.

I don't get to eat lunch out often. Being a one-woman shop, I risk losing walk-in business. But that first day of detecting I decided go across the street to hear any buzz about the robbery.

I enjoy this diner. It's All American, 1950s. Looks just like the pictures my parents used to show me from *Life Magazine*. Chrome stools like the ones the kids sat on at the lunch counter in 1960 which was way before I was born.

Shirley came over as soon as I was seated. "Tracy, what can I get for you?"

"Bacon, lettuce and tomato on white toast, please," I said, "and a glass of water."

"Any fries with that?"

"No thanks."

I leafed through the selections for the old-fashioned juke box. *Let's Twist Again.* 1961. Chubby Checker. What was he like? My mother would know. *Love Me Tender.* 1958. Elvis Presley. Now *there* was a voice.

When Shirley brought the BLT, she stood next to the seat opposite me while I took my first bite. "How's the sandwich?" she asked.

"Great," I told her, taking a good look at her face. "What's eating you?"

"Boys," she said.

As if I didn't know. "Who this time?"

"Brian."

"What's wrong with Brian?"

"Won't talk, won't go out, won't have any fun." She picked up the salt shaker and wiped it down with a napkin.

"Sounds depressed."

"Money troubles."

"A man with money troubles is a dangerous man." I studied her pretty face hovering over the collar of her fifties-era waitress uniform. She looked like she was cast straight out of a movie. "What kind of money trouble?"

"He can't break into the business around here."

"What business?"

"Contracting. It's a closed system."

"How does that work?"

"The contractors all get together and decide who bids on which contract. If you're not part of the in-crowd you don't get to be a player. No bids, no wins."

"So he's shut out."

"All the newcomers are shut out. It's an old boys' network."

"I don't know if that's legal."

"Legal schmegal—it's been that way for years."

I chewed my sandwich, thinking about what she told me. "I'm glad we hairdressers don't have that system. To sort out all those heads would be too complicated."

"There aren't that many contracting jobs."

"Which one did he want?"

"A house. Name of Alcott. No dice."

"I'm sorry."

She sighed. "Anything else, Tracy?"

"Just the check."

I paid and crossed the street to my salon. I found Shirley's name in my Book. Shirley Jones. Brunette. Age 22. Boyfriends: Tom, Dick, Harry. I was glad the problem was not with Harry, my third customer of the day. I added the name "Brian" and wrote down what I'd learned.

After lunch I had a few appointments before Jeff Stockman walked into my salon with a newspaper in one hand and a briefcase in the other.

"Jeff, how've you been?" I said. When I took the briefcase from him, its weight nearly pulled me to the floor. "What's in this thing?"

"Tax advice," he said.

"If I open it up, will I know everything?"

"If all the tax advice in the country were stacked in one place, the pile would be as big as Fort Knox and Dodger Stadium combined. So, no, I'd say you'd know as much as I do. Which is nothing."

Jeff is a humble man. He does everyone's tax returns in town, including mine, and he gets a year's worth of haircuts in exchange for keeping me on good terms with the IRS. Sometimes I think this man is the only thing standing between me and jail for tax evasion. I'm just as honest as the next small business owner but I don't want the government to get more than their fair share. It takes a smart man like Jeff to keep us all on the straight and narrow.

"Would you like some tea?" I asked.

"No."

"Water?"

"No."

"Bourbon?"

"Yes."

I looked at my watch. "It must be five o'clock somewhere." I rooted behind the peroxide and the hair dyes until I found the fifth of Jim Beam I keep just for my tax accountant.

Behind me, Jeff readied two tumblers with ice. After I gave each glass a dollop of Beam, I splashed lime juice and ginger beer into mine. I like a Moscow Mule. Jeff doesn't.

We clinked and continued to put a dent in the bourbon supply as we caught up on Life, Love, the Universe and Everything. Then the clock interfered.

"Better get outa here," he said. "I'm about to have dinner with a really big client and my hair's too long."

I draped him in green, for money of course, and slid a section of hair through two stout fingers, making sure the blond ends protruded just so. "Snip, snip," the scissors said to me. I giggled.

"You tipsy again?" Jeff asked.

"You know I'm a cheap date, Jeff."

People often wonder who does Jeff's hair because it's never a perfect job. Blame it on the bourbon.

"Someone told me," I said, "that the big contractors in this town get together and decide who gets what business. They shut out the little guys who aren't in the 'in' crowd. Is that true?"

"Where'd you hear that?" A clump of hair fell on Jeff's nose and he pursed his lips upwards to blow it off.

"I can't reveal my sources," I said, "but what do you think?"

"There's about five contractors whose business is very good, and lots more who just eke out a living."

"Who are the big five?"

"I can't talk about my clients—it's confidential."

"Oh."

"But you probably know who they are. You see their trucks around and their signs on the jobs."

"Like the one doing Henrietta Sanborn's house? What's his name?"

"Chase."

"He a biggie?"

"$55 million gross revenue." Hair fell on his lips again. He spat. "I'm not revealing anything that hasn't been in the paper."

"It's big business, isn't it?" I said.

"Very big. With this building boom we're having—very big indeed."

I worked on Jeff's back layers for a while. He's a handsome guy with a full head of sandy brown hair that he likes to keep long, but trimmed out in layers.

Jeff took a long pull on his highball. "The same can be said for painting outfits. Only a handful seem to get all the business. I wouldn't be surprised if they fixed the field too."

"Interesting." I went after errant hairs on the nape of his neck. "So it would be very hard for some newcomer to break into the painting business here?"

"I'd say it would be near impossible."

I pruned his sideburns and gave him the hand mirror.

He held the mirror at all angles, inspected the sides, and then the back of his head. "You do good work, Tracy, even when you're tipsy."

I removed the green cape while Jeff sorted through his money. He always leaves me a tip even though his haircuts are free. He knows how much I don't make.

"I'll see you next month," he said, setting his empty highball on the counter.

"Looking forward to it."

I found the broom and swept the clumps of sandy-colored hair from the floor. Contractors fixing the field, workers having trouble breaking into the game, Spiderman with paint on his shoes. I had learned a lot of stuff that day, and I wasn't willing to call it gossip.

But had I learned a lot of nothing? I suspected somebody would think so—a handsome cop who wanted to make detective.

After I finished sweeping, I checked my schedule—no more appointments. I decided to swing by the thrift store to find a present for Jamie. They always have something good—sports equipment, toys, funny hats. I powered down the computer, snatched up my sweater, and locked up.

The church thrift store is everyone's tag sale. The whole town brings stuff in and the whole town takes stuff out. I've seen clients as rich as Mrs. Alcott go in there alongside the most desperate drifters coming off the highway.

"Hello, Tracy," said the lady at the front desk.

"Hello, Doris. Long time no see."

"You were here last week."

"Long time, like I said. Anything new?"

"An artist dropped off a beautiful set of watercolors. You interested?"

"Perhaps." I slipped a shopping basket off the stack by the cash register and headed for the arts and crafts section. There they were. Tubes of them. Cerulean blue, burnt sienna, alizarin crimson. I scooped them up as Sassy Morgan walked into the room.

"Tracy," she said. "Just who I wanted to see. Are you coming to book club tomorrow night?"

"Book club?" I said, easing the watercolors out of sight.

"Don't you remember? We're meeting at my condo on Main Street."

My mind groped for a conflict on my calendar.

"Lots of your friends belong," she said, "Shelley Prothero would love to see you."

I felt a stab of guilt. Shelley's my best friend from high school and I'd been neglecting her. Between my job and her family life we never seemed to find time to hang out. She's one of those caregivers caught between generations with five children and two aging parents at home.

"Candy Samuels has gushed over you. She says if you join us she's going to give you free samples of her latest formula."

My face grew hot. Candy is the local rep for one of those Ponzi-scheme diet-supplement companies. I didn't want any more of her elixirs.

"We'll see you tomorrow night," Sassy said. "The wine will be on the house—don't bring a thing. By the way, what have you got in that basket?" Sassy eyed the watercolors as if I'd mined gold nuggets from a mountain stream.

"Nothing," I said. "I'll see you tomorrow evening."

"Okay, bye bye."

With Sassy gone, I headed for the kids' section. Ice skates—not good for June. Trucks—Jamie had plenty already. Wooden blocks—too old-fashioned. A Spiderman mask. I sprinted back to Doris and handed her the watercolor tubes. "I'll take all these and could I have a bag, please?"

Doris gave me a thrift store bag with the inscription, "One man's trash is another man's treasure."

"Thanks. One sec," I said.

I scuttled back to the kids' stuff, took a pen out from my purse, balanced the Spiderman mask on my pen so I wouldn't touch it with my fingers, and dumped it in the bag. I saw this technique on TV. Then I returned to checkout.

"I have a Spiderman mask here, too," I told Doris.

"That came in today as well."

"Do you know who brought it?"

"Can't say I do. They're a dime a dozen, you know."

"Well, how much is this one?"

"Fifty cents."

I took my spoils and drove home. As I turned into the driveway, I realized I'd forgotten a present for Jamie.

Drat, drat, and double drat.

After dinner, I cleaned the kitchen while Jamie did his homework with Carl. Dishwashing is my Zen time when I try to focus on what I'm doing and forget about work. You might think the life of a hairdresser is as simple as a deep fry operator's. You might believe there's nothing to worry about when all the clients go home, but there's always something. My china plate disappeared under the soap bubbles. They were soft and white. Silver water cascaded down as I pulled it out and watched my hand gliding to the dishwasher rack. The plate stood up like a soldier in line.

It's so hard to be a one-woman shop. Should I try to rent my second stylist's chair again? The last girl didn't work out. What a pothead! Why can't I seem to find a good junior stylist? Maybe I advertised in the wrong place.

I banished these thoughts as my casserole dish swam into focus. I rubbed macaroni and cheese off with my plastic scraper. The crust parted easily from the glass. I flipped the switch of my disposal and the garbage swirled down the drain. My Pyrex sparkled. It had held comfort food and my family had eaten it—the Cycle of Life completed once more. Then Jamie's Spiderman cup bobbed to the surface.

The Spiderman mask. Was it the actual Spiderman mask? Is the theory I've been working on all day true? Who would rob Maverik and leave April unconscious in the beer cooler? A desperate man, that's who—a guy who's down and out, a drifter, a newcomer—someone trying to make it in this town and not succeeding. Like a contractor or a painter—especially a painter. Brian said there were paint spots on the man's shoes. What would Carl think about this theory of mine—that a painter took all the cash and put April in the beer cooler?

Carl needs a good case. He needs a break that will make his career. He's been on the force for three years now and he wants to move up from patrol. Chief Fort Dukes is a stubborn old bastard. My man deserves that job. Maybe the Spiderman mask has prints and Carl will be able run them.

After tucking Jamie into bed and turning in for the night, I cuddled up to Carl. "Guess what I found at the thrift store today," I said. The paper bag crinkled.

"What?" Carl asked.

"A Spiderman mask."

"So?"

I waved the mask in his face. "It's a clue."

"To what?"

"To the Spiderman robbery at Maverik."

He laughed. "Spiderman masks are a dime a dozen."

"But can't you test it for fingerprints?"

"On cloth?" He rolled his eyes.

I pressed on. "There's a label. It's plastic. What if the robber touched the label?"

"Highly unlikely."

"All right then, be that way." I scooted away from him. The one thing that gets a man's attention is withholding the evidence, so to speak.

Carl turned his body toward me. "Okay, it might be a clue. What else have you got?"

"Did you know that the Spiderman robber had paint spots on his shoes?"

"Yeah, April told me that."

"She did?"

"When I interviewed her in the hospital."

"I thought the chief did that."

"He did, but he misses things. I like to sweep up afterwards, if I can."

"That chief is a pain. Mrs. Oscar gave me twenty dollars to pay for his haircut, but he took the money home with him."

"That doesn't surprise me."

"Why not?" I said. "He's the police chief—he should be honest!"

"He's cheap," Carl said. "He picks up pennies off the sidewalk. He turns down expense requests. He's getting addled in his old age too. He probably thought the twenty was his. Now, stop worrying about the chief and pay attention to me." Carl raised the sheets and showed me something arresting.

I pulled the sheets back down. "Did you know that the contracting business in this town is fixed? The painters and builders have an old-boy network and they decide who's going to get which contracts and how much they're going to bid. They won't let newcomers in. I'll bet the Spiderman robber is a guy who can't get a job and is desperate for money."

"You're right, he is," Carl said.

"What d'you mean?"

"I arrested him today and that's what he is—an itinerant painter down on his luck."

"You got the guy? You got the guy and you didn't even tell me?" I launched myself on top of him and pounded on his chest. "You knew all along and you kept me guessing? That's not fair!"

His brown eyes danced. "I drove around the RV Park in an unmarked car and checked license plates. I got a hit on a stolen camper van. We nabbed the guy and found everything inside the vehicle."

"Case closed?"

"Case closed." His hand slid down to my inner thigh. "But you did a great job. You figured it out, my beautiful detective."

A few lovely minutes passed; then I remembered. "One last thing," I said breathlessly. "What are you going to do about those selfish contractors who keep all the business for themselves?"

"Honey, if it will make you happy, I'll go straight to the Attorney General's office tomorrow and whisper in his ear." His breath was warm and moist on my cheek. "I'll tell him there's some people screwing with each other in our little western town and they're having a good old time.'"

Case 2

Bells at the Crossing

• • • • • • • • • •

"We're all glad that Tracy Lemon could join us at book club this evening," Meryl Thompson said. "She's a friend of Sassy's and the owner of The Citrus Salon. Welcome, Tracy."

"Thank you." I smiled at Sassy Morgan, who'd invited me to her book club.

"You'll find that our discussion will be very freewheeling." Mrs. Thompson gestured to the group of sixteen women sitting around Sassy's living room as if she were Queen Elizabeth acknowledging the masses. "Please don't be shy. Chime in whenever you have a comment."

I was about to respond when Mrs. Thompson moved on. "Before we get started, I'd like to suggest we decide on our book selection for next month."

A collective groan rose from the club members, including my friend from high school, Shelley Prothero, who sat across from me. She looked as worn out as Methuselah and I wished I could anoint her with water from the Fountain of Youth.

An elegant lady in a designer dress spoke first. "I think we should read *Spilled Milk*. It's about a young girl who calls social services to escape from her abusive father and then gets even more abused in foster care."

"I don't know if I could stomach a story like that right now," said Shelley. The worry lines on her forehead looked deeper than usual. I wondered what was going on at home.

"Child abuse is an important social issue, Shelley," said designer dress. "One can't pretend it doesn't exist."

"I'm sure we can find a title we all like," said Mrs. Thompson in a placating tone. "How about *She's Come Undone* by Wally Lamb?"

A twenty-something blonde spoke up. "We read that a few years ago, Meryl. Don't you remember? That was an Oprah pick."

"I guess I forgot, Orchid. What book would you suggest?"

"*The Leader in Me* by Stephen Covey."

"What's that about?"

"How to instill leadership characteristics in children."

"That's perfect for you, Orchid, you're a teacher," said Candy Fiber. "But I'm in sales. I'd rather read *The Ultimate Sales Machine*."

Candy Fiber is not her real name, but we call her that because she tries to sell us fiber-based dietary supplements at least once a week. She's involved with one of those pyramid marketing schemes. Her sales techniques are manipulative enough without reading about them.

I turned to the young teacher. "What school are you in, Orchid?"

"Sunshine Elementary. I know your son Jamie. I'm Miss Fisher."

"Let's not read anything dark or serious," Shelley said. "Let's try something fun like a mystery."

"Or a romance," said Candy. "Sandra Brown writes thrillers with the best sex scenes. You'll be creaming your jeans in your chair."

Everyone laughed. Leave it to Candy to say something raunchy. Her flamboyant behavior was known all over town.

But I knew romances wouldn't do. People don't bring bodice rippers to the hairdressing salon. Neither do they bring the classics. They want to be seen reading important books—titles with Oprah's Book Club seal on the cover saying "Winner of the Such and Such Book Award." Then, when they set them aside in sheer boredom, my customers turn to me and talk.

"I like a book that informs me," said designer dress, sniffing slightly.

"We could consider non-fiction," said Sassy. "Your husband's a policeman, Tracy. What's Chief Fort Dukes reading right now? Something about identity theft? Racial profiling? Community policing?"

"I think his reading material is rather dry," I said. "But a client of mine was raving about a science book the other day."

"What's it called?"

"*Packing for Mars.*"

Shelley came alive. "Absolutely hilarious. Space toilets. Space sex. Space stiffs. " She looked at Candy Fiber. "Something for everyone."

"But is it scholarly?" asked designer dress.

"The author, Mary Roach, writes *New York Times* book reviews and participates in scientific studies," Shelley replied, failing to mention the author's scholarly topic was sexual intercourse.

When the group voted unanimously to read *Packing for Mars,* Sassy whispered her thanks. "You've been a real help. Every book we've read before this has been so turgid."

Later I looked up the word "turgid" on dictionary.com. "*1*: swollen; distended; tumid." That sounded like a porno film. "*2*. inflated, overblown, or pompous; bombastic."

I gathered this was more to the mark.

I was sweeping the salon floor when I heard a deep voice. "You have time to cut my hair?"

I whirled around, my broom tracing an arc as if to ward off the stocky muscular man who appeared at my workroom door.

"Now," the stranger added and it wasn't a question. I could tell he was agitated. Blunt fingers plowed through unruly salt and pepper hair. His jowls had a five o'clock shadow left over from yesterday and the day before that. I assumed he'd come off the highway—we get a lot of drifters in town, although how he'd ended up at my salon instead of the barber shop on Main Street was anybody's guess.

I leaned my broom against the wall where I could get it if I needed a weapon. "Take a seat," I said.

He grunted.

I selected a drape—taupe to match his tanned neck—and tucked a Turkish towel over the collar of his brown jacket. "Just a trim or—?"

"Take off at least three inches." He pointed at his head. His fingers were dark—stained with oil or grime.

"You've been letting it grow for a while, I see."

"I've been away from civilization."

Most of my clients require warm towels, aromatherapy and my sharpest gold-colored scissors. This customer looked like his last haircut was done with a pair of pruning shears.

"I think a wet cut is in order," I said.

"What's that?"

"A shampoo, then a deep conditioner." I lifted the ends of his hair. "Your hair is damaged. Have you been in the sun?"

"The sun is outside. I've been outside."

I led him to the bank of shiny black basins where he surveyed the backwards chair as if he was not sure what to do. After he sat down, I maneuvered his muddy work boots onto the foot rest. Then I tipped the chair back so his head dropped into the yoke of the sink and his legs pushed out into an extended position on the foot bar.

"This will feel warm."

He closed his eyes while I massaged his head and his body relaxed. Perhaps he'd never had his hair shampooed by someone else. Perhaps he had and there was a fond memory. I tilted him up, applied a towel to his head, and changed his neck cloth. He gave me a look I imagined was grateful.

"Come back to my chair." When I began to cut, all we could hear was the snip-snip of my scissors and his breathing, which was a little ragged.

"Just passing through?" I asked.

"Yeah."

"Where are you from?"

"Here and there."

"What brings you this way?"

"Work."

I held up a three-inch lock of hair. "Am I taking enough off?"

"More."

I cut some more.

"I saw it," he said.

"I know. Three inches."

"No, I saw it." His brow was furrowed, his face contorted.

There could only be one thing he was talking about. It'd been on the news. "The train wreck?" I asked.

His eyes were black pools where nothing could make waves except a train wreck. There were ripples in there now. They were making spouts between his eyebrows, rivulets out from the corners of his eyes, and creases down his mouth.

"I saw the car the train crashed into."

"Where were you?" I asked.

"I was sleeping in the shed behind the hardware store. No one saw me go in there, so I decided to spend the night. Good a place as any."

"Mm hm," I murmured as if I looked for places to sleep by the side of the railroad tracks on a routine basis myself. "What happened?"

"I heard the horns—once at midnight, again at three, and then at five. The last one was just before dawn. Then the awful noise—the car screeching all the way up the tracks with the engine right behind it. When I looked out, there was a dead baby in the bushes."

I stopped cutting. My scissors hung at my side. My mouth was open. I was staring at his face. He saw horror just behind the mirror. I couldn't see what he saw but I could tell it was living inside him.

"I walked around for hours until I saw your shop. Your sign said Walk-ins Welcome."

"You want a drink?" I asked.

"No."

"Chips? Chocolate? Anything?"

"I don't feel good."

I sat down in my extra chair. "Shouldn't you see somebody?"

"Who?"

"A priest? A social worker? Someone at the police department? My husband says they have counselors there."

"I'm seeing you. You're fixing my head for now. Could you finish it?"

"How high do you want your sideburns?"

"Here." He fingered a spot near the top of his ear.

"You want your nose hairs trimmed?"

"Yeah."

I worked on the forest up his nose. "I don't offer a shave, but I have a razor and some soap," I told him. "You can use the bathroom."

He grunted.

I took that as a yes and found the razor. My soap is organic with jojoba bean and aloe, but I didn't mention these finer points to him. He took the dark gray Turkish towel I offered and disappeared into my powder room.

Ten minutes later he came out looking fairly decent.

"What will you do now?" I asked.

"Move on down the line."

I pictured him following the tracks with his brown coat slung over his shoulder. Of course, he'd probably get in his pickup truck and head off down the highway. But then why was he sleeping in a shed instead of his truck? I realized there was no truck.

We drifted out of my workroom toward my front desk.

"How much?" he asked, reaching into his back pocket.

"Twenty-five."

He gave me thirty and left.

I sank onto an upholstered chair, feeling a little shaky. The accident had made the news on TV and radio—a woman and her nine-month old son were smashed to death by the 6:01. God, I'd heard the train screeching from our house. Carl had left for the police station; Jamie and I were just getting up. Afterwards we heard the sirens.

Carl should know about this guy. I picked up my cell and hit My Favorites, but just then Mrs. Hernandez walked in for her 10:30 appointment.

"You look surprised to see me," she said in her Mexican accent.

"No, no. I was expecting you."

"Somet'ing wrong?"

"No, everything's fine."

"Well, ev'rything not right with me."

"Why not?"

"You know that girl that got killed this morning?"

"By the train."

"She my sister's child's teacher's daughter."

I pondered this connection for a minute. They say there are only six degrees of separation; there appeared to be only four here. "A close friend then," I said with only a hint of laughter in my voice.

"Very close. She married to the best friend of my grocer's son. I see her all the time at the Amando Mercado. She a housekeeper at the Resort."

"You must be in a state of shock," I said.

"It very, very bad."

"I'm sorry. How did it happen?"

"She taking her baby to day care. Then she going to work. Every day she go across those tracks. Why problem today?"

"You're so upset. Are you sure you want to have your hair done?"

"Si, si." She headed for the back of the shop and sat in my chair. "I cannot sit at home. I cannot sit."

I looked at her sitting in the chair. "Would you like some coffee or tea?"

"Coffee, a little sweet."

I fixed her a cup. Then I went to my closet to pick out a cape.

"The turquoise one," she said.

She once told me it matches the color of the Gulf of Mexico where she was raised in a tiny beach town in the state of Tamaulipas. I consulted my Client Notebook where I had notated her children's names, her husband's name, and her hair style information.

"So," I said. "We'll continue to grow out the length of your hair in the front and trim a little at the neck and in the back. You are liking the shape, I take it?"

"Could you use bigger rollers this time so the hair is more—" She groped for a word and settled on "Poof."

With this and her hand gestures, I got the picture. "A fuller look?"

"Si."

I set to work, shampooing and conditioning first, then getting the dryer up to temperature before I finished the cut. Mrs. Hernandez was quiet. I put that up to the events of the morning, but as I rolled her hair she said, "She wasna hoppy."

"Who wasn't happy?"

"The one who got killed."

"Why not?"

"She was too beautiful."

I'd expected to hear men troubles, money troubles or immigration troubles. Or all three. "What do you mean?"

"She was going to be in that beauty contest—Miss Cowgirl. And she had a real chance. But her husband didn't want to let her do it. He said she was making herself a fool, she would never be chosen, and she had no business being married and being Miss Cowgirl."

"It's *Miz* Cowgirl, not Miss Cowgirl," I said. "The contest is open to both married and unmarried women."

Mrs. Hernandez took a sip of her coffee and set the cup in its saucer. "She was unhoppy. A girl who is unhoppy with a beautiful baby and a husband and a good housekeeping job and who is a chica muy hermosa has no business being unhoppy."

I accepted this pronouncement with good grace. "The customer is always right" has always been my mantra. I knew people in this world with many, many blessings could be dreadfully unhappy, but who was I to correct my client?

"Why don't you get under the dryer now, Mrs. Hernandez," I said, "and I will get you a magazine. Would you like to read *Siempre Mujer* or *Hola!*?"

"I cannot read anything," Mrs. Hernandez said, as she reached for both magazines.

I placed her coffee cup on the table beside the hair dryer. "A refresher?"

"Por favor."

With Mrs. Hernandez enjoying a magazine and coffee under the soft, warm air of my best hair dryer, I headed toward the phone to call Carl, just as it rang.

"The Citrus Salon," I said.

"Tracy, this is Martha Farquhar at the Resort."

My favorite customer. Not. Martha Farquhar is the rudest, most imperious woman I've ever met and she's a city councilor as well as an executive at the Resort, our town's main claim to fame.

"Cancel my appointment Friday," she said. "I'm going to a conference tomorrow and I need to see you this afternoon."

My heart sank. She usually demanded an appointment after work which meant I couldn't be home on time to pick up my son Jamie at the neighbor's.

"I can't stay late today," I said. "How about four?"

"Sooner.

Relieved, I scrolled down my computer screen. "Is two o'clock all right?"

"Two o'clock *sharp*."

"See you then," I told Martha, but she had already hung up.

The UPS man walked in the door. I signed for a stack of packages and followed him to the storage room where he unloaded his trolley.

On our way out, Mrs. Hernandez said, "Am I done?"

As the UPS man left, I felt her rollers. "You are."

I brushed out her hair and styled it. The reddish brown highlights in Mrs. Hernandez' abundant hair, make her appear more regal than anyone I know.

"Why do those men always wear shorts?" she asked.

"What men?"

"Those delivery men. Always wearing brown shorts. Even in winter."

"I don't know."

"And why did she kill herself?"

"Kill herself?"

"The beautiful girl," Mrs. Hernandez said. "The beautiful, unhoppy girl. Do you think she did it on purpose?"

"Surely it wasn't suicide!"

"Then why did she stop on tracks? You tell me that, huh?"

I gazed into Mrs. Hernandez' eyes. Her brows had knitted together.

We didn't say any more as Mrs. Hernandez made her next appointment but her question was sitting on the computer keyboard as she handed me her credit card. Her question was standing on my bamboo flooring as we crossed to the front door.

Why did she stop on the tracks?

"Tracy!" said a voice at my front door.

Oh no. It's Candy Fiber. I just put up with Candy Fiber at book club the other night. I don't want to talk to her now.

"Candy! How nice to see you!" I said.

"You doing good, Tracy? Love your hair color! How do you get that particular shade? Just that one little patch on the right-hand side. You're so clever. Not everyone's as good a colorist as you are. And green. Only you can pull it off."

"It's chartreuse, Candy. To match my nail polish. But I didn't expect you until next week."

"A new product came in and I wanted to share. Your clients will love it and so will you. In six days you'll feel like new. 'Zoom Away' is guaranteed to make you lose weight *and* work magic on your complexion, or your money back."

I should be calling her Candy Bilk-U-of-Your-Money. She's signed onto as many pyramid schemes as I've given haircuts—the kind where a person buys inventory and must sell it to make her money back.

Without taking a breath, Candy continued her spiel. "There are no preservatives, no chemicals, and no GMOs in this product, so it's healthy for you. And gluten-free! You don't have to spend too much at first. A fifty-five dollar starter kit will have your clients seeing results by the beginning of next week." Candy pulled out a brochure with before-and-after photos and an order-form on the back. "How many would you like?"

She was poised with her pen on the door sill, so no one could get in or out of my salon. I marveled at this girl's balls. But then, of course, she doesn't have any. Only little tits that she would like to have enlarged at the earliest opportunity so she could snag some guy before he knew what hit him. Conveniently, she was dating a plastic surgeon.

"How's the cosmetologist?" I asked.

"Cosmetic surgeon," she said. "Fabulous. His office bought fifty starter kits!"

"What a score! Then you don't need business from me." I advanced on her, propelling her out of the doorway toward the street. "Let's not block the door, Candy."

"On the contrary," she said, batting her eyelashes. "I need your business, Tracy. You see more people who need these products in one week than the doctor sees in a month."

"Are you trying to say my clients are fat?"

She smirked. "They're a bit overweight, aren't they?"

"Candy, give me a break. I'm not interested in carrying any new products, okay?" I caught sight of the clock. "I have a client coming in five minutes and I have to get ready."

"Well, if you'll try at least one starter kit, I'll tell you what I heard about the big accident this morning!"

I looked at her smug little face. She wasn't kidding. She knew something and she wouldn't give it up without a bribe.

"Candy, you don't know anything."

"Yes, I do."

"What is it?"

"Na uh." She shook her blonde curls.

I wanted to slap her. Instead I said, "I'm not interested. I'm too sad. That poor girl and her baby. Crushed to death by two hundred tons of metal going five miles an hour. What could you possibly tell me that I haven't heard already?"

"She wasn't alone in the car."

"She had her baby."

"She wasn't the only *adult* in the car."

"Who says?"

"Wouldn't you like to know?"

"Candy, if you know something, you should tell the police."

"Nonsense. I'm only repeating what somebody told me who was told by somebody else."

"Then it's not good information."

"There was a *man* in the car. A stocky man with black and silver hair. He was in the car with her and jumped out before the train hit!"

"I don't believe it."

"Choose what you want to believe. Or ask your husband. You'll see I'm right."

I remembered the phone call to Carl I should have made hours ago.

"Candy Samuels!" yelled a voice from a car careening into a parking space in front of my shop.

"Oh, boy, I'm outa here!" Candy scuttled down the sidewalk.

Katherine Putnam leaped out of her car and set off after Candy who disappeared around the corner.

When Katherine returned, I took one look at her florid, pudgy face and knew what was going on. "You didn't try one of her elixirs, did you?"

"Guaranteed to melt pounds off in five days."

"Yikes."

"If I catch that sorry—"

"Didn't get your money back?"

"No."

"Still trying to get it?"

"Yes."

We went into the salon and I checked my Client Notebook. "Last time we talked about an auburn color to enhance your complexion," I said to Katherine. "Did you think that one over?"

Katherine reached into her purse, which contained more stuff than the local thrift store, and pawed around for a few minutes. She finally pulled out a picture of a beautiful model with bright red hair. "I want this color," she said.

"Ahhh," escaped my lips. *How should I react to this?* I settled on: "A truly vibrant shade."

"I saw it on a singer in a band at the festival last week. It's totally radical. Don't you think it will look super?"

On her, yes.

"Very distinctive," I said. "Shades of red. Violet. A little of the auburn we talked about. Auburn would really suit your complexion."

"I want to be different. I want to be—sensational."

"It will be that."

We cruised into the color salon where I opened my book of color swatches. As we discussed the choices, I suggested a weave. Red, auburn and blonde. "Not exactly like the picture but I guarantee it will enhance your complexion. Then if you want to go brighter red next time, we can ease into it."

"Okay. If you think so. But I want to look like that singer. You know she's going to be the next Ms. Cowgirl."

"Oh really?" I mixed the colors and notated the formula in my Client Notebook.

"Yeah, she's a shoo-in now that Angelica Diego is dead."

I looked up from my mixing bowl. "Is that the girl who was killed by the train this morning?"

"Yeah. An absolutely gorgeous girl."

"You knew her?"

"Yeah."

"How?"

"We went to high school together."

I began to section off Katherine's hair. "Why would she do such a thing?" I asked.

"Go to high school with me?"

"Stop on a train track."

"Accidents happen."

I applied color to a chunk of hair and wrapped it in tin foil. "Some people are saying it was suicide."

"Suicide!"

"You don't think so?"

"No way. She had everything to live for. A great husband. A beautiful kid. Not such a great job, but a chance at being Ms. Cowgirl? No way."

"Then what do you think happened?"

"Car trouble?"

"But why would a car pick that spot to stall out? Most train accidents seem so ridiculous. You can hear the train coming. You can see the train coming. Crossings have lights and barriers. Anybody who gets stuck on the tracks is a dope."

Katherine absorbed this information. Then she said, "Some people say someone else was there."

"Who?"

"Someone who stepped on the brake or stalled out the car."

"And forced her to stay?"

"Had a big argument."

"A big stocky white guy with silver and black hair?" I asked, dreading the answer.

Katherine laughed. "No! Where'd you hear that? People are saying it was a woman. Someone saw a woman running away from the train into the shadows."

"Who was the someone?"

"The train engineer."

Now it was definitely time to call Carl. I wished there hadn't been so many interruptions.

"You're done." I put down my painting brush. "Where would you like to process?"

"How long do I have?"

"Thirty minutes."

She thought for a moment. "How about in the spa with the footbath and the massage chair?"

"You got it."

I ran the tub and sprinkled lavender essential oil in the warm water. Then I placed a pillow on the seat of the chair, so vertically-challenged Katherine would be tall enough to enjoy the full range of my automatic deep cushion-rest back kneader.

Katherine eased into the chair and dangled her feet over the tub while I removed her Reeboks and socks. She dipped her feet in with a chortle of delight.

"Enjoy," I said and turned down the lights. Katherine closed her eyes, a little smile on her face.

I strode to my desk and grabbed the phone.

Carl answered on the first ring. "Hello, Miss Headstrong."

"Hello, Officer-In-the-Know."

He laughed.

"I'm worried about the accident this morning," I said.

"Why am I not surprised?"

"There was a man in here. My first customer. He said he saw it happen. Well, I mean, he said he saw the dead baby."

"The baby's not dead."

"Not dead?"

"The baby was saved by a squirrel's nest. You know those things you see in trees? This one was in a shrub, big and wide and soft inside. The baby fell into it and survived."

I bit my lip which was quivering. I put my hand over my mouth to make it stop. *My son Jamie. Her baby. Alive.*

"But he said it died in the bushes," I whispered.

"Not so. The nest was above some brambles and it lived."

"So this man who was here this morning—"

"Stocky? Working man? Black hair shot with gray?"

"Yes."

"He came in and gave a statement. You should have seen his face when he found out the child was alive. Blubbered like a baby."

Thank God.

"So what happened, Carl? What happened to that poor girl?"

"Active investigation, sweetheart. I can't talk about it. Goodbye, Miss Ears."

"See you, Officer Sexy."

He laughed.

I hung up.

Katherine was gone and Martha Farqhuar had arrived—Martha with the big chest, hefty shoulders, and stocky frame. I have always marveled at her girth and her grit. Martha is a presence no matter where she shows up, whether City Council or the Rotary Club. Martha is Vice President of Operations at our town's main claim to fame—the Resort where the rich and famous go for rehab. Martha's in charge of the culinary, maintenance, and housekeeping staff.

I consulted my Client Notebook. Basic bowl cut on her steel wire head with no color touch-ups. Likes her eyebrows waxed to get rid of stray white hairs that tend to give her a pale, *insipid* appearance—her word, not mine. Likes her mustache waxed, too. No five o'clock shadow for her.

My Client Notebook told me that she had no husband, boyfriends, or love interests of any kind. She was working on a memoir about her life with the rich and famous that she planned to publish posthumously, which was her fancy word for "after death." Whose? Hers or the rich and famous? I was never quite sure.

"I would like the usual," she said, after I took her brown coat and hung it in the closet.

"Of course." I brought her an assortment—Hershey's, Belgian, Godiva. She selected Godiva. I draped her in a burgundy cape which hid her lumpy body. After tucking a royal blue terry cloth towel around her neck, I began to trim the hair all over her black and silver head. My snips sounded quite staccato as I marshaled her layers into shape. She eyed me in the mirror.

"You're looking happy today," she said.

I was surprised. Usually she didn't pay any attention to me. "I've just learned that the baby who was hit by the train is still alive."

A flicker crossed her face. "Oh?"

"Yes, he was thrown clear and came down into some kind of nest—a soft landing. Isn't that a miracle?"

"My, my."

"But you should know about him. Wasn't Angelica Diego one of your housekeepers?"

"Was she?"

"That's what I heard."

"She could have been."

"Didn't you know her?"

"I don't know all the people on my staff. There are so many."

"A beautiful girl, they say. She was going to compete for Ms. Cowgirl."

"Oh. *That* one." The way she said it, I felt she was talking about a leather glove. Oh, *that* one. As if there were two and one had been lost but now found.

"Yes," I said. "Apparently she was a front runner, but her husband didn't want her to compete. Said she wouldn't win and shouldn't even try."

"Playing the race card, was he?" she said.

How crass! But was she right? Was that his real objection—that Angelica couldn't win because she was Hispanic?

"These macho Hispanic men," Martha said with some venom. "They think they can run their women's lives. She was a pretty thing, as I recall. And she did have a baby. But – Not so close!"

"Sorry!"

"You nearly took my ear off!"

I wasn't anywhere near her ear. Why was Martha so touchy? "I'll be more careful," I said.

"These girls should be more mindful who they marry," she said. "*He hurt her.*"

I pulled back and caught a glimpse of my horrified expression in the mirror. Luckily, Martha was looking elsewhere. "How do you know that?" I asked.

"Came to work with bruises. On several occasions."

"Really!"

"We reached out to her, tried to help. She would have none of it."

"So you *do* remember her."

Her silence spoke volumes. What had made Martha hide her knowledge at first?

"Of course, you have so many employees to worry about," I said, "but this one sounds like she was in trouble."

Martha expelled more air from her lungs than a beached whale. "She was terrified of her husband and what he might do to her. I tried to make her leave him. Gave her the number for the battered women's shelter."

"But she wouldn't use it?"

"No." Martha was silent for a while.

Don't dry up now.

I changed tactics. "You are so persuasive, councilor. I've seen you in city hall meetings. I know how you make things happen." I poured it on. "Surely she would have listened to someone as wise as you."

"I took her home with me."

My eyebrows were raised, but I hid behind her head so she couldn't see me in the mirror. I shaved the hairs around her collar. Her head emerged from the chair at about the same height as my first customer of the day. I stared at the back of her head. Her thick neck matched the brown of the coat I had hung in the closet. Was that a coincidence? Candy said the engineer saw a woman running away from the tracks—a woman with salt and pepper hair.

"How did she fare at your house?" I asked, pushing my alarm bells down near my ankles. "Were you able to talk some sense into her?"

"She didn't stay long."

I took out the soft plush cosmetic brush I use to dust off hair snippets resting inside ears and on delicate neck muscles. Martha didn't have any— delicate neck muscles, I mean. I had never contemplated what a formidable, muscular body she possessed and suddenly I thought I knew why Angelica refused to stay at Martha's house for very long.

"All set," I said, putting a lilt of gaiety in my voice.

I took off the burgundy cape and removed the royal blue towel. I gave her a hand mirror. "How's the back?"

She took the mirror and moved on muddy, booted feet to observe the back of her head. Then she said with a bitter tone, "Good enough for city hall but not good enough for Ms. Cowgirl."

I gulped.

How did Angelica reject your advances—with polite good nature or noisy screams and a terrified retreat?

"You want to keep your standing appointment next month?" I asked, leading her toward my desk.

"I don't know. I might be busy," she said, not looking at me. "I'll call you."

I took her cash.

She dropped five bucks near the computer and lumbered through the front door.

After I saw Martha Farquhar out, I plucked the hand mirror off the counter with a tissue and dropped it in a plastic bag. Then I locked up the salon and drove to the police station.

The place was bedlam. Strange men in suits huddled in sweaty groups beside our uniforms. Half the men were on cell phones. Our local admins bustled around with print-outs and coffee pots. Chief Fort Dukes stood in the middle of it all looking stunned, but then he looks that way every day.

I found Carl at a computer terminal and waved my plastic bag. "I think I have the fingerprints of the murderer in here," I said.

"Murderer," Carl said. "What murderer?"

"The woman who was with Angelica Diego when she was killed." My words tumbled out. "The woman who ran away from the train tracks right before the engine hit. The woman who parked Angela's car on the tracks!"

"Slow down." He held up his palms as if directing traffic. "You've lost me. Say it again now—slowly."

I told him about Martha Farquhar and, of course, he knew who she was. I told him why I thought she was in the car with Angelica in the early morning hours and that maybe she was even driving. "She stopped the car on the tracks. Maybe she was trying to kiss Angelica and they were having an argument and Martha got out before the train came but Angelica didn't!"

Carl burst out laughing. "What an imagination."

If steam could come out of ears, mine were scalding hot. "Cars don't just get stuck on the railroad tracks," I said. "They get stopped there and the person who does the stopping can be very emotional. There's something going on here—there's got to be!"

"But with *Martha Farquhar*? Get serious. If I tell the Chief that I think Martha Farquhar had the hots for Angelica Diego, I'll get run off the police force."

I thrust the bag against his chest. "Fingerprints don't lie. See if they're in the car!"

"All right, all right." He took the bag.

"Look," he said, hugging me. "I love you very much and I thank you for wanting to help."

"Carl, will you check those prints?"

He gestured toward room. "After I help the Feds. They've all got rods up their asses."

"Let me know about the prints."

"I promise, but Tracy, this is the wildest accusation I've ever heard."

"Goodbye, Officer Skeptical."

"So long, Miss Suspicious."

The next day my three o'clock appointment was Don Westcott. He lives on a forty-acre ranch outside our town. Once upon a time in a big city on the East Coast, he made good money doing voice-overs for radio and television commercials. He socked away some bucks so he could retire early and raise thoroughbreds.

Don has been getting a haircut and a manicure from me every month for years, so there was a lot of data about him in my book: Race horse named Sally Mae foaling. Sire Dapper Dan. Wife having trouble with sun spots; dermatologist fears malignant. Emcee again this year for the Ms. Cowgirl beauty contest.

"How's your wife?" I asked, as I draped Don's angular body with a charcoal-gray cape.

"Much relieved," he said. "The diagnosis was benign. She's covering up now and wears sunscreen all the time and a hat. So do I."

I placed Don's new Stetson on the top shelf of the closet and slipped on a green bracelet to remind me it was there. People will leave their heads behind if you let them.

"Nothing like a scare to get you to do the right thing," I said. "Our western sun is strong."

"Ozone layer's thin all over the world."

"Same as usual today?" I asked.

"Yup."

Don reached into his briefcase and pulled out an iPad. As I got to work, he scrolled through to the website of the New Mexico Horse Breeders Association. I read the headlines over his shoulder. "Penalties announced for Class 4 Drug Aminocaproic Acid; the latest look at the career of Sparkling Moolah."

Sparkling Moolah. What a great name for a race horse. I wondered if Don was thinking of racing again. He scrolled down and enlarged the type on the screen:

Studies have shown that lungs don't bleed from hard exercise when horses are given Aminocaproic Acid, but use of the drug in New Jersey and New Mexico results in stiff fines.

Don looked up from the iPad and examined himself in the mirror. "A little more off the top."

"Too heavy up there?"

"I don't want to look like a bubble top at the competition. Trim some more, but watch our 'Little Secret.'"

"Will do." I knew he was talking about his comb-over. His bald spot was the reason he was never on-camera but his voice is remarkable. It flows like chocolate syrup colliding with a maraschino cherry; just a little bit of bass to give the tenor texture with occasional high notes that make important words distinct.

"How does that look?" I asked.

"Good," he said.

"How's Sally Mae? She had her foal yet?"

"Yup. A filly."

"Nice. No health problems?"

"None."

Then why was he reading that article?

When I was finished, he inspected his hair in the mirror, turning his head from side to side. I couldn't offer him the hand mirror because it was at the police station with Martha Farquhar's fingerprints on it.

He fumbled at his neck.

"Let me take care of that." I removed the brown sable terry cloth and the charcoal-gray cape.

He set his iPad down on the counter before we went into the spa. I made a mental note: "Three Green." That meant the green bracelet would remind me he had three possessions to take with him when he left—the iPad, the briefcase and the hat.

Don sat down at my manicure table. I prepared a bowl of warm, perfectly temperature-controlled water with marbles in the bottom. Marbles make the water look special.

"Got a new horse trainer," Don said, putting his right hand in the bowl while I turned my attention to the left.

"Anyone I know?"

"Friend from out of town. New Mexico."

"Oh?"

"He was big in racing down there."

"You woo him away? Offer him some moolah?"

"He got a bum steer."

"What happened?"

"Gave a horse the wrong drug on race day. He got fined and the owner fired him."

"Bad scene."

"Had to leave in a hurry. There's no reasoning with some people."

"You're right about that." I pulled out my medium clippers and nicked any hang nails I could see.

"He drifted around for months real down," Don said, "and ended up here this week."

"How do you know him?"

"Racing."

I put the left hand in the warm water and began on the right.

"He's a nice guy," he said, "who didn't deserve what he got. Drug's not outlawed in other states. He just wanted to protect the horse."

"Sounds like he has good instincts."

"We met in Vietnam. Good guy to have around."

Don served two tours in Vietnam, one in combat and the next one on the army's radio station. *Good Morning, Vietnam* is his favorite movie.

"Did you guys get in some tight spots together?" I asked.

"Nah. I didn't meet him 'til my radio stint, but he got stung badly there too."

"What happened?"

"Witnessed a massacre. Women and children. Dying babies. Still has nightmares about it."

I digested this information in silence. *Could this be my first customer of yesterday? That could explain his reaction to the baby.*

"May I have some water, Tracy?"

"Sure. Sparkling or spring?"

"Sparkling."

"Ice?"

"No thanks."

I headed for the refrigerator where I keep the Pellegrino and poured him a glass. Then I poured myself one, returned to the spa, and placed the two glasses on the manicure table. He took a long draught. I followed suit.

"Darndest thing about that beauty contestant," he said, putting his empty glass down.

"Isn't it, now? Did you know her?"

"Yes."

I covered his fingertips with warm moisturizer and massaged it into his cuticles. "What do you think happened?"

"I think she was just in the wrong place at the wrong time."

"But how do people miss the train horn and the stop lights and the bells at the crossing? Not to mention the bar coming down?"

"Young girls listen to loud music in their cars. She could have stopped to attend to the baby. It was dark. Pre-dawn. Just one inattentive moment and wham!" He clapped his hands together. Moisturizer spattered.

I pulled a tissue and wiped the moisturizer from my face.

"Sorry," he said.

I applied more cream and massaged up to his elbows. "I think I may have met your friend," I said.

"Oh?"

"Stocky guy, salt and pepper hair, deep tan, brown coat?"

"Yeah."

"He came in for a haircut that morning. Said he'd seen the baby in the bushes."

"You're kidding." Don's eyebrows pushed up against his comb-over.

"He was pretty shook up, but he went down to the police station and talked to Carl."

"That was brave. He's had a tough time with cops lately."

"People said they saw him running away from the train crossing just before the engine hit." I watched Don's face in the mirror. "But I think it was someone else."

"Who?"

"Someone who was driving Angelica to work and stopped on the tracks to scare her. Someone who ran away while Angelica was trying to get her baby out."

Don stared at me. "Her husband?"

"No."

"Then who?"

The phone rang. I let it go to voicemail.

"Who do you think?" I asked. "Someone who has salt and pepper hair about the same length as your friend and wears a similar brown coat."

"I can't think of anyone," Don said. "Unless you're talking about Larry Big Pouch. He's one of the Ms. Cowgirl contest judges."

This was not the answer I expected. "What's his story?"

"Native American. Comes into town from the reservation for the contest. Promotes the participation of all ethnic groups, not just Indian. But would he be involved at all? Judges don't have any contact with contestants before the day. It's just not done."

I didn't doubt for a minute that a lot of things that just aren't done are done. I had heard stories about the preposterous, the nonsensical, and the unthinkable from many people sitting in that very chair, and all the stories were true. I cleared my throat. "Does the Tribe have a horse in the race this year?"

"Yeah." Don laughed. "Tina White Horse. Larry's wife's sister's daughter."

"A close relative."

He laughed again. "They're all close on the reservation."

This was getting interesting: Here was a young Hispanic mother who incurred the wrath of her husband for entering a beauty contest, the displeasure of her boss for spurning her advances, and fear from a judge who wanted his niece to win the same contest.

I loved this lineup of suspects and I was itching to interview them all, but then I caught sight of my face in the mirror. I looked quite nasty. Could any of these people have really caused the incident on the railroad tracks? *Don't get carried away, Tracy.*

I wiped the moisturizer off Don's arms and hands, then buffed his nails. He had long fingers and manly hands.

"Were you ever a hand model?" I asked him.

"Always stayed behind the camera," he said. "My voice was the moneymaker."

"Must have been fun."

"Never had to do any heavy lifting. Worse thing was a script where I had to say 'tweedy striped wrap' half a dozen times."

"What's so bad about that?"

"You say it."

"Tweedy stwipe wap." I giggled.

"See what I mean? Say Redwood Road real fast."

"Wedwood Wode."

Don examined his hands with an appreciative smile.

He moved to my desk, made an appointment for the next month, and paid with a credit card. "Are you coming to the beauty pageant?" he asked.

"Wouldn't miss it," I said. Don likes an audience.

I spied the green bracelet on my wrist and grabbed the Stetson from the closet. He remembered his iPad. I saw him out the door, cleaned up the manicure station, and swept up the hair from underneath the chair. There was Don's briefcase.

Drat.

My computer said that Margaret Pyle, back office maven of Fu Tsu's Hardware and Auto Supply, was next.

Margaret Pyle is larger than life. She wears a teased-up hairdo, left over from the days when she was a cheerleader and every one of her boyfriends was a local linebacker. What Margaret can't do in the bookkeeping department she manages to do in the meat department. It was twenty years since the beginning of her first marriage and only three months since the ending of her fifth.

"Yoo hoo!" Margaret swept into the salon, the smell of perfume permeating every nook and cranny within seconds.

"Hey, Margaret, how's tricks?"

She plunked her large handbag down on the sofa. "Tea with honey," she said, "and a big bag of chips."

"How do you keep that figure?"

She sashayed down to my drape closet, her voluptuous, big-boned body parting the air. She extracted a gold cape embroidered with her initials—MVP.

The V stands for Vera, but of course, she maintains the initials stand for something else.

I gathered the tea, the chips and a gold terry cloth towel I keep for her behind the cookie jar. The cookies are reserved for my son, Jamie.

"I'm conducting an investigation!" she said as I draped her.

"At the hardware store? Sounds important."

"It is."

I pulled off the hair band buoying up her white-gold tresses and began the hardest part about working on Margaret—combing out her teased crown.

Knit one gnarl two.

She gritted her teeth.

"You have nothing to say about this." I pulled on her hair again.

She scowled even more.

"If you didn't tease your hair every day, we wouldn't have this trouble."

"What are you?" she asked. "My mother?"

"I'm your hairdresser and it hurts me to see how much you damage your hair. It's a wonder you have any left."

Margaret is blessed with abundant hair, but it breaks off as fast as she finds a new man. The roots are brown, the ends are dry, and the style is vamp. We have this discussion every single time. It always ends the same way—I untangle her hair, mix the bleach, burn the roots, and run the blonde through. I bought a new dishwasher with what I earned from Margaret last year.

The torture session over, I dipped my paint brush into her formula. "So what's this about an investigation?"

"I've found something fishy," she said.

"What?"

"Wrong orders."

"What do you mean?"

"Computer reports show that the right car parts are ordered, but not as much stuff has gone out the door as we should have sold. Wu says he hasn't been entering wrong orders so who has?"

"Hu?"

"He hasn't either."

Wu and Hu are brothers. Each has an equal share in the hardware store which was started by their father, Fu.

"Who do you suspect?"

"It has to be Hu, Wu, Humphrey, or Juan Diego. They're the only ones who use the ordering system."

"Okay," I said as I painted Margaret's roots. "How does that work?"

"A customer calls up and asks for a part. If it's not in stock, we order it over the net."

"How could someone monkey with that?"

"I don't know."

"How would you do it if you were the thief?"

She rubbed her chin. "I guess I'd go back into the system later and change the order."

"Can anyone do that?"

"Any one of those four. But why would they? What's in it for them?"

"What was ordered?"

"Car batteries. Spark plugs. Air filters."

"Stuff that can be sold under the table?"

"Sure, but if their order was missing, customers would complain."

"Not if the quantity was changed," I said. "Two car batteries instead of one. A dozen spark plugs instead of six. Could it happen that way?"

"I guess so." Margaret scratched the top of her head. "Oops."

I wiped the platinum dye off her fingers. "Earlier you mentioned 'Juan Diego.'"

"What about him?"

"Is he by any chance, related to the Angelica Diego who died on the train tracks this morning?"

"He's her husband. He hasn't been to work since it happened."

"Check to see if there's extra stuff waiting around for him to pick up."

"You're kidding."

"He's one of the suspects, right?"

"Yeah."

"Then check it out. If half was picked up by a customer and the other half is still there, then maybe he's your guy. And look up the start date of all the orders you're worried about and the employee hire dates for him and Humphrey."

I gathered a shower cap tight around Margaret's ears and parked her under the hair dryer.

"More tea?"

"Yeah. And more chips."

Thirty minutes later, I checked Margaret's highlights. "Looking good."

She moved to the sink and then to my chair for styling. "Can we fix your hair without the rat's nest?" I asked.

"Not a chance."

Puffed and platinum, she twirled around in front of the mirror, let the gold cape swirl off her hourglass figure, and undulated up to the front of the salon.

"Put it on my account," she said. "With a twenty percent tip."

"I think I'll up the quantity. Two hair colors and two cuts."

"Knock it off."

"Call me."

"I'll let you know what I find out."

"Ciao.

"Chow," she said.

After the door shut behind her, I turned on every ceiling fan, hoping to banish the heavy perfume.

"Hello, Love."

I whirled around. There he was. The handsomest, sexiest policeman on the planet, standing at the front door of my shop holding my plastic bag.

"I just came to tell you that the fingerprints on your hand mirror were not found in the car."

My movie of Martha Farquhar driving Angelica to the tracks faded to black.

"And there's more," he said. "Angelica was on her cell phone."

"With—?"

"Her husband, who she dropped off at the hardware store, *and* –" He looked at me.

I steeled myself. "What?"

"The baby was placed in the nest."

My mouth dropped open.

"The docs said the force of impact would have killed the baby if he was thrown into those bushes. The baby was put there."

"How?"

"We're still trying to find that out. We want to talk to your friend again."

"The salt and pepper man?"

"Yeah."

"He's a horse trainer. Don Westcott's hired him, and there's something else you should know."

"What?"

I told him about Margaret Pyle and her forensic accounting. "We think Angelica's husband might be selling car parts on the side. Margaret's checking to see if there are car parts waiting in the back store room that are duplicates of sold orders."

My cell phone rang and I swiped it right away. "It's Margaret," I mouthed, then signaled yes to Carl—there were duplicate orders waiting to be picked up.

My husband opened the front door. "There were new car parts in the back of Angelica's car, too."

We stared at each other.

"Goodbye, Miss Helpful," he said and left.

I leaned on the front door. My knees were weak.

In my mind's eye, I saw Juan Diego calling on his cell with a command to his wife. "Stop where you are. I've left car parts on the back seat." Visions of his blows, his anger, his blame made her screech to a halt with the music thumping. He wrenched the back door open just as the bells clanged and the barriers started down. A huge headlight coming fast, out of the dark, the panic. He yanked his son out. "Go! Go! Go!" But she didn't, couldn't or wouldn't go. He sprinted back to the hardware store, shocked and confused. And there was the nest, ready for him to stash the baby until he could think of what to do.

Was that how it happened? A big accident by a wife beater who was stealing car parts for extra cash?

Over the next 24 hours, the police did their work. They brought Juan Diego in for questioning and searched his house. After they found a black and white striped hoodie, a thick brown coat, and closet full of brand new car parts, he confessed. He'd ordered her to stop so he could get the car parts. She didn't realize the car was on the tracks—the whole thing was one big accident. He was charged with one felony count for thievery, but not for manslaughter.

Breaking the case made Chief Fort Dukes a hero. He was all over the evening news for a week. The crowd went wild when Don Westcott introduced him at the Ms. Cowgirl contest.

"Chief Fortdoux," Don said, pronouncing the name Fort Dukes as everyone does. "How'd you know what went down?"

"Good detective work, Don," he said, grasping the microphone. "You see I—"

Don reclaimed the microphone. "Let's hear it for the chief!" Then he dampened the crowd with his palms down. "Now we'll observe a moment of silence for Angelica."

People bowed their heads. I caught a glimpse of Mrs. Hernandez fussing over a baby carriage. With the father in jail for theft, she was caring for the son until Angelica's sister could come from California.

Don broke the silence. "The judges have made their decision." He gestured to the beautiful contestants, lined up on the stage in their cowgirl outfits. "May I have the envelope please?"

Larry Big Pouch rose from the judges' table and approached with three pink envelopes clasped against his thick chest, his rugged profile topped with a shock of black and white hair.

Don took an envelope, slit it open and read out loud.

"The Second Attendant is—" The high school band leader cued the drum roll, then Don pronounced, "Miss Red Wing." Applause.

The red-headed singer that Katherine Putnam admired crossed the stage to receive her spurs. A young girl draped a banner over her shoulders. She waved to the audience and took her place below the dais.

Don slit open the second envelope. "The First Attendant is—"Another drum roll. "Miss Tina White Horse."

Larry Big Pouch's raven-haired niece strode across the stage with a huge pearl-white smile shining from her flawless face. She thanked Don prettily for her spurs.

"And now the contestant who will be Ms. Cowgirl for the next year." Drum roll. "Mrs. Su Tsu!"

The wife of Hu Tsu minced across the stage where a young boy covered her shoulders with the traditional Ms. Cowgirl ermine vest.

"I want to thank my family, my friends, and my husband for all their help. I couldn't have done it without you," said Ms. Cowgirl. She wriggled her shoulders. "I just love this fuwwy white wap."

Case 3
A Maddening Adjustment

• • • • • • • • • • • • • •

Mondays are my catch-up days—Jamie is in school and the salon is closed. I tackle paperwork and housecleaning; then Jamie and I spend time together when he comes home from school. I make a point of doing whatever he wants to do. The Monday after the Ms. Cowgirl contest, he wanted to go fishing.

We went out to the garage and collected rods, a tackle box and waders. He climbed up on a stepstool next to the deep freeze and reached under the lid where we keep plastic bags full of bait. He pulled one out and tossed it in the car.

Our river runs through the whole valley which is lush and green compared to the surrounding hills studded with desert sagebrush. We parked in the spot where the river is shallow but the pools nearby are deep for casting.

Jamie handled his rod very well. His father taught him how to whisk it back and settle the artificial fly right on the top of the water. I like drop fishing myself—just bait the hook, drop the line, watch the bobber, sit back, and enjoy the day. Fly fishing is too much work for me, but Jamie was having a ball.

He caught two trout. I caught nothing, but then I never do. Each time he snagged a rainbow, I leaped up, grabbed the net, and watched him play the fish. The trout glistened in the sun as it descended into my net.

"Wait 'til Dad sees this!" he said.

"Wait 'til Dad *eats* this!" I imagined how proud Carl would be and my heart glowed.

When the sun began to set, we packed up and headed for the car. "I met someone who knows you," I said, as Jamie pulled his waders off. "Miss Fisher. From your school."

"She's mean."

"Excuse me?" Jamie's head was down and I thought I hadn't heard him correctly.

"Miss Fisher is a mean teacher."

"Why do you say that?"

"She yells when she's mad and she's mad all the time."

"Nobody's mad all the time."

"She is."

I pondered this for a while. "Was she mad today?"

"She was really mad today. For no reason."

"Did one of the boys do something wrong?"

"I just wanted a drink."

Okay, so she was mad at you. "What happened?"

"I got in line at the water fountain and when it was my turn, she said 'Time's up' and I said 'But I didn't get a drink' and she sent me to the principal's office." Jamie's lower lip quivered.

"I bet that didn't make you feel very good."

"No."

"What did the principal say?"

"She likes me. She told me I'm practicing hard and I'm going to be the best soccer player on the team. And then she said some people have bad days."

Bad days indeed. Had Orchid had a bad day? She seemed so sweet at book club, drinking her wine, and suggesting a leadership book for kids.

Jamie said something I didn't quite catch.

"What, sweetheart?"

"She gets mad when we don't do what she says and she makes us put our heads down on our desks. She makes us fold our arms and sit there forever with our faces hidden. To punish us."

I was shocked. "Does your teacher agree with this?"

"It's only when she's out of the room."

Jamie's excitement over catching the trout had gone. I wanted that childish glee back in my life. "Well," I said, "the principal thinks you're great and I think you're the greatest. We're not going to worry about Miss Fishbait."

He giggled. "Miss Fishbait, Miss Fishbait!"

I was a bit aghast at the disrespect I'd wrought, but Orchid Fisher sounded disrespectful herself. It was good to hear Jamie laugh again. We climbed in the car with our two rainbow trophies and drove home. For several days I dithered back and forth on whether I should call Jamie's principal. The head down on the desk routine was dreadful, but I decided not to make waves.

I heard a shout over the noise of my blow dryer. People often wonder who styles a hairdresser's hair. The answer is: I do.

When Kayla Prothero burst through the door of my workroom, I took one look at her head and erupted. "What happened to you?"

"I tried to straighten my hair."

"Looks like you fried it."

Kayla's teenaged wail rose and faded like an ambulance hurtling down the highway.

I pictured her bending over an ironing board with her mother's steam iron trying to make her naturally frizzy hair swing as straight as a cheerleader's. Her head looked like a Brillo pad.

"This calls for a deep protein treatment," I said, taking Kayla by the hand. "The Portuguese Pump-up." I brandished a white and gold bottle.

"What's that?"

"A luxurious hair treatment that will restore the protein damaged by your flat iron," I said, as if the instrument had done the job all by itself without intervention by a human hand. "But it's not for the faint of heart."

"Is it dangerous?"

"To the purse." I whispered a figure and she squealed. "The Pump-up is an eight-step process. It takes two hours, but when we're done, you'll have beautiful, silky hair."

"All I've got is this babysitting money." She pressed a handful of bills into my palm.

I unraveled the ball. "This will do for today, but you'll owe me three hours of babysitting. Will that work?"

"Anything. Just make it go away."

As I squirted the first of eight Portuguese-speaking potions onto her scalp, I parroted the description on the back of the bottle. "This special formula prepares each hair shaft for the Professional Pump-up Potion." Kayla scrunched her eyes. The fragrance of "Mediterranean Florals" filled the salon.

After dispensing the contents of another gold bottle labeled "La Bomba," Kayla became quite chatty. I learned about the date with the captain of the football team that instigated the do-it-yourself hair straightening.

"How's your mother?" I asked, when she took a breath. Kayla's mother Shelley was my best friend in high school. She married her teenage sweetheart the same year Carl and I tied the knot. I remembered how stressed-out she looked at book club two weeks before.

"Mom's so confused," Kayla said. "She's going through Grandpa Prothero's medical bills."

I didn't need to consult my Client Notebook to know what Kayla was talking about. Shelley Prothero is one of those caregivers caught between generations. At 34 she had five children between the ages of six and sixteen and, until last year, two sets of aging parents between the ages of 70 and 85.

"How's your other grandpa?" I asked.

"He's on his way out, too." Death was a known quantity in the Prothero household. Grandpa Prothero died last year and so did Shelley's mother.

"Is Medicare taking care of the bills?"

"Yeah, but it's hard for Mom to make sense of it all. She's even had me try. There are numbers called diagnosis codes and dates of service and stuff with initials. Mom found three boxes of unopened bills when she dismantled Grandpa Prothero's house. She's had papers all over the bedroom floor for weeks now."

"What's she trying to do?"

"Match the stuff that's paid with the stuff that was done."

"I take it that's not easy."

"Near impossible. Medicare has their codes, doctors have their medical terms, hospitals call it something different. Mother is tearing her hair out."

I hoped not literally.

Kayla's wail returned. "I wanted to buy her a massage with my babysitting money, but now I've gone and spent it."

"Don't worry about your mom, Kayla. I'll take care of her."

"Will you?"

"Of course. Let's go back to the sink for a rinse now. Then you'll get Rigor de Mascar—a powerful enriching mask. Yours will be the most gorgeous hair at the ball, Cinderella."

Kayla twisted in her chair. "Oh, Tracy, you do take care of me!"

With Kayla out the door, I texted Annabelle Davina. She's my salon masseuse. Annabelle went to the hippy school of hard knocks where she learned to turn her New Age, crystal-toting, incense-burning know-how into dollars and cents. I scheduled a massage for Shelley the next day at eleven a.m.

As we emojied off, Mrs. Beale walked in the door wearing a neck brace.

"What happened to you?" I asked.

"A pickup truck rear-ended me." Mrs. Beale's head was rigid and her lips hardly moved.

"Looks bad." Morsels of egg and toast dotted the shiny black plastic of the neck brace, which looked like a high-tech torture instrument that had found its way into a high school cafeteria.

"Will you be able to remove the brace for your haircut?"

"Yes, but we'll have to cut dry. I don't think I can lower my head onto the sink."

Good—another injury to Mrs. Beale's neck was a risk I wasn't about to take. I consulted my Client Notebook. "Age: 47. Shoulder-length page boy, tendency to split ends. Husband: Personal injury lawyer."

I chose a peach colored cape and a matching terry. "Let's get you all spruced up," I said, sponging the brace clean after she removed it. "Would you like some tea, water or a probiotic drink?"

"Water would be nice." Mrs. Beale's voice had a high staccato rhythm. "My husband insisted I go straight to the emergency room. 'There's no fooling around with whiplash,' he said."

"What did they do?" I asked, handing her the ice water which she sipped with her chin in the air.

"An MRI and CAT scan. I was feeling okay, but the body releases so much adrenaline I didn't realize I had a problem until later."

I began to clip the hair on the side of her face where it angled toward her chin.

"The other driver was at fault," she said. "All my medical bills will be paid by their insurance." Mrs. Beale took another sip of her ice water with a slight jerk of her neck. "Ow!"

I stopped cutting.

"Just a twinge," she said, as visions of her attorney husband danced in my head. "There's muscle pain all down my back and my right arm. Even my jaw hurts."

"What are you doing for the pain?"

"My neighbor has been raving about that young chiropractor on Main Street. Whiteside. She says he does wonders. I'm going to try him out."

I shuddered. The first time I visited a chiropractor, he stood at the head of his exam table and wrenched my neck to the right. I asked him not to do it again, but he wrenched my neck to the left. I haven't darkened his door since.

"Have you been to a chiropractor before, Mrs. Beale?"

"Never."

"Some of my customers swear by chiropractic adjustments, but others believe it's alternative medicine that doesn't work for everybody."

"The insurance covers it," she said, her voice more staccato than ever. "That's good enough for me."

I handed her the mirror. "Take a look at the back."

Mrs. Beale eased out of the chair and inspected her hair, turning her whole body. With a noise of approval, she reached for the neck brace. All stretched up again like a heron with its beak in the air, she stalked to the front desk where she plucked a wallet from her purse, bending over from the waist to view her array of plastic.

"I hope you feel better soon," I said, as I processed her credit card.

"Thank you.

"Let me get the door for you."

When she backed her car out of my parking lot, I breathed a sigh of relief, as all thoughts of her litigating husband drove away with her.

Margaret Pyle strode through the salon looking like a platinum blonde bimbo out of a Swedish porn movie. That was not unusual. Her teased bouffant hairstyle was gone. For years, she'd styled her luxurious white-gold mane into a long blonde flip with a teased up crown, reminiscent of white go-go boots and mini-skirts.

"I met a man." Her wicked brown eyes crinkled as if this were the funniest thing that had happened to her in the last six minutes.

"So what else is new?" I said. Margaret Pyle meets men every day at Fu Tsu's Hardware and Auto Supply.

"His name is Barry," she said. "He does not like teased hair."

This was news. Margaret has never kowtowed to the personal preferences of any man. Husbands Number One through Five have had to bow to her "my way or the highway" policy regarding just about everything.

"Why change now?" I said out loud before I could stop myself. "I'm not complaining. Teasing damages your hair."

"You've never promised me a three-week all-expenses-paid trip to Venice."

"To quit teasing your hair?"

"Sto praticando già il mio italiano," she said.

"Which means?"

"I'm practicing my Italian already."

"Who is this Barry?"

"He's a doctor. When we're on our first ride on the canals I'm going sing 'Stavo solo scherzando.'" She gesticulated like an opera singer.

"What does that mean?"

"It means 'I'm just teasing.' We're going to Venice and when we come back, so will my usual hair style."

"That'll go over big."

"The man can take it." She hefted her humongous pocketbook onto the coffee table and dropped her shapely derriere onto the sofa. "So—why did you want to see me?"

What Margaret couldn't do with an Excel spreadsheet would fit into a flea's overnight bag, and our mutual friend Shelley Prothero needed her expertise. All thoughts of the doctor who didn't like teased hair flew out of my head as I explained the reason I asked Margaret to stop by.

She got the problem right away. "So you want me to do some moonlight accounting—organize Shelley's medical bills and EOB statements and find out who owes what?"

"EOB statements?"

"'Explanation of Benefits. That's the name of the statements Shelley gets from the insurance companies and Medicare."

"Can you give her a good deal?"

"No charge. Shelley's my friend too; I'm happy to help her."

"Good." I expected no less. We all went to high school together.

"When's she coming to have her massage with Annabelle Davina?" Margaret asked.

"Tomorrow at eleven. I figure you can drop by on your lunch hour after her massage is over."

"Will do." She reclined deeper into the sofa and scratched her thigh. It was a totally absent-minded gesture that looked languid, lazy and incredibly sensuous—just the kind of thing that drove men crazy. I hoped this guy Barry would last longer than the last one. Margaret tended to fold 'em not hold 'em.

The next morning Annabelle Davina arrived around ten o'clock for organic tea and pumpkin bran muffins which Jamie and I had baked the night before. Annabelle is tall—about five foot eleven. She folded her long, flat-chested body into an upholstered chair and sipped her mug of tea with a dreamy look.

"I have been channeling energy for my patients," she said. "Energy is all around us. It is intelligent and conscious."

I looked around. I saw my hair products, my computer, my area rug, and my masseuse folded up into a soft chair much too small for her tall body. Maybe she had a point. This was all intelligent and conscious stuff produced with a lot of energy. But why was Annabelle talking to me like this? She knew I didn't believe in energy work.

I recalled the afternoon I spent at the Psychic Fair, held at the local Best Western, where women came from miles around to have their Tarot cards read, their hands hennaed, and their tummies stuffed with organic, gluten free, GMO-prohibited goodies. I paid twenty dollars for "energy work" which consisted of some fairly onion-laden breathing transmitted from a lady who hovered her hands over my body for fifteen minutes. I had felt nothing and told Annabelle so.

But today Annabelle assumed an innocent, sincere aura enhanced by her doe-like eyes whose lash extensions appeared to have been purchased at Lash My World. "I make the energy flow," she said. "My own intellect is not involved. I see without knowing. The intention of the Universe is to make whoever I touch better, complete, and whole."

I raised my eyebrows. "Annabelle, come off it. This is me you're talking to. Shelley doesn't need energy work."

"It is the most beneficent thing."

"You sound like a commercial from a New Age shyster," I said, getting up and going to my computer. "Shelley is hurting; she needs a full-body massage, not some flimflam stuff."

Annabelle detached herself from the upholstered chair. "A massage was the first thing on my mind."

That wasn't obvious to me. "Shiatsu or Swedish?"

"Whatever she wishes."

"Swedish, then. Let's get the massage room ready."

As we tucked in the sheets, warmed the massage lotion, ensured the heating pad was the perfect temperature, and chose the most relaxing music, I wondered why my blood was boiling. This was Annabelle Davina, the loveliest, most selfless, most soulful post-hippy hippy ever. Why was she promoting energy work?

I excused myself from the massage room and went to the front door where Shelley was coming up the path. Her shoulders were slumped as if she were carrying the weight of the world. "I'm so glad you're here," I told her, hugging her, then holding her out in front of me. The creases in her forehead looked like a river delta; I wanted her forehead to resemble a smooth sand dune.

"Kayla told me what you did for her," she said. "Aren't kids a treasure?"

"Teenagers," I said. "We got her fixed up, and Jamie is looking forward to an evening of fun with his favorite babysitter."

"I'm glad you didn't discount the price," she said. "Kids need to know how much things cost."

"So true."

"And I want to pay for my massage."

"Not an option." I commandeered her arm and led her to the massage room.

"Annabelle!" Shelley said. "I haven't seen you for so long."

"Too long," said Annabelle. I could see the sincerity in her eyes came from within. I wondered what I'd been worried about and felt a pang of guilt.

"I'll leave you two alone," I murmured, and shut the massage room door with a gentle click.

Shelley emerged an hour later. The Mississippi River Delta on her fore-head was less noticeable. I gave her a glass of ice water. She sank into one of my upholstered chairs.

"Yoo hoo!" Margaret swooped into the salon looking like a cockatoo, in her clinging pink sweater and lime green skirt. Her heels clacked on the bamboo floor before she hit my pretty patterned area rug. Descending on Shelley, she gave her a big smack and left a lipstick print on her shiny massage-oiled cheek.

"I can see you've had a nice time," Margaret said. "Not as good as sex though. Does that man of yours service you at all?"

From anyone else this question would be invasive but Shelley and I have known Margaret forever, and we expect no less.

"It's too much trouble," Shelley mumbled into her ice water.

"Get yourself a vibrator, girl," said Margaret. "The little bullet kind—takes all the work out of it for Jack and he will make you smile."

Shelley cringed and I laughed.

"Margaret is here to do you a favor, Shelley," I said, "but not of the sex therapist kind." I shot Margaret a warning look, which was lost on her because she was inspecting her perfectly sculpted acrylic nails. "Margaret is going to do some forensic accounting on your parents' medical bills."

Margaret grinned as if the prospect of all that paperwork was as entic-ing to her as chocolate mousse. "I'm going to organize them and figure out what's what."

"But there are hundreds of papers," Shelley said. "Stacks and stacks." The furrows over Shelley's brow returned, making her forehead look like a cornfield before sowing.

"I'm sure they've made you see double," Margaret said, "but I have my methods. Shelley, you have to understand that more than half of Medicare bills have mistakes in them. Unreasonable medical costs can be appealed and you can win. Hospitals have been overcharging to compensate for the uninsured and you can negotiate with them. We'll get a handle on your family's medical costs and everything will be under control."

"I thought we were going to go bankrupt," she whispered, tears filling her eyes.

"Not if I can help it, Shelley," said Margaret. "I'll need the policies of all your insurance carriers that were in effect before Medicare kicked in, information about any supplemental insurance, and all the paperwork. I understand there are three boxes?"

"Yes, but that's only from Jack's parents' stuff," Shelley said. "I have files from my parents, too."

"All right, bring it all to the hardware store this afternoon."

Shelley looked at Margaret with a relieved expression.

"And bring me any appointment books or calendars too."

"What do you mean?"

"Anything that documents when your parents and Jack's parents went to the doctor."

"I drove them to all their appointments."

"Do you keep a calendar?"

"Yes. I have a little black date book for every year."

"I'll need those." Margaret rose to go. "Give me a week or two. Then we'll meet again."

Shelley hugged Margaret. "Thanks."

"Wait a minute." I wiped Margaret's lipstick from Shelley's cheek, pleased to see her looking so happy.

After Margaret and Shelley left, I collected the water glass and tea mug before I realized Annabelle was still in the massage room. From the door, I could see her seated on the table in the Lotus position. The lights were dim and the spa music was off. Her back was straight, her hair was straight, her nose was straight. Everything about Annabelle seemed straight.

"Annabelle?"

"Tracy." She uncoiled her body and slipped off the massage table. "I have an idea for you."

"What's that?"

"I'm working for a chiropractor giving massages and doing energy work. He wants to be full service and offer his patients manicures and pedicures. He'll give you referrals if you tell your clients about his chiropractic services."

"A bit of reciprocal marketing?" I said.

"It's a nice idea." Her lash extensions fluttered. "Your spirits will complement each other and it will cost you nothing."

"Who is this chiropractor?" I asked.

"His name is Whiteside."

"That's the second time I've heard his name this week. Mrs. Beale mentioned him yesterday."

"He's young and hip and very popular. My appointments have tripled since I joined his practice."

I wondered how Annabelle's usual tie-dyed style fit in with a chiropractor's clinical white, but then this guy Whiteside sounded far more modern than the chiropractor I visited.

"I'll think about it," I said, giving her cash for Shelley's massage. "Thanks for coming, Annabelle."

"You're welcome. I think Shelley feels a lot better."

"I know she does."

I saw Annabelle out the door. Then I turned the "Back in 30 minutes" sign over, locked the front door, and went out to lunch.

After lunch Heather Desmond arrived at one o'clock. My Client Notebook said: Age-52. Retired from California real estate market. Raises chickens, goats, llamas. Hair color: Ash blonde. Cut: Neck length, feathered ends, no bangs.

Heather reached into her bag and pulled out a plastic tub that I knew was filled with the most delicious, creamy hors d'oeuvre spread I'd ever tasted.

"Goat cheese," I said. "My favorite."

"I almost brought you some wool—it's shearing time for the llamas—but I didn't think you wanted to wash and card and spin all that stuff."

I shook my head.

"You could take it to Spinderella and Spinderfella in the big valley," she said. "Wouldn't you like to knit a pair of mittens for winter?"

"Even if you gave me a skein of wool from your beautiful llamas, I wouldn't have time to knit. In fact, I don't know how."

We talked about the decline and resurgence of women's traditional handicrafts—knitting, embroidery, tapestries, and tatting. When Heather Desmond left the salon, she looked eager to do all those things.

A few minutes later Sarah Binford breezed in smelling like the out-of-doors. This was a darned sight better than the last time she came in, when she smelled like a short order cook. I had to wash her hair twice to get the deep fryer grease out of it.

"Sarah, you look fantastic."

She'd transformed from a barrel-chested square on legs to a trim size six in Reeboks. "I have a new career," she said.

I swathed her in a rose cape which matched the color in her cheeks. "Doing what?"

"Live Signage Marketing."

"What's that?"

"I'm one of those people who jump up and down and wave signs to get customers to patronize a business."

"You're kidding."

I always wondered who would be desperate enough to do a job like that.

"Today I wore a clown costume and got several families to choose ABC Pizza over Jocko's. Yesterday, I wore a Statue of Liberty outfit and you should have seen the cars peel off and go into Sam Acorn's Tax Prep instead of that national chain."

"Isn't all that jumping around exhausting?"

"Not anymore." She poked her arm out from under the cape and held up her bicep for me to feel.

"Impressive," I said.

"I canceled Pilates and I'm saving hundreds of dollars. I've never felt so good."

"You look terrific."

"I've got several more customers. Woodie's Car Wash, Blain's Farm and Fleet Mechanics, and Amando's Mercado. I'm going to hire people to help me soon. Live Signage Marketing is hot. It's a growth industry."

I turned the salon chair to the right and gazed at her with a practiced eye. Sarah had naturally curly hair that she wore in a short bob. She used to look like a kewpie doll with a fuzzy beanie on top of her head, but fifty pounds lighter, she now looked more like a bubble head Barbie.

"Sarah, I would recommend a slight adjustment in your hairstyle. Let's allow the back and sides to grow a little more so the shape is more elongated. Your curls will wrap around your neck rather than float above your ears. I think it will be very flattering."

"How much longer?" she asked.

"Almost shoulder length." I produced my iPad from under the counter. "Let me show you some pictures."

We browsed curly hair styles for a few minutes. "Okay, let's do it!" she said.

"You'll look sensational."

I shaped the hair as agreed and we were silent for a while until she piped up. "I saw a weird thing happen yesterday."

"Mmm?" I had a hair clip in my mouth so that's all I could say.

"I was waving my sign outside of Sam Acorn's and there was a fender bender—happened right in front of me. Two cars collided at the turn signal. It was clearly an accident. They pulled over to the side, but the weird thing was, another car stopped and a guy ran out to give each of the drivers a business card. Then he drove away."

"How weird is that?" I said, thinking it was weird indeed.

"Very weird," she said, "until I found out what the card said. One of the drivers threw his in the gutter."

"Litter bug."

"It was from Whiteside Chiropractic."

I absorbed this information with interest.

"You know those accident lawyers?" she said.

"Ambulance chasers?"

"I think he was like them."

Jamie sat at the kitchen counter painting me a picture. "Mom, can we have Tater Tots for dinner?"

"I'm not buying Tater Tots any more. We don't know what's in them. I'm only buying real potatoes."

"There's potatoes in Tater Tots."

"And sugar and salt and fat, too."

Jamie had used up his allotted hour of video games so I let him paint with my new watercolors. I want him to be creative. Computer games have their place, but they're somebody else's idea of fun—a game designer somewhere who dictates what children do and see.

When the back door opened, I greeted my husband.

"Stop kissing!" said Jamie.

"I'll kiss you too!" I puckered my lips and leaned toward him.

"Mom!"

I roughed up his hair instead.

Carl bumped Jamie's shoulder with his fist. This was a guy thing. No touching without it looking like a knockout in the eighth round or a quarterback going for the first down. Fists, elbow bumps, head butts, arm wrestles. A real kiss? Never.

"Dad! Let's throw the football."

"Okay, I'll get changed."

Carl disappeared upstairs and I pulled out ingredients for dinner. Spaghetti, garlic, onion, yellow peppers, fresh tomatoes, sweet Italian sausage, Italian bread.

Carl re-appeared only to escape out the back door with Jamie and the football. I prepared the meal alone. It was a traditional arrangement—men playing, women working.

Over dinner, I sought the answer to the question stewing in my mind all day—was it legal to solicit business at the scene of an accident? I told Carl what Sarah had witnessed.

"There's no law in this state against that kind of marketing," Carl said, "but there have been some big cases against it recently. One was in Minnesota."

"What happened?"

"Two car insurance companies sued a big chiropractor in the Twin Cities. Apparently, the clinic used accident reports to find people and call them to solicit appointments. They even sent cars to pick them up."

"Sounds helpful."

"It was so helpful that the Minnesota legislature made 'runners and cappers' illegal." Carl twirled spaghetti on his fork and stuffed it in his mouth. "Good dinner."

"Yummy," Jamie said, tomato sauce all over his face.

"The suit accused the chiropractors of submitting more than one million dollars in bogus insurance bills over two years," Carl said.

"Wow," I said.

"Mom, what does bogus mean?"

"It means false or fake," I said.

Carl turned to his son. Being a policeman, he was always careful to explain morality. "When a bad guy says something untrue or does something wrong, that's bogus, Jamie. It hurts people. It touches everyone's lives in a bad way."

"We all pay for insurance fraud," I said. "Our rates go up."

"What's insurance?" Jamie asked.

"Insurance is a way for everybody be protected against the cost of an accident or an illness," I said. "Everyone pays a little bit so people who need to pay a lot are taken care of."

"It's a way for a lot of people to help out a few people who are unlucky, Jamie," Carl said. "And you never know who's going to be unlucky. It could be us, or it could be one of our friends."

I thought of Shelley who was terrified that her family would go bankrupt when insurance didn't cover all the bills.

"Time for bath and a story," I said.

Jamie took his plate to the sink. Carl took his. Then they rinsed them and put them in the dishwasher. I have the most helpful men in the world.

My first appointment the next morning was Harriet Carpenter, a friend of Mrs. Beale's—the lady with the neck brace.

"I've heard so much about you, Tracy," Harriet Carpenter said, as she sank down on my sofa next to my bowl of fake fruit from Bali.

When people sit there they cannot see the innards of my salon—not the hair washing sinks, nor the haircutting chairs, nor the small refrigerator where I keep the juices and the ice for their drinks. The front area of my salon looks like a well-appointed living room where I get to know a new client.

"Amazing we've never met before," I said, taking in Harriet Carpenter's manicured hands, her coifed and frosted hair, and her well-tailored business suit.

"We came to town five years ago but I only just moved near Penny Beale. I'm renting a condo in her complex."

"Would you like a cup of tea, some ice water or a probiotic drink?"

"The drink, please."

"Kale lemon or turmeric ginger?"

"Goodness." She hesitated. "The ginger."

When I gave her a glass, she touched it to her lips. "Delicious," she said, then parked it on a coaster on the coffee table.

"What brought you to our town?" I asked.

"I manage Whiteside Chiropractic."

No wonder she convinced Mrs. Beale to visit the clinic.

"I've known Dr. Whiteside for years. We started out in Scottsdale where we ran a very successful practice."

"Why did the doctor move here?"

"Weather—too much heat in Arizona—and he loves skiing."

"Everyone loves skiing around here," I said, which was a little white lie. The cowboys I know don't ski. The housewives I know don't ski. The tradesmen I know don't ski. Few of the policemen ski. Only the newcomers in our gated communities ski. It has become a rich man's sport.

We began to talk about her hair. Harriet Carpenter wanted to keep her frosted look and have me follow the lines of the cut already in place. She wanted her eyebrows waxed and the hair plucked out of the mole on her chin. We did all that and the entire visit took an hour and a half.

The whole time, she told me nothing about herself. She was one of the most closed persons I had ever met. From her coifed and hair-sprayed style to her starched blouse and dress-for-success suit, she gave off an untouchable aura.

When she proffered her credit card at my salon desk, she said, "I do hope you'll consider the offer that Annabelle gave you yesterday."

"Annabelle?"

"We think the world of Annabelle. Such a presence. Such composure. She makes our clients feel better just being with her."

I didn't say anything.

"I do think businesses can prosper by referring clients to each other." She smiled at me but not with her eyes. "You're in a position to know about the health and well-being of so many people, as are we. Their total happiness is of utmost importance to us. Their health *and* their appearance. We can refer to you and you can refer to us. Isn't that a natural thing to do?"

Her voice was almost mesmerizing. I felt as if I were listening to a recording prepared to soothe and persuade me, and even put me to sleep. I said yes without thinking. *The most natural thing in the world.*

Then I woke up. "But I'm afraid I can't make referrals for something I've never experienced."

"Of course. Come by for an evaluation at a deep discount." She handed me a coupon. "I know Dr. Whiteside would love to meet you."

"Thanks."

"Goodbye." She moved toward the door. I leaned back in my desk chair, a little stunned. The probiotic drink sat on the coffee table. Full. I wondered if she actually tasted it at all.

Margaret Pyle burst in my front door carrying a red leather briefcase. This particular briefcase retailed for three hundred dollars—I knew because I was with her when she bought it at the Leather Emporium.

"I've come to my senses," she said, sweeping everything off the coffee table and shoveling file folders out of the briefcase.

Margaret's bouffant hairdo was back, loftier than ever.

"Why the hair teasing?" I asked, sitting down next to her.

"I'm about to show you why." The acid in her voice could have disinfected all the combs in my salon. "I organized Shelley's bills by date of service. Then I matched the Explanation of Benefits from the insurance companies with the medical providers' statements. Here's what I found."

Margaret extracted an Excel spreadsheet from a stiff-backed folder. "Before he went on Medicare, Jack's father had a herniated disk. The hospital charged $56,000, the anesthesiologist $4,300 and the orthopedist $133,000. All that was covered by the insurance company, except a $117,000 fee for an out-of-network assistant surgeon. The hospital is still trying to collect that fee."

The amounts were staggering—more than $400,000 for one operation, and the hospital was trying to dun Shelley and her family for more than twenty-five percent of the bill.

"But that doesn't explain why the teasing is back," I said, just to be clear.

"There's more," said Margaret.

I listened up.

"The orthopedist referred Jack's father to a chiropractor here in town. Over the course of two years, lots of X-rays were billed. I asked Shelley about the exorbitant number and she said Jack's father hated X-rays—he was very leery of radiation—and would never have agreed to them."

"Fraud?" I asked.

"Yes. " Margaret gave me a *listen to this* look. "Jack's mother is still going to the same chiropractor. I compared the dates of service with Shelley's calendar. There are lots of cross outs and dates where appointments were re-scheduled, but the chiropractic office billed for them all."

I understood why Margaret was looking at me like a prosecuting attorney. "Greedy little office," I said.

"And here's the difficult part. They're billing for massages that Shelley's mother doesn't get—she says she has 'energy work' done, whatever that is."

A deathly feeling came over me. "Margaret, what's the name of this chiropractor?"

"Whiteside."

I gulped.

"*Barry* Whiteside," Margaret said, emphasizing the first name as if she were saying 'Toad.'"

I gazed at her with sudden comprehension. "That wouldn't be the Barry you've been speaking Italian with? The one who doesn't like teasing?"

"It would."

"I guess Venice is out then?"

"*Arrivederci.*"

My eyes swiveled up to Margaret's bouffant hairdo. "I always said that hairstyle becomes you."

"You're damned right." She patted her hair. "So what are we going to do about Shelley?"

"Well, the first thing is, we need to get Annabelle out of there."

"Annabelle?"

I proceeded to tell her about our friend's gainful employment in the energy field. "She shouldn't go anywhere near that place."

Margaret eyed me with a crafty gleam. "But she could be a plant!"

"You've got to be kidding," I said. "She's too sweet to be a spy. This is a job for professionals."

"I'm sure you have someone in mind."

"Carl works with an agent from the local FBI field office. Would you talk to her?"

"You betcha."

I looked down at the pile of insurance statements and spreadsheets. Who would believe they told more tales than the story of a family burdened with end-of-life cares? Then I remembered Harriet Carpenter. Now *there* was an untold story.

"Margaret, someone else may be involved in all this."

"Who?"

"Barry has a business manager. Have you met her?"

"No. Barry and I meet in bars."

I suspected that was not the only place. "Her name is Harriet Carpenter," I said. "She came in the other day and suggested we do some reciprocal marketing."

"You mean, I scratch your butt if you scratch mine?"

"Exactly."

"Did you take her up on it?"

"I said I couldn't recommend something I'd never tried and she offered me twenty percent off my first consultation."

There was dead silence as Margaret rose from the sofa to her full six-foot height and squinted down at me.

"No!" I said.

"It won't hurt," she said.

"Yes, it will," I said.

"You owe it to Shelley."

"But—"

"He's milking and bilking our friend!"

I was feeling as hog-tied as a heifer at a livestock auction. "All right. I'll go," I said. "But I don't know what good it would do. I doubt I could tell anything from just meeting the guy. The FBI's got to put someone inside who can really snoop."

"So what are we going to do about that?"

"And what are we going to do about Annabelle?" Margaret gathered up her files and dropped them into her three-hundred dollar red leather briefcase.

"How about if I invite Annabelle over to our house next week?" I said. "You can bring your briefcase."

"Will Carl be there?"

"I'll make sure he is."

"Sounds like a plan," she said.

"But keep quiet about my snooping at the chiropractor's office."

"Why?"

"Sometimes Carl sees me as helpful and sometimes he sees me as meddling."

"How are you meddling?" asked Margaret. "You're just going to the chiropractor."

I marveled that Margaret didn't get this. Men's egos are easily disturbed. What would be seen as help from a perfect stranger would be seen as Interference from a well-meaning wife. Carl had laughed at my ideas about the Spiderman robbery and scoffed at my theories about the train wreck. He's reminded me often about how wrong I was about our esteemed city councilor, Martha Farquhar.

"I'm learning to go more slowly," I said. "It's Carl's business, not mine."

"Tracy," said Margaret, "I'm surprised at you. Where's the spirited girl I knew in high school who sashayed in from Colorado and stole the heart of the school's Most Valuable Player? He worships the ground you walk on."

"I know, and I want to keep it that way."

Jamie pushed cauliflower around his plate as if he could hide the fact that the florets were still there after fifteen minutes of shuffleboard. I'm not the kind of cook who boils cauliflower until it's mushy and tasteless; maybe that was the problem.

"Jamie," I said, "if you push your cauliflower around anymore they will have run the Indianapolis 500."

"I hate cauliflower."

"They're delicious."

"No, they're not!"

"Jamie," Carl said quietly. "Speak to your mother with respect."

"I don't care for cauliflower," Jamie said. "May I please be excused?"

"Not until you eat three bites," I said.

"Is there any more steak?" Carl asked.

I got up to slice more ribeye. When I returned, the florets were gone.

"Good job," I said to Jamie, eyeing my husband. I suspected he scooped the florets off Jamie's plate and washed them down with beer, but I let this be their little secret.

"When are Margaret and Annabelle coming?" Carl asked.

The doorbell rang.

"Right now."

Jamie took his plate to the sink. I answered the door. Carl stood up when my friends entered. We chatted about the usual and then Margaret plunked her red brief case on the coffee table while Annabelle folded herself into a deep armchair.

"Tracy thinks you should know what I've found, Carl," Margaret said, removing her files from their handsome red leather environs. "And you too, Annabelle." She walked them through the Whiteside insurance fraud. Carl leaned over the paperwork and questioned her in detail. She provided clear answers.

When Carl was finished, Annabelle spoke. "So Barry Whiteside is billing $140 for my energy work?" Her voice was so soft we could hardly hear her.

"That's right," said Margaret.

Annabelle sat up from the depths of the armchair like a crane unfolding her wings. Her face beamed with a beatific light, as if she were channeling from another world. "I feel a shift in the Universe," she said. "A planetary declension is dragging an energy force through a primal divide."

Carl stirred. Margaret looked dazed. I hung onto every word.

"We are hurtling into a state of fear, greed, and deception," Annabelle continued, "in which I can no longer perform my energy work at Whiteside Chiropractic."

Carl reached out and patted Annabelle's shoulder. "That's the right thing to do."

"I had no idea."

"You weren't to know."

I was proud of my man—a compassionate cop who knew how to make citizens feel calm in the face of calamity.

"And to think I gave him a good discount." Annabelle sounded less other-worldly.

Margaret's eyes de-glazed. "How much?" she asked in decibels far louder than Annabelle's.

"He pays me seven dollars a patient."

Margaret snorted. "A 2,000 percent markup to $140 dollars! That's a tidy little profit."

I marveled that Margaret could calculate percentages within seconds but that's why I'm a hairdresser and she's an accountant.

"In exchange for such a deep discount over my normal $15 dollars an hour," Annabelle said, "he was going to take me on an all-expenses-paid trip to Venice."

The room turned 2,000 percent hotter than it was a moment before. I could see steam coming out of Margaret's ears. Before she had a chance to say something dumb I stood up. "Would anyone like a cold drink?"

Margaret followed me into the kitchen. "That S.O.B.—is he boinking Annabelle too?"

"I doubt it. Annabelle is dating that bass player in the Grateful Dead tribute band."

"Then what's he offering her a trip to Venice for?"

"Probably just a perk—something to dupe poor Annabelle into giving him a discount."

"Two thousand percent." Margaret balled up her fists. "I'll give him 2,000 percent!"

"Calm down. They'll hear you."

"I don't care if they do."

"Drink this and listen to me." I poured several fingers of bourbon onto a sugar cube and added a splash of water. "I know what to do on my chiro visit now."

She took a sip of bourbon, then shot the rest.

"If he offered you a trip to Venice and he offered Annabelle a trip to Venice, who else has been offered a trip?" I slid my eyes at her sideways. "Think carefully now; this isn't a trick question."

A gleam appeared under my forensic accountant's mascaraed lashes. "His office manager."

"I'll bet Harriet Carpenter is studying Italian at this very moment." I poured two glasses of white wine and a mug of beer. "All I have to do is mention your trip and let jealousy rear its ugly little head. She'll turn state's evidence and presto. Mr. Travel Agent loses his passport."

When the day of my discounted appointment arrived, I put a "Back at 2:30" sign on my salon door and drove to Whiteside Chiropractic.

The waiting room was furnished in blues, tans and browns—tasteful colors but perfectly boring. The receptionist had a China doll face—blond hair, blue eyes, and perfect little white teeth. I bet she was studying Italian too.

After filling out a sheet on a clipboard, (Did I have insurance? Did I have secondary insurance? Did I have supplemental benefits? Did I have chiropractic benefits?) I was ushered into the nether regions of the practice where the walls were adorned with pictures of spiny skeletons that made my bones hurt just looking at them.

I sat on an exam table and glanced around the room—cool and medical, just like every clinic. Why was the temperature always so cold? Why was the hum of the HVAC system always so loud? Why did a room like this always feel so lonely?

I slipped off the exam table and heated my hands with hot water at the sink. Then I browsed the rack of magazines: *Health*, *Parents*, and *National Geographic Traveler*. I riffled through *National Geographic Traveler* and stopped at a story called *Made in Italy*. There was Venice, complete with pictures of gondoliers and St. Mark's Plaza.

The door opened behind me and I whirled around, but not before he caught a glimpse of the four-color, two-page spread. "You've been to Italy?" Whiteside asked.

"Never," I said, stepping away from him.

He was dark haired with even features and a virility I could feel. He smiled at me. "It's the most romantic city in the world. Are you married?" His eyes twinkled as if he'd made a joke.

"Yes," I said, a bit too quickly.

"Make sure you take your husband to Venice sometime. Guaranteed to put the zing back in any relationship. Now what's going on with you?"

He guided me through a practiced set of questions. "Any pain here? Here? You're standing a little awkwardly. Are you on your feet much in your job? Yes? What do you do?"

"I'm a hairdresser."

"That explains it," he said, probing lumbar vertebra L7. "Hairdressers have the worst spines in the world. Occupational hazard. Without proper alignment, you can't function at your peak."

My teeth clenched as his hands drifted from L7 closer to my derriere.

"I'm going to recommend a full set of X-rays so we know what we're dealing with." He faced me. "And a full body massage. The masseuse will find all those tight spots—you have them, don't you?" His white teeth glimmered. "And then a small adjustment based on what I see in the X-rays. How does that sound?"

He didn't wait for my answer but opened the door and took me down the hall to his radiologist. I got the works—front, side, and rear. Then I was taken to a dim room smelling of patchouli where a bearded masseuse poked and pummeled with a running commentary about knots and toxins.

Back in the exam room, Barry Whiteside asked me to lie down. I climbed up on the cold, draped table, steeling my nerves for the inevitable. He rounded the corner by my neck, took hold of my head and wrenched it to the right.

"Ow!" I said. "Don't do that!"

He did it again.

Outside in the reception area, I was handed an invoice for $350.00—80 percent to be paid by my insurance company and 20 percent to be written off by Whiteside Chiropractic as my "complimentary service." Tucking the paper in my pocket, I asked the China Doll receptionist for Harriet Carpenter. She ushered me to her office.

"Harriet," I said, my neck listing to starboard as I approached her desk. "How wonderful to see you."

She glanced up from her computer with a perplexed expression.

"I'm Tracy Lemon, the hairdresser. Remember? You wanted to do some reciprocal marketing?"

"Oh, yes." She shot me a porcelain smile brighter than an Audi's headlights.

"I've just had an appointment and sampled all your services." I lowered my frame into her guest chair. "I'm very impressed."

"Marvelous." Her fingers flew over the keyboard and a machine on her credenza pumped out a dozen color-printed pieces of paper. "I have just the thing for our first promotion."

She thrust the papers into my hands. One set were coupons for 20 percent off a manicure at The Citrus Salon; the other set was for 20 percent off an introductory exam at Whiteside Chiropractic.

I didn't need to be an accounting whiz to calculate that 20 percent off a manicure at The Citrus Salon would net me $12.00 and 20 percent off a first visit at Whiteside Chiropractic net them $280.00.

"What a great idea," I said. "I'll be sure to send a lot of business your way." I looked Harriet in her plucked eyebrows. "And that Dr. Whiteside is so personable. So attractive; what a great guy!" I clasped the coupons to my heart. "Now I know why my dear friend Margaret Pyle is so taken with him. Have you met her? No? They're quite an Item. He's taking her on a trip to Venice."

Harriet's eyes narrowed, the creases at the bridge of her nose became as black as ash on the first day of Lent. Her dark eyes smoldered. Her lips twisted up and collided with the hairs around the rim of her nostrils.

"Did I say something wrong?"

"Dr. Whiteside's trip has been canceled," she said.

"Oh, that's too bad." I stood up. "When did that happen?"

"Recently."

"Margaret will be so disappointed."

"I dare say."

"Is there no rain check?"

"His wife is terminally ill."

"Wife! Dr. Whiteside is married?" I let my voice rise on the last word like a rocket from Cape Canaveral.

"She still lives in Scottsdale. He's been commuting every weekend by private jet."

"Dear me." I fanned myself with the coupons. "I didn't know. Margaret didn't know. I'm glad you told us." I turned to go.

"I wouldn't want your friend to labor under any delusions," she said, advancing on me.

"None of us, Harriet, want to labor under any delusions." I opened the door. "Thanks for the coupons. Bye bye."

I shut the door, and skipped down the hall.

Three weeks passed. I was running inventory on hair accessories for the high school prom when Annabelle walked in with a young black woman. She had a 'Fro and a muscular body. If I had to compare her with anyone famous, I'd say she looked like Angela Davis, the Sixties civil rights activist who's sometimes mentioned in one of the pictorial news magazines.

"Tracy, this is Rasheeta Jackson," Annabelle said. "I'm training her to be my replacement at Whiteside Chiropractic."

I smirked at Rasheeta and she smirked back.

"Energy work is so fruitful," I said. "Have you been investigating its benefits for long?"

"My search for true meaning began a few weeks ago," she said, "when I sought the insurance of a higher power, the ethics of the common man, and the true profits of a bonehead."

I winked at Annabelle. "You two can do energy work at my salon anytime."

She and Annabelle disappeared into the massage room and soon spa music emanated throughout the salon. Annabelle was teaching an apt pupil—Rasheeta, a Federal Bureau of Investigation insurance fraud investigator.

It turns out Medicare, Medicaid, private insurance companies, and the FBI all employ expert health care fraud investigators. When Carl brought Shelley Prothero's bills to the attention of our local FBI agent, Rasheeta and her colleagues set up camp right down the street from the cop shop.

That evening Margaret came over to our house for dinner. I told her the latest news about the FBI undercover agent and swore her to secrecy. "Don't tell Carl I told you about Rasheeta."

"My lips are zipped," she said.

Carl came in from the deck bearing meat from the grill. "What's that you said?"

"Just discussing the Whiteside case."

As we sat down to a meal of ham steak with potatoes, grilled onions, and cauliflower, Margaret said, "I always felt he was a two-timing S.O.B."

I rolled my eyes heavenward, but not for her to see.

"It pays to be suspicious," Carl said.

"What does suspicious mean?" asked Jamie.

"It's like that word 'bogus,' Jamie," I said, casting a glance at the cauliflower on Jamie's plate. "You don't trust it." The white florets had been pushed under his ham steak.

"If something's too good to be true, be suspicious," said Margaret.

I caught Jamie's eye.

"I'm going to eat all my cauliflower tonight, Mom," he announced.

"Highly suspicious," I said, looking at Carl. "Highly suspicious."

Case 4
The Cat in the Suitcase

• • • • • • • • • • • • •

Checking my calendar a few weeks later, I saw an appointment with Ralph Abramowicz. I opened my Client Notebook. Age: 37. Beard trim. Layered cut. Never married. From New York. Skier. Night staff at the Resort.

The Resort is our town's big draw—the most prestigious de-tox ranch west of the Mississippi and east of California.

Ralph sauntered in just past one o'clock. Muscular and bearded, he greeted me with a big wide grin revealing natural white teeth. When I offered refreshments, he settled for a probiotic on ice after glancing ever so briefly at my fake harvest from Bali. Ralph was the only customer who mourned the passing of my bowl of fresh fruit.

I draped him in sable brown, then set to work.

"How's Jamie?" Ralph always asks about my son. He loves children. I couldn't figure out why he'd never married.

"Doing well in school. He's on the soccer team and goes to Make-It Club every Thursday afternoon." I pulled out my cell phone. "Check this out."

Ralph admired the picture of Jamie with his robot made from recycled materials. "Is that an operational arm?" he asked.

"Complete with a retractable rope for tying up bad guys."

"Awesome." Ralph laughed. "Shows some real creativity." He looked closer at the picture. "That's a lot of duct tape!"

"Give a boy some duct tape, coffee cans, and cardboard tubes, and he'll have hours of fun."

"Right on, Tracy. You're such a good mother."

I glowed with pride. Ralph made this compliment with such sincerity I felt as if the world were painted-rose colored and I were Glinda, Good Witch of the South.

We lapsed into a companionable silence as I re-cut layers grown long over the past month. "How's work for you?" I asked.

"Good. Fairly quiet at night. A lot less stressful than the day shift."

"Is the Resort full?"

He sighed. "We're always full."

"The celebrity magazines often cover prescription drug abuse among the rich and famous."

He laughed.

"Why do people get addicted to pills, Ralph?"

"If I knew that, I would have the antidote."

I laughed.

"But I can tell you about my own experience with prescription pain-killers," he said.

I held my breath. Ralph was about to tell me his deepest secret and I was all ears.

"I started when I was fifteen. My father had a knee operation so the doctor gave him a prescription for a strong narcotic. Kids at school had been getting high and I wanted to be like everybody else. They told me it felt tingly and blissful. So I took one. It was everything they said. I felt as if I were floating away. All my teenage troubles were gone. The next day after school I got high again.

"Pretty soon Dad's prescription ran out and so did his need for painkillers. I had to figure out where else to get them. That's when I began stealing. I would go through medicine cabinets in my friends' houses. I found pills everywhere. I went to bed high and I went to school high. My grades went to shit. My parents couldn't understand what the problem was.

"But then one night in my senior year I went to a party. It was classic; the parents weren't home and we took over the house. Kids were drinking beer and slobbering all over the furniture. Girls and guys were draped everywhere—on the sofas, in the beds—and I was with my friends and a vial of OxyContin. We each took several pills and chased them down with beer. I was floating away as usual but my friend, Isaac, was zonked. We put him in a bed and partied on until the cops came at about three in the morning. Everyone scattered except Isaac."

Ralph lifted his head. I had stopped snipping a long time before.

"His heart had stopped."

My jaw dropped.

"That was the end of pills for me and the beginning of a new career. Of course, it didn't happen overnight. I confessed to my parents and they supported me. They sent me to a place like the Resort but for kids, and I recovered. I vowed I would help whoever I could to get free of drugs, and I've kept my promise. So that's a long answer to a very short question."

I didn't know what to say. Luckily, Ralph kept talking. "But why? Why do people get addicted to drugs? I'll never forget how one of my counselors gave me the answer. He asked me to think of that first high when I was floating the farthest away. He reminded me that all you can think about is feeling that way again. Only it's physically, chemically impossible. Your brain has changed and you need more drugs to repeat the first high, but you never come close. That's why I think I'm effective at the Resort. The patients know I've tried drugs and I've found out they don't work."

He stopped talking. There was silence for a while.

"I never knew," I said.

"Of course you never knew. I never told you. But, Tracy, I've told this story many times. I'm not ashamed to tell it or who knows. Because it's made a difference in so many people's lives at the Resort, just as it did when my counselor walked me through it. Because he too had been there. You see?"

"Yes," I said. "I see."

Soon after Ralph left, Harry came in for his usual cut and blow dry. He was the twenty-something friend of April—the girl who was left unconscious in the beer cooler at the Maverik gas station.

"Did you hear about the guy who went berserk in the cemetery?" he said, as I draped him in beige.

"Is this a joke?" I asked. Harry didn't usually make jokes.

"No, no, it's for real," he said.

"Okay, I'll bite. What did he do?"

"He destroyed a dozen old headstones at the pioneer cemetery, and then—get this—he left his cell phone behind.

"You've got to be kidding."

"The police knocked on his door and he admitted right away he did it, but he had a reason: Headstones prevent resurrection; dead people can't go to heaven with all that weight on top of them.

"Now I know you're kidding."

Harry shook his head. "You can't make this stuff up."

I started giggling and ended up coughing. "Don't make me laugh." I held a towel to my mouth. "My allergies are kicking in."

"He couldn't believe the police arrested him because he had such good intentions, so he put up a fight. They got him for resisting arrest *and* criminal mischief. I'm surprised Carl didn't tell you about it."

So was I. We would have laughed over this one. So why didn't he mention it?

The minute Carl came in the door that night, I asked about the graveyard vandal. "Why didn't you tell me?"

"It slipped my mind," he said, "because there was something else in the cemetery that got my attention."

"What was that?"

"A suitcase with a dead cat in it."

My eyes widened.

"It was behind a gravestone and when I opened it, there was a note inside with a dead cat." He grimaced. "Its throat was slit."

"Whoa."

"I don't remember the exact wording but the note started with 'Please bury my sweet cat. There's nowhere to put her but here.' The last two lines were smudged but legible. We're having that analyzed, but it looked to me like a child's handwriting all messed up with tear stains."

"A child?"

"Probably a girl."

"And what were her last two lines?"

My husband's brows furrowed. "I know he didn't mean it. I know he loves me and he didn't mean it."

Carl went upstairs to change. I got a cold beer out of the refrigerator and a glass mug from the freezer. *I know he didn't mean it. I know he loves me and he didn't mean it.*

When Carl returned to the kitchen, I handed him the cold beer. He took a long pull, grabbed me by the shoulders, and clutched me to him. "Did I ever tell you how wonderful you are?"

"Not today," I said.

"Well, you are." He took another pull from his beer and kissed me on the mouth. I tasted the nut-brown ale and felt the heat rising under my skirt.

"Where's Jamie?" he asked.

"In the den."

"Later then."

"Promise?" I said.

He grinned.

I began washing dishes left over from breakfast. "So what about this cat?"

"Ordinary orange and white tabby. Bled out before it was put in the suitcase."

"An act of cruelty?"

"Not torture. The cut was deep, so death would have been swift."

"A warning?"

"Possibly."

"An act of vengeance?"

"Possibly."

"Come on, give it up."

"Experts say there's a correlation between animal abuse and child abuse."

I submerged my frying pan in the dishwater. Sausage grease rose to the top, infusing the white bubbles with a brown oil slick. "So you think whoever wrote this note might be a victim, too?"

"Can't be ruled out."

Now there were two people whose attention was disturbed by that suitcase.

On Wednesday, my first appointment was Hawk Reynolds. Hawk was wearing a biker T-shirt that said "Riding the Good Life." Tattoos crawled up his arms and around his neck. I was sure there were tattoos elsewhere on his body, but I'd never cared to investigate. All I did was shave his head.

Hawk Reynolds might have looked like a biker, but he was big business. His tow truck operation removed all the wrecks on our interstates. He got calls from the cops in the ski town next door where there was no place to park. Hawk really cleaned up when they had the international film festival over there. With 40,000 people packed in a canyon that could only fit 20,000, he towed cars night and day.

"How are things going?" I asked, draping his burly shoulders in black.

"Jeez, my guys make me crazy."

The men who drove Hawk's wreckers looked like a bunch of bikers too. Not one of his so-called "staff" came to my salon for grooming, although they needed to.

"What's the matter?" I asked.

"No one wants to own up to keeping a slideback out overnight."

"You mean unauthorized?"

"Yeah. We got a lotta trucks so it wasn't like we couldn't do business. I figure if they went on a little bender or even a walkabout with some girl, I wouldn't break their balls. But that tow truck was missin' overnight and no one would admit they had it."

"Maybe you should persuade them with these," I said, pulling a pair of electric hedge clippers out of my cabinet. The noise accelerated as I pretended to discipline the bad boys.

Hawk laughed, as he did every time I pretended hedge clippers were my shaving instruments of choice. He cheered up right away and I wondered why his drivers didn't own up to a boss who was as easy going as he was.

Martha Farquhar came in a few hours later. She's earned a place at the top of my list of Least Favorite Clients. She's gruff, opinionated, and self-absorbed, not to mention that she has a really bad hairstyle I can't do anything about. She's rejected every suggestion I've made to soften the lines of the steel bowl on her head.

Martha is vice president of operations at the Resort and a city councilor. She hiked into my back workroom and dumped herself onto my chair, reached into her briefcase, and pulled out a sheaf of papers two inches thick.

"Good morning, Martha," I said. "Would you like something to drink?"

"Coffee."

When I brought her a cup, she was already reading the packet that all city councilors review to prepare for their next meeting. The pages were printed on both sides and filled with dense copy.

I had to attend a city council meeting once and I was amazed at the amount of repetition in these documents. For some legal reason, many of the pages are repeats, repeats and nothing but repeats.

I draped her in ice blue nylon and wrapped her neck in a royal blue terry. She moved the papers up and out of the way as I arranged the drape around her meaty body.

"Shall we consider angling your hair down around your neck instead of the neck shave and horizontal blunt cut we've been doing?" I asked.

"Nope."

Hope springs eternal, but in reality nothing could improve Martha's mannish look. My eyes roved to the page and I caught the title: "Pet Cemetery Issues." I stopped snipping and read the first paragraph.

*The state defines a cemetery as '. . . any place dedicated to and used, or intended to be used, for the permanent interment of **human remains**" (emphasis added). Under this definition pet interments are not allowed on dedicated land in cemeteries. Disposition of pet cremains are allowed, subject to individual* *cemetery rules. The law is silent about pet memorial markers in cemeteries, but individual cemetery rules can allow, regulate, or disallow such markers.*

I cleared my throat. "Martha, I can't help but notice that you're reading about pet cemeteries."

"What a horror!" Martha's voice reverberated throughout the salon as if she were addressing an assembly of one hundred. "Did you hear about that pet cemetery in Long Island? They found piles of dead animals. People said the smell was putrefying. They think the town's water supply is contaminated. We don't want a pet cemetery here!"

Martha, why don't you tell me how you really feel?

"I can see why a pet cemetery might be troubling," I said, "but we have so many pet lovers in this town. Wouldn't a pet cemetery appeal to a lot of voters?"

"They can bury their pets on their own properties." Martha's ample chest rose.

I continued the bowl cut. Black and silver cascaded down on the icy blue, like sleet on a heaving sea. "We certainly do have a lot more condos and apartment buildings now, don't we? Our town is really growing, isn't it?"

"Yes, it is," she said, "and that's not a good thing. When I was a child, we didn't even have stoplights."

About a hundred years ago.

"Where are all those apartment dwellers going to bury their pets?"

"They can take 'em to the vet."

"And what does he do with them?"

"Incinerates 'em," she said. "All together."

"Cremation?"

"Joint cremation. And if you want your pet's cremains, you get two scoops!"

I started to laugh and ended up coughing.

"Have you ever been in a pet cemetery?" she asked.

"No."

"I have. My sister buried her little Shih Tzu last year. She was gaga over that dog. 'Come to mumsy wumsy,' she would say. I had to go to the funeral where she gave this eulogy—

> *A little piece of heaven was you,*
> *My very own angel t'was true.*
> *I cherish the day you were mine,*
> *I only wish God gave more time.*

"I thought I would puke," Martha said.

I was coughing again.

She plodded on. "The cemetery had sections with names like Sleepy Doggy, Kitty Corner and Feathered Friends. There were people weeping and carrying on about their pets. I wanted to tell 'em all to get a life."

I remembered how hard Martha Farquhar was on Angelica Diego, the beautiful young Hispanic mother who died on the railroad tracks. *Where were you, Martha, when the hearts were given out?*

I placed my scissors on the counter, picked up my electric barber's trimmers, and shaved the back of Martha's neck. "All done," I said.

She inspected the job. "Now do the mustache."

I rolled my portable waxing station over to her chair. She tilted her head back and I applied the wax on the wide black area below her nostrils, then patted down the pull strip over top of the wax. Her eyes were closed, so she couldn't see the glint in my own as I seized the end of the strip. I ripped the wax off.

"Ow!"

"It hurts to become beautiful," I said, smiling wickedly. There are times when my job is supremely satisfying.

My afternoon schedule was heavy with teenage appointments. There is always much angst over teenage hair. It's either too long, too short, too kinky, too straight, too brown, too limp, or too full. With all the doctoring teens want, it's amazing their hair survives adolescence.

Carl called in the midst of all the mayhem, asking if he could send a police consultant over for a cut and blow dry.

"Male or female?" I asked.

"A woman, Rachel Arbuthnot. She's here to help with the cat case."

My ears perked up.

"She's a veterinarian."

I was about to ask why we needed a consultant when we have a perfectly competent vet in town, but Carl said, "Look, Tracy, I've got to go but can you help her out? She says she's been on the road for weeks and when she found out you're a hairdresser, she begged for an appointment.

"I'll slip her in at six if you can relieve Jamie's babysitter."

"It's a deal," he said.

Rachel Arbuthnot turned out to be an attractive, athletic-looking thirty-something with a pearly white smile, light pink lipstick, and matching pink nail polish. Her hair was a mop of brown with caramel highlights that had grown out half way down.

"Thanks for fitting me in," she said. "I've been away from home for weeks."

"Would you like your highlights restored?" I asked.

"I don't want to put you to any trouble," she said. "It's late and you need to get home."

"No problem," I said. "You'll feel much better."

Rachel looked relieved. "Well, if you've got the time."

While I mixed her formula, she chatted amiably, asking me about my work, my family and my husband. I felt she was truly interested in my answers.

"So what do you do, Rachel?" I asked.

"I'm a forensic veterinarian," she said. "I work all over the country for the ASPCA, assisting law enforcement in animal cruelty cases. That's the main concern of the American Society for the Prevention of Cruelty to Animals, but sometimes I'm called in to do forensic analysis in human criminal cases."

"Like what?"

"There was a case where a burglar was attacked by a pet cockatoo. The burglar killed the cockatoo with a fork but not before the bird took a big chunk out of the burglar's scalp. My DNA test linked the tissue on the cockatoo's claws with the suspect's DNA."

Rachel didn't need much encouragement to say more.

"Then there was a murder case. The killer stepped in dog business on the way into the house and left traces on the floor. I was able to match the dog-do on his shoe with the dog-do in the house.

"There was also a case where a woman was walking her dog when a man stopped his truck and asked for directions. I'm sorry to say he abducted and raped her. She could not identify the guy in a police lineup, but she remembered that her dog had lifted its leg on his truck tire while they were looking at the man's map. The police swabbed the suspect's tire and I matched the specimen to her dog's DNA."

I wanted to give Rachel a high five, but her hands were under the drape and mine were busy brushing on hair color. After a while, I said, "The cat in the suitcase is an interesting case."

"That's why I'm here," she said. "Tomorrow the medical examiner and I will try to determine what kind of weapon was used to cut the throat and check for traces of human DNA in the suitcase."

"Could the murderer's skin be on the claws?"

She nodded. "And likely blood if he was scratched."

"Perhaps you'd find the note writer's DNA too," I suggested.

"Perhaps. What the detectives need to do is find the scene of the crime. I could tell them if blood at the crime scene matches the cat's. Then we would know more about the perpetrator, provided the crime scene is a place where the cat killer hangs out."

Cat Killer. I shivered.

The top of Rachel's head was now covered with aluminum foil packets and she was ready for processing.

"At my salon," I explained, "you have a choice of a chair massage and warm footbath or a warm massage table with cucumbers on your eyelids. These are both relaxing things to do while you're processing."

"I think I would just like to read a book," she said, pulling a textbook called *Clinical Pathology for the Veterinary Team* out of her book bag.

"All right."

I rinsed the brushes and put away the aluminum foil. After twenty minutes I peeked under one of Rachel's wrappers. "You're doing well. About ten more minutes."

Rachel looked up from her book.

"Rachel?" I said. "I'm worried about something. There was a note in the suitcase."

"I know, but I haven't seen it yet."

I described the note and the memorized words. *I know he didn't mean it. I know he loves me and he didn't mean it.*

"Those are classic words," Rachel said. "Victims often try to excuse the actions of their abusers. And an abusive man will attempt to control his woman by hurting the animal she loves."

"Do you think that happened to this little girl?"

"Very possibly. Do you have a women's shelter in town? Maybe she and her mother are already there."

The next morning, I finished marceling Mrs. Oscar's hair and escorted her to the door, when Mrs. Argosy arrived for a cut and style. My Client Notebook said: 55+, husband in real estate, owns a duplex in the big valley, layered cut 4". I rooted through my comb collection to find the one with inch measurements imprinted on the side.

Mrs. Argosy's hair looked like bird feathers that had been mangled by a cat. "Oh, Tracy," she said. "I needed to see you two weeks ago."

"Why didn't you call? I would have fit you in."

"I didn't have time. We've had the most awful experience."

I sat her down in my chair and swathed her in turquoise. "Dry cut today, then wash, okay?" My brush curried her head with sure strokes; then I measured four inches with the comb and began shaping. "Now what's been going on?"

"You know we have a duplex in the big valley."

"Right."

"One of our tenants was arrested."

"What for?"

"Meth."

"Meth cooking?"

"No, thank God, meth using. It's the first time we've ever had to evict someone. I felt awful."

"How did this happen?"

"About a year ago one unit was empty, so we advertised, and I got a call asking, 'Do we accept housing assistance from the city?' I wanted to do my part, so I said, 'yes.' We met the family—a young mother and her two children. They seemed very nice.

"I went to the Housing Authority where the caseworker explained the program. The tenant pays a small percentage and the city subsidizes the rest of the rent."

"Sounds like a sweet deal."

"Things went okay for a year, but then the rent from the mother didn't come in on time. It was only ten dollars so I didn't go after her like I should. Then it stopped coming entirely, so I called the housing authority. They sent the caseworker out and she discovered the mother stoned on crystal meth. Tracy, the children were locked in their rooms!"

"How awful."

"I had to evict her, Tracy. My hands were tied. She'd violated the terms of the lease and I had to make them leave. Some tough-looking boys helped her move out. I think her brothers. We hovered over them until they cleaned everything up. The next day the front plate glass window was broken. I think they came back to give us their opinion."

"Did you file charges?"

She shook her head. "I just wanted to be shut of them. Then the caseworker chastised me for not notifying her immediately when the rent payment was late. When she found out I hadn't inspected the place for six months, she said I was lucky it hadn't been turned into a meth lab."

"Gee."

"She went on and on about meth labs—the caustic chemicals, the explosives, the cat urine smell."

"Cat urine?"

"They use some kind of ammonia. The fumes penetrate everything and ruin a property. She said an apartment with a basement was perfect for a meth lab and why didn't I inspect more often?"

"You caught it from both sides, didn't you? The punk brothers *and* the caseworker."

"She made me feel as if I was the one who broke the law."

Mrs. Argosy's shoulders were slumped. Her mouth was turned down like the yoke of a divining rod quivering over the spot where a well should be dug.

"You deserve a scalp massage with almond, jojoba, and geranium oil," I said. "You'll feel like a tropical flower afterwards."

Mrs. Argosy tottered to the sink and I tried to make those downturned lips point upwards with every stroke of my fingers.

No good deed goes unpunished, I thought. That's the way of the world.

After lunch, I checked my computer calendar and saw that Paddy Hamburger had a four o'clock appointment. Patrick J. Hamburger is our town's most feared news reporter. He lives to uncover wrongdoing, and if there's none, imply there is. He has a nose for news and is a skilled writer, but his headlines rile people up.

Instead of saying "Proposed Playground Too Expensive," his headline will say "Council Nixes Kiddie Fun." Another reporter might say "City Staffers Go on Research Trip," but Paddy's headline will read "Taxpayers Pay for Costly Junket." Paddy's title for the cat story, which Chief Fort Dukes announced to the press the day before, was "Chief Flummoxed by Suitcase Murderer."

Paddy had long hair which curled down his neck and sideburns that extended way below his ears. I draped him in a blood red cape with a black terry at his neck. I figured someone who provoked people as much as Paddy should be wearing a challenging color.

"Same thing as usual, Paddy?" I asked.

"Yup."

"So what's with the pet cemetery issue?" I asked, as I clipped Paddy's wet curls. Last night's city council meeting had turned into a free-for-all with two factions facing off—one group *for* the pet cemetery and one group *against*. The *for* people came with dogs and cats and hamsters. There was even a pet turtle. At one point, between the dogs barking and the cats yowling, no one could be heard and the mayor had to clear the room.

"It's the old guard versus the newbies," Paddy said. "People who've been here for generations have plenty of land and don't see the need for a pet cemetery, but residents in the condos and apartments have no property and they need a pet cemetery. So do the wealthy at Blue Cliffs."

Blue Cliffs was the first gated community built in our little western city. There are more pets in Blue Cliffs than there are maids.

"Every land parcel under consideration has a problem associated with it," Paddy said. "This town is in the middle of a major river watershed and it's against state law to bury an animal within a half mile of a dwelling or a quarter mile of a running stream. The councilors are grousing about the cost of the cemetery, too."

"But wouldn't this be an enterprise project that makes money for the city?" I asked. "Pet burial is big business. I bet you know how much a pet funeral runs."

Paddy grunted. "Nearly a thousand for the plot plus a yearly maintenance fee. The cheapest casket starts at $250, and you'll need to pay for the headstone, the flowers *and* the limousine."

I grinned into the mirror, but Paddy didn't crack a smile. He was a humorless kind of guy.

"What about cremation?"

"Dog owners pay by the pound. Cats are less expensive. Private cremation costs $150 to $300 and common cremation costs $60 to $150."

Not cheap for working class families.

"The upper class can afford it," Paddy said. "Our town is booming and they've got money to spend. We even have a national pet chain store now."

"The old guard is going to have to suck it up," I said.

"Over their dead bodies." A glimmer of a smile disturbed Paddy's lips. "They're going to be as obstructionist as possible."

I shook my head. "Their way of life is vanishing, isn't it?"

"There are far fewer dairy farms and cattle ranches in this county now," Paddy said. "And we're getting a Hooters."

I stopped cutting and stared at him. "No!" My head filled with visions of skimpily clad waitresses with mounded flesh in front and swishy butts behind.

"You're right, I'm kidding. We're going to have a Chili's."

First Walmart, then Petco, now Chili's. All the open land taken up by development; all the Mom & Pop businesses taken over by chains. When I was growing up our small town had a population of 5,000. Now the city proper has 15,000 residents with just as many in the county. Was this progress? Maybe the obstructionists had a point.

"Do you have a pet, Paddy?"

"No. Do you?"

"Jamie would like a dog but Carl and I work too much."

"What does Carl think of the cat in the suitcase?"

"Is this off the record?"

"Everything we talk about is off the record, Tracy."

I didn't believe that one bit. "I want to know what you think first," I said.

"I've been researching veterinarian crimes on the internet. There was a woman in Florida who took her sick dog to a vet to be euthanized, but the vet kept the dog alive for days doing blood transfusions for other dogs."

"Jeez."

"This suitcase case could be a vet gone wrong."

"But our vet is the nicest, sweetest guy in the world," I said. "He runs the animal shelter—don't tell me you suspect *him* of slitting the poor cat's throat!"

Paddy didn't say a word.

What a muckraker. He would give Mother Teresa the evil eye. "And how do you explain the note?"

Paddy turned so suddenly, my scissors poked his nose. "What note?"

"Forget it." I bit my lip. There was no mention of the note in the newspaper.

"What note, Tracy?"

"No note. Never mind." I wished I could cut out my tongue.

"Did Chief Fort Dukes hold out on me?"

I said nothing.

"Tracy?"

"It's off the record, right?"

"Always."

"There was a note in the suitcase with the cat."

I clammed up and finished his hair in silence.

Let him go back to the chief and do his dirty work. I bet Paddy's next headline would read: "Chief Withholds Key Evidence" or "Cat Wrote Note Before Slit Throat" or "Hairy Source Close to Cat Reveal's Murderer's Secret."

But the headline over Paddy's next story read "Forensic Analysis Reveals Cat's Secrets," a title that was quite civilized. There was a sidebar about Dr. Arbuthnot that was also respectful—"ASPCA Vet Ferrets Out Pet Cruelty."

A picture of the note topped the front page. "Please bury my sweet cat. I want to bury her but we have no money and there's nowhere to put her but here. I know he didn't mean it. I know he loves me and he didn't mean it."

The message was written on lined paper by a childish hand. There were circles dotting the "i"s and balloons for the tails of the "y"s. The rest was simple block printing like a young girl's. I could tell this without being a handwriting expert, but a police handwriting specialist had concluded the same thing.

Paddy's sidebar went on to say that Dr. Rachel Arbuthnot had examined the cat, and the suitcase. She typed the blood and documented the DNA. In her opinion the murder weapon was a hunting knife. Fingerprints lifted from the handle could not be identified. The blood under the cat's nails was human; so was the DNA. She also found a long dark human hair that could belong to the little girl, or the cat killer.

The sound of a hardball hitting a bat at a Little League game is one of the sweetest sounds in the world. A kid gets a chance to round the bases and the crowd cheers. I watched Jamie take practice swings and hoped he'd connect with the ball. One glance at Carl's face next to mine spoke volumes about hope and pride.

"Ball two." Our umpire said that a lot, along with "Outside!" or "Low ball." Pitching is the hardest skill to learn.

It was the sixth inning and the pitcher from the opposing team appeared to be tiring. The score was tied, the bases were loaded, and this was the last inning for the eight-to-ten year old division.

"Ball three." In a minute, Jamie would walk, a runner would go home, and the game would be won.

Across the diamond, the opposing coach slapped the back of his tallest player, propelling the boy onto the field. The current pitcher loped off the mound, and we all clapped. That's how we teach sportsmanship in this League.

The relief pitcher wound up and let fly. "Strike one!" said the umpire.

This guy was good.

"Strike two."

My heart sank.

Crack.

Jamie's hit to centerfield bounced beyond the outfield player. Parents rocketed to their feet as our runners tore for home. My eyes pinned on Jamie as he ran for second base. The outfielder threw long and hard, but Jamie made it to third. The pitcher scooped up the ball and shot it towards the catcher, who whirled on Jamie and tagged him.

"Safe!" cried the ump.

Our crowd went wild. Fathers clapped Carl on the back. Players rubbed Jamie on the head. The game was over despite the fact there was one more batter up. No matter what happened now, the score was four points in our favor.

"Our son's a winner tonight," I said to Carl.

He draped his arm around my shoulders. "You are too. Guess what happened today?"

"What?"

"Charges came down in the Medicare fraud case."

"I hope they threw the book at that crooked chiropractor," I said. "Shelley thought her family was going bankrupt."

"The chiropractor and his assistant each got four felony counts of Medicare fraud. That means they could go to prison for five to ten years for each count."

I thought of FBI agent Rasheeta Jackson. She must be feeling satisfied, now that she'd finished all her "undercover energy work." Annabelle Davina would be happy too, although she was not the gloating type.

"Harriet Carpenter turned state's evidence against Barry Whiteside and is trying to trade her sentence down." Carl shook his head. "I've seen plea bargainers before but she seems downright vindictive."

I smiled into the bottom of the grandstand.

"She's gone after him with a vengeance, as if they were never friends," he said.

"Perhaps they weren't friends."

He cocked his head at me.

"Perhaps they were lovers, and he done her wrong."

Carl got the picture.

"What about all the money his patients paid?" I asked. "Will Shelley's family be reimbursed?"

"The prosecution will present all that during trial," said Carl. "I wouldn't be surprised if Whiteside's required to pay restitution. The FBI discovered millions socked away in foreign accounts."

The wheels of justice turned slowly but I could envision a time when the Protheros and others like them would be made whole.

"You done good, honey," Carl said.

Our eyes returned to the field. "Strike three," shouted the umpire. Our kids threw their hats in the air. We clambered down the metal benches as the teams shook hands.

"By the way," Carl said. "Paddy Hamburger came to the station today. He knew all about the note in the suitcase even though we kept that under wraps." Adrenalin spiked through my body. "I noticed he had a fresh haircut."

Carl looked at me with a question in his eyes.

I took a deep breath. "Paddy's such a conniver. He made it sound like he was going to accuse our local vet of killing the cat. I was so mad, it slipped out."

"Why would Paddy think the vet did it?"

"Because of some cruelty case in Florida."

"No wonder he asked about vets. I told him we've canvassed the vets in the area, to learn about any other pet abuse cases and inquiries about pet burial services."

"You don't suspect our veterinarians, do you?"

"No," Carl said. "We're focusing on the link between animal cruelty and domestic violence. I've been to the women's shelter, and the youth resource officer is working with the Department of Child & Family Services and the schools to try to identify the note writer."

"Dad!" Jamie rushed up beside us, all dust, sweat, smiles. "Did you see me, Mom?"

"Of course we saw you," I said. "Congratulations, sweetheart!"

"You done good, Jamie," his father said, Carl's highest accolade for excellence.

Time passed with no movement on the case. Then Carl's cell phone rang one Sunday when he was off duty: two llamas butchered at the historic Burbridge Homestead.

After Carl left, I placed the farm's name. Heather Desmond and her husband had purchased the homestead five years before when the old dairy farmer passed away. *Not her llamas—she'll be crushed.* I decided to stop by Monday on my day off. I could take Heather a gift to return the favor of the marvelous goat cheese.

The next afternoon, Heather met me on the spacious front porch of the Victorian farmhouse. "Tracy, how nice of you to come."

"I've brought some Elégance products for your face."

"You shouldn't have."

I gave her a sympathetic look.

"Life goes on, Tracy," she said with a sigh. "Life goes on."

"I'm truly sorry about what happened."

She sank onto her sofa looking like a small, huddled child. "My poor Zoom, my poor Zelda. I raised Zoom from a little cria. I bottle fed him when he was born and he couldn't stand to nurse. I watched him grow up. We called him 'Zoom' because he would zoom around the pen—so *fast*, Tracy. He was a joy to watch."

"You've often talked about him."

"And Zelda. She was a good mother. She dropped a baby every year. Imagine being pregnant all the time. Did you know a llama's gestation period is eleven months? She gave birth all by herself and never complained."

I wondered how a llama would complain but I didn't think it was a good time to ask.

"They would eat out of my hand." Heather offered me some imaginary grain with wonder on her face. "They'd pick it up with their finger lips. So soft, so sweet. And they didn't spit."

"Ever?"

"I never did anything to make them angry. They loved people. They were curious about us humans. They would stand in the corral when we had parties and watch all my guests in the backyard having fun, gazing at us with their amazing big eyes and their long lashes."

I gave Heather a hug. "I'm so sorry."

"Tracy, it was horrible. I woke up Sunday morning and milked the goats as usual. The chickens had given us six fresh eggs for our breakfast. Then I went to fill Zoom and Zelda's water bucket."

She sniffed. I hung on her next words. They were long in coming.

"I looked into the back field and saw them on the ground. I could barely see them that far away but I could tell they weren't moving. I thought they were just sleeping, so I filled the bucket and turned away, but just then my husband let our blue heeler out the back door. He rushed into the field and barked at them. They didn't get up, Tracy, they just didn't get up!"

Heather was weeping now. I gave her a tissue.

She buried her face in it. I waited until she resumed. "I opened the gate to the field. When I got close, I saw that their throats were slit. There was so much blood," she whispered, "so much strange blood."

"Strange?"

"Llama blood is bright pink-red, almost florescent. And it beads up in strange globs."

I tried to picture this and couldn't. "My husband Carl is working on your case, Heather. He'll catch the person who did this."

"But why, Tracy, why? It's so senseless." She lifted her face to mine and I could see the anguish there. "They didn't do anything wrong. They didn't do anything to anybody. They were so innocent."

Early that morning Rachel Arbuthnot had determined the llama's throats were slit with a hunting knife, the same type of weapon as the cat in the suitcase. Carl was reviewing all the animal cruelty cases tried in adult court over the past five years, but the juvenile cases were sealed and hard to access. Carl and Rachel were extremely frustrated. They needed a break in the case.

"The police will find the killer," I said with a confidence I didn't feel. "Now let's get you fixed up. How about a soothing eye cream treatment and facial massage? That will make you feel better."

As I directed Heather to lie down and began to clean her face with organic skin care cleanser, I thought about how much Heather deserved justice. So did Zoom and Zelda. So did the cat in the suitcase.

But how?

I wished I could review all the court cases myself. I wished I could question the school counselors and all the teachers. Surely some kid in the school system was in a world of hurt. All that negative stuff had to come out somehow. Children acted out their pain on the playground. Pre-teens had hurtful exchanges in hallways. High school kids bullied and taunted each other. Negative feelings like this needed some kind of release valve or they blew. If the cat killer was a teen, how would his actions at school tip a teacher off? If the note writer was a young girl, how would her pain reveal itself? A teacher or a counselor must have seen something.

But there were seven schools, thousands of children, and only one guidance counselor at each school. High school guidance counselors only saw a student for ten minutes twice a year, their focus on college placement. It was an unreasonable expectation to think that the school staff could see any warning signs because they only saw part of the picture.

After wiping off the cleanser I applied eye repair cream to erase the puffiness and redness caused by tears. With a fragrant probiotic moisturizer, I began to massage Heather's chin and cheeks. The light repetitive motion made Rachel sigh with contentment while my mind wrestled with the problem.

Where were parents in all this? Maybe they were working too hard to see what their children were doing. Most people around here have three jobs just to make ends meet. Parents work all day, nights and weekends. There are lots of latchkey kids. The father could be absent; the mother could be a drunkard. Or there might only be grandparents.

The possibilities boggled my mind.

I moved to Heather's ash blonde hair. A scalp massage is always soothing. Heather's eyes were closed, her body relaxed, as I created swirls with the balls of my fingers, a light pressure all over her head.

My thoughts turned to hair color. Ash blonde dye is actually dark brown. Red hair dye is light pink. Dark brown hair dye is light tan.

Nothing was as it seemed, just like the case. The cat killer could be the most well-liked kid in the school. The note writer could be from a wealthy family, not a working class family. The llama killer could be a man not a boy.

We just didn't know.

Heather was ready for toner to brighten her face. I wiped the moisturizer off with a soft serenity contoured pad. "Now I'm going to apply a spritz of chamomile tonic. You'll feel a slight tingling sensation and you'll love the fragrance."

Heather kept her eyes closed as I pumped the aromatherapy finishing layer, and there was the wisp of a smile on her lips. Her face was no longer red and swollen but clear and rosy.

As I put the facial products away, we chatted about goat cheese, blackberry jam, sun-ripened tomatoes, apron making, and the difference between fresh eggs and store-bought. We stayed away from llama shearing, wool spinning, and sweater knitting which were Heather's favorite topics. She appeared refreshed and tranquil, but I knew she was hiding her grief.

That's what we do, we humans—we hide our grief, we hide our hurt, and we fool the world most of the time.

A few days later my one o'clock appointment was Tina White Horse. I mulled over that name before I remembered. Tina ran for Ms. Cowgirl. She made First Attendant and is related to Larry Big Pouch, who is a mover and shaker on the reservation.

Tina entered the salon looking radiant. She had long black hair stretching down her back with a hint of blue cresting in the waves. Her eyes were almond-shaped and her skin was flawless.

"Tracy Lemon," she said, striding into the salon and shaking my hand. "I've always wanted to meet you."

"I remember you from the Ms. Cowgirl contest. You look fabulous."

"Thank you." She dropped her eyes, then looked back into mine.

"So you're here for a pedicure?"

"I'd like a pedi with a flower."

I nodded. "Come pick out a color."

I ran warm water into a footbath while Tina browsed through my polish selection. She chose light pink, perfect for a girl her age. I placed the bottle on my nail polish caddy, which I'd rolled out from the closet along with my pedicure stool.

This caddy contains everything I need to create a ground, refreshed and self-possessed person. My pedicures remove spent skin, groom the nails, massage the calves, relax the feet, strengthen arches, and dress toenails up so that a woman feels special. A girl could be pug-nosed, droopy-eyed or bed-headed, but when she looks at her painted toes, she feels pretty and feminine.

Tina removed her sandals, slid onto the recliner, and slipped her feet into the footbath. I let her soak for a few minutes while I readied my nail clippers and emery boards. I picked up her right foot and placed it on a salmon-colored terry covering the footrest.

"Your toes are so pretty," I said, as I removed old polish.

"Thank you."

I submerged the right foot and picked up the left. "You have wide, athletic-looking feet."

"I ran barefoot on the reservation as a child. I think that builds up strength."

"Foot doctors say so, too," I said, swiping a cotton ball over the little toe. "That's why those running shoes with the separate toes have become popular. They're like skin. Have you ever tried them?"

"No, when I go home I still walk barefoot everywhere."

I returned her left foot to the pool.

Tina selected a setting on the automatic back massager and round balls underneath the leather began to knead her lower back.

"I take it you're not living on the reservation right now?"

"Just part time," she said. "I have a job here in town at an after-school program."

"Really? Where?"

"JR Ewing Elementary."

"I didn't think any of the elementary schools had an afterschool program. My son Jamie goes to a neighbor's house when he gets off the bus."

"This is the first year. JR Ewing has a lot of latchkey children so the district started a pilot program. I run the activities."

I clipped each toenail and used an emery board to file the nails, then squirted pink cuticle softener on her toes. It looked like pink icing. I waited for the cuticle to soften.

"What kinds of things do the kids do?"

"Gymboree comes over to teach gymnastics and Yoga 4 U does stretching. Arts-Kids comes every week too."

"What's Arts-Kids?" I began to push Tina's cuticles back with an orange stick.

"A professional artist gives the kids an expressive arts project. It's intended to help kids release their frustrations through art."

"Like art therapy?"

"Not exactly, because they don't ask the kids to paint or draw how they feel. They give them materials let them be creative any way they want."

I nodded. Jamie always feels good about himself when he's free to create without any direction from me.

"A lot of these kids have trouble in school," Tina said. "They're told all day 'Don't do this, stop that, you're wrong, do it this way.' Some have dyslexia and ADHD; others are going through some tough life events—divorce, death in the family, alcoholism."

I raised my eyes from her toes and looked at her. *What about animal abuse?*

"I suppose you see some interesting things in their art," I said, "things kids won't talk about but they might draw instead."

She laughed. "One kid is obsessed with Ryu Hayabusa. I can't even pronounce that name. He's a ninja character in a video game. The boy made a Ryu mask, a Ryu light saber, and a Ryu jet pack. We had a cartoonist come and work with the kids, so he even made a Ryu comic strip."

I laughed. "What about the girls?"

"Girls love to draw flowers and hearts and big yellow suns with rays shooting out of them. Gender differences are so pronounced. The boys will draw guns and cars and the girls will draw puppies and kittens."

"I have a little boy myself. Jamie loves to draw soldiers with gore dripping out of their chests."

"Then you know what I mean. It's all in character. I only worry when it's out of character. Like one little girl. She's now drawing kitties with their heads cut off. That's a bit worrisome."

"Who is this little girl?" I asked.

"She's a fourth grader. I think she lives in the West Side Apartments. Her mother works at McDonalds and there's a half-brother. He picks her up sometimes."

"What did you say her name was?"

"I didn't, but it's Charlotte."

Tina's toes were ready for polish but her muscles still needed work. I dipped into my wide-mouthed jar of sea-salt scrub and rubbed it up and down each of her calves. After I rinsed her legs, I picked up each foot and used a file to remove the callouses on her heels.

"I bet you love putting up displays of the kids' artwork," I said, wondering if I could drop by and see this little girl's drawings.

"Most of them take their art home, but we do have some work on the wall right now. It gives the children a sense of pride."

"I'd love to see them," I said.

"We're always looking for volunteers. If you're interested, you can come any time. Maybe you'd like to help out."

"How about today?" I said.

"School gets out at three-thirty. You can come then."

"Great."

I rinsed Tina's feet one last time and applied warm moisturizer from the bottle I keep in my electric warming cupboard. I massaged each of her calves. She closed her eyes and I could see her relax. People don't realize how much tension they carry in their calves until they receive a massage like this.

I rinsed Tina's legs in the footbath and patted them dry. After I replaced the salmon terry with a yellow one, she put both feet on the footrest again. I applied a base coat and then pink polish on each toe.

"Now for the flower." A Vietnamese pedicurist taught me how to paint flowers. I don't know why Vietnamese girls are so good at this. My flowers aren't bad, but they're not as good as Cin Dee's.

"That's so cute!" Tina said.

"I'm glad you like it. You'll need to let that dry for at least forty minutes. Would you like a magazine and a cup of herbal tea?"

"Yes, please."

"I also have ice water or a probiotic drink. There are chips and chocolate too."

Forty minutes later, Tina was done with her tea, her Hershey's kisses and the latest issue of *Elle*. She paid with cash, added a nice tip, and walked out the door looking down at her toes in her sandals. I could read the happy set of her shoulders and the lift in her step.

I picked up my cell. I knew Carl would leap at any new lead, no matter how shaky. He said he'd meet me at the school.

"Don't wear your uniform," I said. "We're potential volunteers."

"Plain clothes. Don't worry."

We met Tina in the school lobby. "This is my husband, Carl. He's interested in your program, too."

Tina smiled and beckoned us to follow her. Backpacks were stacked in one corner of the room. Kids sat with a volunteer or a teacher, bent over textbooks, pencils in their hands. "The children do their homework first," Tina said. "Work before play.

She took us to the gym where counselors from Gymboree were setting up shop. They'd brought a trampoline, balance beams, and tumbling mats.

"The kids must love this," Carl said.

"You mentioned there was art?" I said.

"Arts-Kids isn't here today," Tina said.

"But I think you said there's a nice display of their work."

"Over here." Tina said.

Carl and I followed Tina to a hallway that circled the library kiva. The artwork was quite expressive. Wide sweeps of watercolor interspersed with figures—human, animal, and fantasy. Each child's name was written in the lower right hand corner of their paper. I looked for the one we wanted. *Charlotte.*

It was there—a watercolor with a tiny, tiny figure in one corner. Our noses almost touched the wall, as we strained to see. It was a headless cat with drops of blood cascading from the neck. I would've missed it, if I hadn't been looking for it. In the other corner, surrounded by a field of red, was the cat's tiny head. It had ears, a triangular nose, and tears descending from each eye.

"Is this Charlotte's picture?" I asked Tina.

"Yes. A bit disturbing for a girl. She went through a tough spell about a month ago. Emotional. Teary. Wouldn't join in. Not much better now."

"Is she here today?"

"No. Her attendance has been spotty."

I glanced at Carl.

He nodded.

I blathered on as Tina showed us the rest of the program. Children were working on computers; others were gathered around a nutritionist who was talking about carrots and celery.

We said our goodbyes and I walked out of the school in a daze.

Carl and I stopped on the sidewalk.

"Thanks," Carl said. "You've been an amazing help."

"You're welcome," I said, looking up at him. He wiped the tears from my eyes and saw me to my car. I drove away.

Carl brought home everything he learned about Charlotte and her family.

"They moved here about a year ago from a ranch that bordered the Ute Reservation," he said. "When they lost the ranch to the bank, the father left for parts unknown. The mother got a job at the Resort but didn't make it through the probationary period. She's been fired from McDonald's, too. She drinks. Heavily.

"I convinced a judge to order the release of the half-brother's juvenile record. There were complaints against him at the age of ten. Shooting razor arrows at livestock. Strangling chickens. As a teen he slit the throats of a whole herd of goats. The biggest trouble was on the reservation where he killed eagles for their feathers. That's a federal crime with a fine of twenty-five thousand dollars."

"How could they afford that?"

"They couldn't. That's why they had a second mortgage," he said. "With this background, I got a warrant to search their home at the West Side Apartments. We found a bloody shirt under the boy's bed. Rachel Arbuthnot was able to link the blood on the shirt to Heather Desmond's llamas.

"We also found the hunting knife and the corner of the kitchen where the cat was butchered. Blood had penetrated cracks in the tile floor. Rachel said it matched the cat's blood type and its DNA. The blood under the cat's nails matched the half-brother's blood. The strand of hair in the suitcase was Charlotte's."

"That poor little girl," I said. "What's going to happen to her?"

"The intake with Children and Family Services has already taken place. She's been placed in foster care, and she's being interviewed by therapists at the Children's Justice Center this week."

"She's just Jamie's age, Carl. Imagine being torn away from her family, even a family like that, and going to live with perfect strangers."

Carl hugged me. "I know, but don't worry. The professionals can handle it, Tracy. It's for the best."

Case 5

Floating Away

• • • • • • • •

Sassy Morgan wriggled her toes inside a of tub fragrant spearmint water. Her hand popped out from under *Packing for Mars* and reached for her cup of spearmint tea. A timer was ticking away but only I could see it.

"How much longer?" she asked.

"About ten minutes."

"This book is hilarious, Tracy, I don't want to put it down."

I checked the temperature of the water and added more hot.

"All the tests to figure out how humans will react to floating away in outer space. An astronaut thinks he's going to vomit in his space suit, then gawks at the blue planet below him just as urine is dumped from the space ship. 'What a sight to behold,' he says." Sassy giggled. "And it's not just the anecdotes, it's the writing. Mary Roach is a master wordsmith. Are you going to read the book?"

"I'm not sure I have time for a book club, Sassy."

"Not even for the wine?"

Margaret Pyle belongs to a book club—only for the wine. I shook my head.

"That's too bad, because I'm worried about something."

"What?" I said.

"After everyone left book club last month I got ready for bed and my sleeping pills were gone. I have insomnia so I've been taking Ambien and the bottle had vanished. I couldn't find it anywhere."

"You think someone in book club took it?"

"That's what I'm guessing."

"Who?"

"I have no idea. I can't imagine why anyone would take my pills. They can all just go to the doctor and get their own."

My mind took an inventory of the faces circled around Sassy's living room. Meryl Thompson, Candy Fiber, Orchid Fisher, Shelley Prothero, and the elegant woman in the designer dress.

Shelley. Surely not Shelley. She had looked like death warmed over that night, but we'd tackled her problem since then. Margaret was helping her negotiate the out-of-network charges at the hospital and the chiropractor, Barry Whiteside, had been indicted for insurance fraud. Why would Shelley resort to drugs? Besides there were ten other women who could have taken the pills.

"How long have you known everyone?" I asked.

"Seems like forever. I can't believe any of them would steal."

"I wonder if other hostesses have had this happen."

"Not that I know of."

"Why don't you ask around?"

The timer dinged.

Sassy slipped on her sandals and padded over to the sink. The whooshing sound of the rinse water filled our ears. The plastic rollers clacked as they hit the porcelain. In the styling chair, I worked on her body waves in silence. When she was dry, her luxuriant curls cascaded halfway down her back. She left a big tip. I watched her glide out the front door into the summer day.

When I returned to my salon desk, I made notations in my Client Notebook: Ambien for insomnia, stolen pills at book club, floating away.

I'd heard that phrase before—floating away. Ralph Abramowicz from the Resort used it to describe the feeling of drug-induced euphoria. *Was a member of Sassy's book club floating away?*

That night, after I read Jamie a story and finished the dishes, I slipped into bed with the handsomest, sexiest policeman on the planet.

"Tell me about prescription drug abuse," I said.

"I'd rather talk about that teddy you're wearing." Carl fingered the lace around my bodice with one hand and slid the other one down the soft, white silk to my thigh. His hand disappeared under the teddy. We didn't talk much after that.

In the morning, I leaned back on the pillows as he put on his Kevlar vest. "So tell me about prescription drug abuse."

"Why do you want to know?"

"I have a customer who thinks a guest stole Ambien from her medicine cabinet."

"Ambien's a powerful drug. It's a sedative that relieves anxiety so people can sleep. It's not as habit-forming as Valium or Xanax. Did she report the theft to the police?"

"I don't think so. She's not sure who did it."

"You'd be surprised what people do to get high." He shrugged into his blue shirt. "I think it's the number one problem with teens and young adults."

"Why?"

"When kids combine alcohol with pills, they can die."

I pondered this for a minute.

Carl pulled his firearm out of the safe and snugged it into the holster around his waist. "Then there's suicide. Men settle for a gun, but women tend to end it with an overdose, especially young women in their twenties."

"Not a pleasant thought for a nice day," I said.

Carl strode over to the bed and kissed me fully on the mouth. "Have no fear—no suicides or drug overdoses for me today. The chief is making sure my Saturday is full of parking tickets and motorists with car trouble."

"Just petty crimes and head cases," I said. "For both of us."

He laughed, but I knew Carl was annoyed—Chief Fort Dukes continued to ignore his application for the detective opening and it was bugging him.

My first appointment Saturday was with Noela Salazar, the director of the girls' section of the Juvenile Justice Center. You'd never peg Noela for the job. She seems too little and too kind. But under her crisp pink shirtwaist, she has nerves of steel. I imagined the things she saw all day – teenage girls in the throes of hormonal changes, street kids with volatile personalities, young souls damaged from rape.

"How goes it, Noela?" I said.

She gave me a wan smile. A slightly upturned mouth. A brief raising of the eyebrows. "Fine."

We repaired to my workroom and I draped her with a light pink cape. She looked like a mound of pink candy with a tarnished silver button on top. I began to cut.

Typically, Noela is not chatty. She keeps to herself. But that day, after a while, she spoke. "I heard something of interest yesterday, Tracy, and I wonder what you think of it."

I snipped the steel-and-dark hairs at the base of Noela's neck as she continued. "There was a conference at the Capitol and the keynote speaker was a physician. He said that if you wanted to design a culture that produces anxiety and is bad for the self-image of girls, you'd make it look like the United States."

"Wow." I stared at Noela in the mirror.

She returned my gaze. No drama. No facial commentary. Just a steady look.

"That's quite the indictment," I said. "Who was this guy?"

"Someone whose clinic helps people deal with stress."

I returned to snipping.

"So what do you think," she said. "Is he right?"

I felt flattered. A woman like Noela Salazar, who must have seen more stressful things in the last week than I saw that month, was asking me for my opinion. I was happy to oblige. "American girls measure their self-worth too much by their appearance. I should know—I make half my living off the supreme anxiety of teens who are having bad hair days."

This prompted more of a smile than I had ever seen—a sliver, kind of like a crescent moon before it becomes new. The smile vanished and Noela said, "We've been seeing more young girls from well-to-do families who have low self-images."

"How do they end up in juvenile court?"

"Drug offenses."

"I suppose rich kids can buy any drug they want."

"They're not buying them; they're stealing them from medicine cabinets."

For a moment, all we could hear was the sound of my scissors.

"Drugs are a coping mechanism," Noela said. "Some girls have learning disabilities and they struggle in school or they don't handle social situations well. They want to feel better, so they get ahold of painkillers—Vicodin, OxyContin, Percocet."

Just like Ralph Abramowicz. He came from a fairly wealthy family, too. I revolved Noela's chair around and checked the hair length on each side. "What's done for these girls?"

"We have a detox center in the facility. Unfortunately, the girls go through withdrawal. They get panic attacks. They throw up. One girl had a seizure. All of them are on suicide watch."

I made a face and glanced at Noela in the mirror. Again, her serene eyes met mine.

"The mood swings are the toughest to deal with," she said. "I have to hand it to my staff. They deliver the best, most compassionate tough love in the world."

At that moment a voice screeched from the front of the salon and seconds later Candy Fiber dashed through the door of my workroom. She was wearing clogs and the clatter drowned out Noela's next comment.

"I'm sorry, Noela. What did you say?"

I leaned down to hear and missed it again because Candy was shouting. "Tracy, you'll never guess what I've got for you!"

She plunked down a cardboard display so tall Noela could no longer see her reflection in the mirror. The headline on the display said: "I lost ninety pounds with Blubber Burner! This diet delight is a Miracle!"

A picture of an absolutely humongous woman wearing flowered trousers dominated the left side of the cardboard. A svelte woman, wearing the same flowered trousers, dominated the right side. She stretched the waistband out about a foot to show how much weight she'd lost.

I compared the faces. Since one was scowling and the other was smiling, it was hard to tell if the two Miss Blubber Burners were really the same person.

Noela laughed for the first time in all the years I'd known her. "Such a character," she said.

I didn't know if Noela was talking about Miss Blubber Burner or Candy Fiber, but it didn't really matter. Both were over the top.

"Tracy," Noela said. "I think we're finished here, aren't we?"

"Pretty much." I removed the neck towel and pink cape.

"Your hair looks nice," Candy said to Noela. "But you look a little pale. Have you ever tried a dietary supplement?" Candy smiled her most winning smile.

Noela fluttered her hand and said in a voice Candy strained to hear. "Most diet supplements do not contain the ingredients advertised on the packaging." Then she shouldered her purse. I marveled at her self-control. I wanted to grab that purse and brain Candy.

After I saw Noela out the door, I returned to my workroom where Candy had moved Miss Blubber Burner so she could see herself in the mirror. I've given up on telling Candy she is rude, obnoxious, and self-centered. Nothing penetrates. She has a narcissistic self-image, and that is another problem altogether.

"What are we doing today, Candy?" I asked.

"You know those green hair streaks you had the last time I was here?"

They were chartreuse. "Yes."

"Well, I want some too. Only purple."

We spent the next ten minutes sifting through color books. There was no purple. There was periwinkle, plum, violet, amethyst, and wine. There was even a tone called violaceous—which Candy picked out right away. I spent the next thirty minutes weaving her hair.

Candy spent the same thirty minutes talking about the benefits of dietary supplements, deals on dietary supplements, and her sales success with dietary supplements. I tuned everything out. I was just about to turn up the sound system so we couldn't hear each other when I remembered Fen-phen.

"Speaking of diet pills," I said, interrupting her in mid-sentence, "wasn't there once a diet pill called Fen-phen? What do you know about that?"

Candy's expression turned sour. "I would never sell Fen-phen. You can't even get it anymore."

"Why not?"

"It caused heart problems. A malfunction of the heart valve."

"Young women died didn't they?"

"They had to take it off the market. There are still product liability suits over it."

"What about addiction?"

"Girls I know who used Fen-phen were never addicted. They liked the energy it gave them and the weight loss, but they weren't addicted."

My eyebrows shot up. "You know girls who used it?"

"Yeah."

"Who?"

"You wouldn't know them. They're gone now. Moved away." She dismissed them with a flick of her hand.

"Did *you* take Fen-phen?" I asked, looking at her in the mirror.

She gazed back at me. Then she grinned, shrugged her shoulders, and rolled her eyes. "Of course, Tracy. We *all* did. It was *no big deal.*"

The thought flit through my mind that something that can kill you might actually be a *big deal*. I pressed my point. "What do you use now?"

"Come on, Tracy. Is this the third degree?" The grin hadn't left her face, but she shifted in her chair and I could see she was uncomfortable. "I take *dietary supplements!*"

Candy Fiber. Miss Motor Mouth. The Energizer Bunny. Never a Dull Moment Candy. Sugar High Girl. *Could she be on drugs?*

At two o'clock I placed my "Closed for Special Event" sign on the salon door. I went to the closet where I store my heavy-duty chromium-steel garment-rack, assembled it, and parked it next to the salon desk.

Roxy Rafael arrived and heaved her professional make-up artist's case onto the credenza near the plate glass windows. She positioned two upholstered chairs so natural light would fall on my clients' faces. She opened the top flap of the case and revealed a clear plastic see-through compartment stuffed with brushes of every size and shape. Two pull-out drawers contained powders, shadows, glosses, lipsticks, creams and foundations.

Annabelle Davina slipped through the front door, her tall, erect body a serene presence as she drifted towards my massage room. The sound of spa music emanated from the open door as she prepared the massage table.

The ambience was broken when the front door slammed. "I've arrived, girls," a voice announced. "Now Life can Begin!" Cholly Chockworth swished in, dropped his purse on my sofa, and bussed me on the cheek. "Where do you want me, darling?"

Cholly was multi-talented. He could style hair, paint nails and serve champagne, all in a way that made a girl feel pampered and fussed over as never before. He had perfected a running patter about everyone from movie stars to royalty that made girls giggle hysterically. His favorite topic was Chief Fort Dukes, who can't get it right about anything in our town, especially his public comments about our gay community.

"Can you start with the manicures until you're needed elsewhere?" I asked.

"Of course, dear. My pleasure."

Cholly sashayed into the manicure salon and re-arranged three tables in a semi-circle around a rolling chair. Then he retrieved his large handbag and pulled out a gorgeous selection of red, pink and coral-colored fabrics which he spread over each table. Finally, he arranged several different nail polish choices along with glazed ceramic soaking bowls and charm-clad champagne flutes whose colors also matched the decor. He looked around for the champagne. It was missing.

I glanced at the clock and realized we had only ten minutes. Where was the champagne?

Just at that moment, Tony Lazar materialized outside the front door, pushing a hand dolly stacked with a case of champagne and a tub filled with ice. I breathed a sigh of relief.

We were ready.

The bride and her entourage arrived at exactly two-thirty. The salon filled with young, beautiful twenty-somethings carrying dress bags, shoe bags and hat boxes. Some had their heads wrapped in scarves with rollers underneath. Others had already done their up-do's and were there for massage, manicure, and make-up. Madeleine, the bride, had requested an elaborate coiffure—an intricate braided confection swept up and around her head, the back contours interwoven with lustrous seed pearls.

Wedding Party Prep is my specialty and why so many brides book my salon on their Special Day.

Cholly began to direct traffic. Before long, all the dresses were hanging from the garment rack and the hat boxes were lined up on my workroom counter. Each bridesmaid had wrapped herself in a silky fuchsia robe and the bride was wearing a white satin wrap with appliqued pink roses. Every girl had a full champagne flute.

Annabelle beckoned to the Maid of Honor who followed her into the massage room. Roxy invited two bridesmaids for make-up consultation. Cholly commandeered the rest and I took the bride under my wing. When Madeleine and I re-emerged from my workroom an hour later, I was surprised to see Sassy Morgan.

"Hey, Tracy."

"Sassy! I didn't know you were coming!"

"I didn't either." She winked at Madeleine. "Prepping at the Citrus Salon was the bride's Big Secret. Madeleine, you look marvelous!"

The bride glowed.

"And look who else is here—Orchid Fisher." Sassy accepted a refill from Orchid who had emerged from the nail salon with a bottle of champagne.

"Would you two like to be the first bridesmaids to have your headpiece arranged?" I asked.

Sassy glanced at Orchid. "Sure."

We went into my workroom where Sassy took the chair at my station. Orchid set the champagne bottle, a flute, and her purse on the counter.

I picked up one of the hat boxes and removed a delicate headpiece made of feathers, pearls, and gossamer lace.

"Enchanting," said Sassy.

"Beautiful." Orchid poured the last of the bottle into her champagne flute and drained it.

"In a few minutes you'll both be wearing a headpiece like this," I said, brushing Sassy's luxurious waves.

Orchid excused herself, taking her champagne glass. I noticed she also took her purse. "The powder room is back here on the right," I said.

"I don't need the powder room," she replied.

When she disappeared out the door, I brought up our last conversation. "Sassy, have you had a chance to talk to the other book club hostesses?"

"I've been meaning to call you," Sassy said. "I spoke with three other women and they checked their medicine cabinets. Two were missing pill bottles but neither noticed until I called, and one said her pills were stored in a bedroom drawer not a medicine cabinet."

"Whoa," I said. "That means the person who's taking the stuff is doing more than a quick search of the bathroom."

"She's searching the place," Sassy said. "But wouldn't that take time?" Sassy's question was tentative. I assumed she was thinking out loud. "We would miss her during the book discussion."

"Maybe she comes back on a different day," I said.

The significance of this statement dawned on Sassy. "You mean the thief returns and breaks in?"

"Do your friends lock their doors?"

Sassy paused for a moment. "They live in fairly secure neighborhoods. They don't always lock their doors. I don't either. If I run out the door on an errand, I figure I'll be back in ten minutes so I often leave my door open."

"But that's a random thing," I said. "The person would have to know someone's routine. Like if you went to yoga or Pilates every week or picked up your kid from school."

"We all know each other's routines. We've been together for so long. I tell you what, we'll ask Orchid what she thinks."

"Why?"

"Because she knows everybody too."

I stopped working on Sassy's hair. "Sassy?"

"Yes?"

"I don't know how to tell you this, but—"

Sassy caught my eye in the mirror. She was no fool. "*Everybody's* a suspect," she said.

"Until we know what's going on, my husband would be the first to tell you that. Even Orchid. Even the hostesses you talked to. They could be covering something up." I began brushing Sassy's hair again. "*Especially* Orchid."

"You're not serious." Sassy turned in her chair and looked at me. "Why?"

"Because prescription drug abuse is very common among teens and young adults."

"You mean people my age?"

"Twenty-somethings."

"I don't like this," Sassy said. "I don't like being suspicious of a friend."

"It sucks, doesn't it?"

"Yeah."

"How much do you know about Orchid?" I asked, weaving the headpiece into Sassy's hair.

"She moved here after college to ski. Couldn't get a job in the fancy ski town next door so she got a job here. She's a teacher's aide in an elementary school."

"I know. Sunshine Elementary. That's where Jamie goes." I remembered Jamie's opinion of Orchid. *Miss Fisher's mean,* he had said. "What about boyfriends?"

"She's a loner. Not many friends. She dates, but there's no one special."

Orchid reappeared at the workshop door with a fresh champagne bottle. Her face was flushed with laughter. "Cholly's a riot!"

Orchid looked more animated than when she left the room. She placed her purse back on the counter along with the champagne bottle.

"There," I said, stepping back from the chair.

Sassy picked up the hand mirror and surveyed the back of her head. "Exquisite."

I turned to Orchid. "Now it's your turn."

Orchid gave me a giddy grin. "Righty-o."

My nose itched to take a look inside that purse, but I didn't dare.

Time passed quickly after that. A parade of girls came through for their headpieces. Madeleine's wedding photographer arrived and monopolized the activities with candids and poses. Then dressing began. When they were all assembled for their final Citrus Salon photograph, I felt this was one of the prettiest wedding entourages I'd ever prepped.

Absolutely gorgeous girls.

The bride looked radiant and Sassy looked sensational, but Orchid's pupils were dilated and her attention was hard to get. As they flowed out to the waiting limousines, I pulled Sassy aside. "Call me next week."

I watched them drive off with a huge smile on my face. The salon was a wreck but there was a twelve hundred dollar check in my pocket and my heart was full: another bride successfully launched by The Citrus Salon.

Monday when Jamie came home from school I announced we were going to the recycling center because my car was full of plastic champagne flutes and glass bottles.

"Awesome!" Jamie said.

Kids love to go to the recycling center in our town. Not only is there a warehouse full of used toys, but the candy jar in the office is always full of fireballs and gummy bears. Jamie darted around the house, collecting recyclables. I sorted through the bins in the garage, making sure cans were in the metal bin, paper in the paper bin, and plastic in the plastic bin.

Our recycling center is the biggest meet-and-greet place in the city aside from The Watering Hole on Center Street. As we slid into a parking spot, I waved to Don Westcott who was backing out. I nodded to Martha Farquhar as she barged by with a box of cardboard, but Martha ignored me as usual.

My son began to unload our stuff right away.

"Jamie!" cried a familiar voice.

Tinker Bell, wearing a T-shirt with big letters saying STAFF, grabbed a full bin from Jamie's hands. Tinker was no taller than Jamie and they seemed to be equals in the sophistication department. They ran to the plastics sorting tent, giggling all the way; then disappeared into the office, heading, I presumed, for the candy jar.

I caught sight of Shannon, who managed the center's operations, and asked him if there were any Styrofoam peanuts I could use to ship a package.

"Sure," he said, leading me to the back of the warehouse. Our recycling center is big on re-use—they keep stuff around that people could buy for very little money—plywood, two by fours, lighting fixtures, kitchen cabinets, toilets, sinks, and packing materials.

Shannon scooped some peanuts out of a bin and poured them into a plastic bag. "Need any moving boxes?"

Stacks of flattened U-Haul boxes towered over us; everyone appeared to be moving *into* our fair city, not out.

"Check out all those computer batteries," said Shannon. "We've had a run on them lately."

"I thought you didn't take hazardous material," I said.

"We don't. Someone left these while we were closed." The pile was a mile high.

"Do they work?"

"The lithium's been removed."

We walked out of the warehouse and I heard Tinker talking to Jamie in her funny voice. "Put your paper in the paper bin, Jamie."

The paper bin was as big as the back of a semi-truck. As Jamie attempted to hurl the bag into the open window, Shannon gave it a boost but paper still fell out. He stooped and picked up a canceled check.

"Tracy, don't be so trusting," he said, tearing up the check. "Stuff like this shouldn't go in a recycle bin. That's why we have a shredder."

"Do you worry much about mail theft here?"

"We have security now." Shannon pointed to a camera perched up on the corner of the warehouse.

"That's impressive."

Shannon laughed. "It's not hooked up or anything, but it looks official. Somebody dropped the camera off, so we decided to put it up as a deterrent."

I looked around for Jamie. "Time to go!"

He waved bye-bye to Tinker Bell.

"So long, Tracy," said Shannon. "I just might come in next week for a haircut."

"Please do," I said, knowing full well that Shannon wasn't about to visit my salon. He had a thing going with my major competitor. She was blonde, single, and a 38D.

When we arrived home, Jamie helped me return the bins to the garage; then scooted inside and rummaged around in the refrigerator for a snack.

"Don't spoil your dinner," I said, as he drew out the layer cake I'd made for Sunday's dessert.

"Aw, Mom."

"Carrots and celery."

"Those are for guinea pigs."

"Cucumber sandwiches."

He screwed up his face.

"Peanut butter and crackers."

Jamie returned the cake to its spot in the fridge and headed for the pantry.

The doorbell rang. Jamie hurtled towards the back door with a knife covered in peanut butter.

"Can Jamie come play in my tree fort?" called a voice from the back deck.

I rescued the knife before the peanut butter separated from the blade and embedded itself in the door sill.

"Sure," I said.

Jamie ran off with his friend, loaded with enough peanut butter crackers for a small army.

I dressed a pork roast with olive oil and rosemary and popped it in the oven; then settled down in front of my computer screen and typed "foster care" into the search field.

The words called up several choices:

"Make a Difference and Become a Foster Parent Today"
"Family of Infant Who Died in Foster Care Files Claim Against County"
"Opioid Crisis Straining Nation's Foster Care System"

I clicked on the last one and discovered several worrisome statistics: Foster care needs around the country had skyrocketed by almost one-third because the parents were addicted to pain pills. Babies were addicted because of the birth mother's addiction. There weren't enough foster parents to care for the 5,000 children who needed foster care in our state.

I clicked on "Become a Foster Parent" and was treated to all sorts of exhortations:

"Share your strength and your home . . . "
"Make a commitment to help and heal . . ."
"Enrich the lives of abused and neglected children . . ."

The same rosy thoughts had been dancing in my mind ever since I learned about Charlotte. Carl and I were in a position to foster a child. We had a comfortable income, a nice home, good health, and would pass a criminal background check. I thought Jamie would enjoy having a sister, although I planned to consult a pediatrician about that assumption. Carl had said "Leave it to the professionals," but I didn't want to be discouraged from looking into it.

I clicked on "Avenues for Adoption." There appeared to be two choices: Fostering a number of children including a "specific child" (Charlotte) before adoption, or going through months of training before being allowed to adopt the "specific child," who would be available for other families to adopt while we were going through training.

The first option meant we would need to incorporate many more children into our lives than I had anticipated and the second option meant we might be disappointed if Charlotte were chosen by another family before we finished our training.

Either way, Charlotte would be placed in foster care with perfect strangers for a number of months. That made no sense to me if a family was willing to take care of her right away.

The back door slammed.

I left the computer and found Carl in the kitchen pulling the layer cake out of the refrigerator.

"That's for dessert," I said.

"There was no sign on it."

"Does it need to say Keepa Ya Hands Off? Maybe I should have written that in icing."

Carl shoved the cake back in the refrigerator. "What's for hors d'oeuvres?"

"Peanut butter and crackers."

He shook his head.

"Cheese and crackers."

He shrugged.

"Beer and crackers."

He smiled.

I poured the beer while he changed clothes. I would ask him the latest news on Charlotte when he came downstairs. And when could I meet her? I wanted to be the one to rescue this little girl. I wanted to fix things and work it all out.

Beer froth ran over the top of the glass. I wiped up the beer with a paper towel, then arranged some cheese and crackers on a cutting board.

Carl reappeared in the kitchen. "How was your day?" he asked, hoisting his mug faceward.

"Bookkeeping all morning, recycling with Jamie after school, then researching foster care and adoption."

A shadow crossed Carl's face.

"What?" I said.

"Charlotte has an aunt and uncle who are going to take care of her," he said. "They're working with the state now. It's called kinship care." Carl must have seen the look on my face because he said, "Tracy, the aunt is the mother's sister. Her goal is to restore Charlotte to her mother once she's gone through rehab. The caseworker is on top of it."

I grabbed the cheese and returned it to the refrigerator so he couldn't see my tears. My heart had been set kind of set on this idea. A little girl Jamie's age would have been fun to take care of. I had enjoyed dreaming about it.

"There's quite a bit of trauma there," Carl went on. "The half-brother threatened to slit her throat if she didn't stop bugging him. He murdered her cat to prove his point. Charlotte has nightmares about it."

An awful thought entered my head which I voiced to the cake inside the refrigerator. "Was she sexually molested?"

"No. But she was terrorized," Carl said. "It will take a long time to get over that. I'm not sure we'd be up to the challenge. Or Jamie. We need to think of the effect on him."

I nodded.

He set his beer on the counter and took me in his arms. "So you see, it's for the best."

The refrigerator door swung shut as I repeated, "For the best."

Sassy Morgan called on Wednesday. "I need you to come to book club again," she said. "Even if you can't join, come to the next meeting. I'm worried about more medicine thefts."

"When is it?"

"Thursday night two weeks from now."

I scrolled down to my calendar. "I'm free."

"You'll have to read the book," she said.

"*Packing for Mars*?"

"That was last month. It's called *Wild* by a girl named Cheryl Strayed who hiked the Pacific Crest Trail."

"Is it turgid?" I asked.

Sassy laughed. "No, you'll like this one."

I wrote down the details. "Sassy, let's tag team a little. If someone gets up during the discussion, one of us will follow the person to see where she goes. Okay?"

"Okay, Sherlock," she said.

"Try to be casual about it, Watson."

"Get another hors d'oeuvre? Pour a glass of wine? Is that the idea?"

"Just say you have a bladder infection."

Sassy laughed.

"And sometime during the evening, tell Orchid you've had some dental surgery and you're off the painkillers the dentist gave you."

Stone silence on the other end of the line.

"Sassy?" I asked.

"Isn't that entrapment?"

"Whoever is taking pills is addicted to them and that means they're hurting, Sassy. Someone's life is taking a dive. They need to get help before something bad happens."

"All right."

"I have my doubts about Candy too, not just Orchid," I told her. "So I'm going to mention to Candy that I've got meds for dental surgery, too. We'll see what happens."

Book club was held at the home of Mrs. Goodrich, the elegant woman in the designer dress who lived in our town's first gated community. Every huge home in Blue Cliffs is right on the golf course. They have breathtaking views of our snow-capped mountains and their own personal putting greens. Half the inhabitants have retired with millions made from hedge funds; the other half are executives in Fortune 500 companies.

As I drove past the palatial estates, I felt a bit uncomfortable. These homes had names like Durango Manor and Lookout Lodge. My house is just called House.

A sign on the door at the book club address said "Walk In" so I did. Female voices bounced off lofty ceilings somewhere in the back. I followed the noise to the kitchen where a dozen women were clustered around a large island. The kitchen boasted two ranges, two sinks and two dishwashers.

"Tracy's here!" shouted Candy Fiber. "Tracy is the *best* hair colorist!" She patted her purple locks.

I had to admit Candy's hair made me look good. I had balanced her natural color with just enough violaceous to make it daring but tasteful. Candy poured me a glass of Shiraz. I took a tentative sip. This was not the cheap stuff.

Orchid stood by a plate of goat cheese, grapes and water crackers, drinking rosé. Sassy was perched next to her on a bar chair, giving me a thumbs up. I assumed she'd told Orchid about her dental work.

After everyone arrived and was properly watered, Meryl Thompson shooed us into the Great Room. The sofa was so deep I couldn't lean on the back cushion and make my feet touch the floor at the same time, so I propped some pillows behind me. We all looked uncomfortable but ready for some studious discussion.

I held *Wild* in my hand. My wine glass sat on the vast coffee table in front of me and I tried to reach it but Candy plunked herself down next to me and saved me the trouble. I managed to mention my fake dental troubles to Candy before the moderator cleared her throat.

Meryl Thompson extracted some printed notes tucked between the pages of her book. "These questions are from Oprah's website. You all know Oprah loved Cheryl Strayed's book and they made it into a movie."

"Starring Reese Witherspoon," said Candy.

The moderator cleared her throat again and read verbatim. "When Cheryl discovers the guidebook to the Pacific Crest Trail, she says that the trip was an idea, vague and outlandish, full of promise and mystery. Later, her soon-to-be ex-husband suggests she wants to do the hike to be alone and get off drugs. What do you think her reasons were for committing to this journey?"

She put her papers down and glanced around the room.

No one said a thing.

I shifted on my pillows. The answer was perfectly obvious—Cheryl had fucked up her life and had no idea what she was getting into. She was out of control. But I didn't say this—I just squirmed in my seat.

Finally, a middle-aged woman said, "She's reaching an age where she must birth herself from the confines of child personhood to adult personhood and go on her own, very intimate journey, just as the archetypal hero goes on his quest to slay his dragons and returns victorious."

They all put that comment in their pipes and smoked it.

Orchid raised her hand. "I think she wants to get away from drugs. She needs to go to a place where there are no temptations and only hardship. She's afraid to go on and afraid not to go on. She is afraid."

Candy said, "I think she wants to off the husband and she needs to get far, far away so she doesn't wring his neck."

Everyone laughed.

"Interesting comments, all of you." Mrs. Thompson beamed, as if we were her children. She consulted her notes again: "Walking on the trail during the first few weeks, Cheryl writes, 'My mind was a crystal vase that contained only one desire. My body was its opposite: a bag of broken glass.' Throughout the book she talks about blisters, dehydration, exhaustion and hunger. How—and why—did this physical suffering help her cope with her emotional pain?"

I watched the faces around the room. Orchid looked tired and listless. Candy looked buoyant and sunny. Sassy looked worried. Another woman looked glazed over. The rest were talking and seemed to be tracking with the discussion.

Mrs. Thompson allowed the conversation to wane before she let fly with the next question: "Cheryl's pack, also known as Monster, is one of those real-life objects that makes a perfect literary metaphor: Cheryl has too much to carry on her back and in her mind. Are there other objects she takes with her or acquires along the way that take on deeper meanings? How so?"

This was surely a turgid question. I rolled my eyes at Sassy to see if she agreed with me. She raised her hand to her mouth and giggled behind it.

People began to talk. They were deep in the throes of reading a lot into a little, when Orchid rose from her chair. Sassy's eyebrows shot up. I struggled up from the passel of pillows sucking me down like a kids' plunge-pile in a McDonalds PlayPlace.

In the kitchen Orchid was pouring herself another glass of wine. I got busy with the cheese and crackers, waiting to see where she'd go next. She headed back toward the Great Room.

"Orchid," I called.

"Yes?" She turned back, right next to a pillar of wall ovens.

"That was very perceptive of you—your remark about the drugs. How did you know that?"

"I have friends . . ." she said. "They'd do anything to get off drugs."

"I guess they're having a hard time."

"They've tried and tried." Her mouth turned down. "It's their prison." She toddled off to the Great Room. I grabbed a couple of grapes and followed.

"In the beginning of the book," Mrs. Thompson said, "Cheryl's prayers are literally curse words—curses for her mother's dying, curses against her mother for failing. How does her spiritual life change with prayer? What is the meaning of God?"

The group worked hard on spirituality. Words like "nature," "meaning," "mysticism," "exorcism," and "otherworldliness" rippled around the room. I was happy to let them wallow in this discussion.

When spirituality had run its course, Mrs. Thompson broached another topic: "Cheryl wrote: 'The thing about hiking the Pacific Crest Trail was how few choices I had and how often I had to do the thing I least wanted to do. How there was no escape or denial.' In what ways have her choices helped and/or hurt her up to this point?" Mrs. Thompson actually said "and/or." She was a very precise facilitator.

Sassy spoke first. "I think the most difficult thing for me to understand was Cheryl's involvement with heroin. We all know what a hard core drug that is and how it leads to addiction. I'm sure Cheryl knew that. So why did she do it? Why put yourself in peril like that?"

I held my breath, waiting for Candy or Orchid to answer. The room was so silent you could hear the ice maker in the refrigerator filling with water.

"I used heroin once," said a voice from deep within a sofa next to Mrs. Thompson.

All eyes turned to the rail thin, elegant woman in the designer dress, our hostess Mrs. Goodrich.

"I had a C-section when my daughter was born and became dependent on prescription pain killers. When Percocet wasn't enough, I wanted something stronger. We were living in New York City at the time, so heroin was easy to get. I became addicted and my husband found out. He took me to the Resort and they saved my life. That's how we ended up living here."

Everyone started talking at once. Some women wanted to hear more; others fled to the cheese and crackers—I guessed this confession was too personal for them.

I followed one woman; Sassy followed another. They ended up in the kitchen, scarfing down hors d'oeuvres and pouring more wine. All except Candy Fiber. She had disappeared.

Sassy motioned up with her forefinger and pointed her thumb to her chest. I took that to mean she would go upstairs while I searched the lower level. No Candy.

The group was re-convening. Orchid had stayed in her chair, body pitched forward, still hanging on to catch every word the elegant lady was saying. Candy returned. Sassy returned. The group discussion continued but I zoned out. I'd had enough of school for the day. *Wild* was not a turgid book, but Oprah's questions made it so.

The evening ended with one final sortie from Mrs. Thompson: "At one point, Cheryl tells herself, 'I was not meant to be this way, to live this way, to fail so darkly.' It's a moment of self-criticism and despair. And yet, some belief in herself exists in that statement. How do the things Cheryl believes about herself throughout the memoir, even during her lowest moments, help or hurt her on the Pacific Crest Trail?"

One woman spoke in a fairly self-righteous tone. "Cheryl must have had a low opinion of herself because she slept with real low-lifes. I can't understand how she could do that."

The woman whose eyes had been glazed over earlier in the evening was engaged now. "That was during a tough period when God had dealt her some pretty bad cards—especially her mother's death," she said. "On the trail, she believes she can make it. She *wills* herself to make it. And she does."

I put in my two cents. "Cheryl Strayed was not meant to walk the Pacific Crest Trail. She was meant to write a book. It could have been about anything. She couldn't give up that vision of herself. Being an author was her dream and *that* was why she did it."

No one seemed interested in my observation.

We finished our wine and said our goodbyes. Orchid and Candy left. I walked out the front door with Sassy. "Where did Candy go during the break?" I asked.

"She went to the master bathroom and snooped through the medicine cabinet."

"She didn't!"

"She did and when I confronted her, she said – 'Just seeing if our hostess needs a re-fill.' She pulled one of her dietary supplements out of the cabinet and opened the bottle."

"The balls of that girl."

"I'll say," said Sassy, shaking her head and giggling as she walked away.

Nothing happened for an entire week and then Sassy Morgan called. Her house had been burglarized. The thief jimmied the back door, but nothing was taken.

"That's because there was nothing to take," I said. "You didn't have dental surgery so there were no pain pills. This can't be a coincidence."

The next evening Carl came home and told me there had been three burglaries in a neighborhood not far from ours. The thief entered the homes by forcing the back door open with a tool, probably a crowbar. Again, nothing was taken.

"Did you check to see if any prescription pills went missing?"

"It was the chief's case," he said.

Carl and I looked at each other. Of course, the chief would forget to ask about prescription drugs. Carl knew how worried I was about Orchid. "I'll see what I can find out." He headed back to the police station.

I sat down at the kitchen table. Orchid's words came back to me: *She's afraid to go on and afraid not to go on. She is afraid.*

I called Sassy. "Have you heard from Orchid lately?"

"No, why?"

I explained about the break-ins. "I can't help thinking about her. Getting drunk at Madeleine's wedding, maybe even high. What she said at book club about 'friends' on drugs. Her reaction to Mrs. Goodrich's story. I just think we owe it to her to stay in touch."

"Especially after these break-ins."

"What if she did them? What if she scored and she's floating away right now? Maybe forever. Do you know her number?"

"I'll call her," Sassy said.

Ten minutes later she called back. Orchid's cell phone had gone to voicemail over and over.

"Do you know where she lives?" I said.

"Yes."

"I'll pick you up in five minutes."

I took Jamie to my neighbor's house. By the time I arrived at Sassy's, she was pacing her front lawn.

Orchid rented a cottage in a modest neighborhood. Her car was in the driveway but there was no answer to the doorbell. The front door was locked.

We circled the house, peering through the windows. The curtains were drawn. I banged hard on the back door. It, too, was locked. Sassy found a sash window slightly open in the rear.

"Let's use it," I said.

She shook her head. "We would be breaking in."

I took my cell phone out of my pocket and tapped on my Favorite.

"You're doing what?" Carl said.

I put him on speakerphone and explained again.

"Tracy, you can't break into a house on a whim. So what if she seems depressed at book club? Lots of people are depressed. And they drink too much. Do you see anything through the window?"

"No."

"Then I can't come over. The chief gets mad if officers go around kicking in doors. I've no warrant and no probable cause of any wrong-doing."

"Okay," I said. "You're probably right. See you at home, sweetheart." I tapped the little red stop button.

Sassy and I traded looks.

"I'll get that lawn chair and you do the job," she said.

We used the Leatherman I keep in my glove compartment to cut the screen. The casement window was hard to raise but I got in. Sassy climbed in after me. We were in a laundry room.

Sassy called Orchid's name and ran through the tiny house straight to the bedroom. Orchid was lying on the bed. We couldn't wake her.

"Her pulse is weak but she's still with us," I said. "Call an ambulance."

Sassy used her cell, then rushed outside to meet the medics.

I called Carl. Then I looked around. There were three pill bottles on the bedside table with a note. I leaned over and read it.

Please forgive me, whoever finds me here, and tell everyone not to do what I have done. Pills are a prison and I'm in it. I'm not strong enough to ask for parole. I'm sorry.

"Oh, Orchid," I whispered. I bent over the comatose figure on the bed. "Don't die now. There's so much to live for."

I could hear a siren approaching. Then the room swarmed with EMTs taking over, checking vitals, running an IV, strapping Orchid on their high-tech wheeled bed, evacuating her to the hospital.

Carl arrived and I showed him the note. He bagged it along with three empty pill bottles. The rest of the forensic team scoured the house. Carl and I drifted out to the front lawn where Sassy stood looking stunned.

"You two did good," Carl said. "That girl would be dead now if it hadn't been for you."

"Is she going to be all right?" Sassy said.

"I heard the EMTs talking—her chances are good."

Sassy's shoulders didn't straighten. "Are we going to be arrested?" she asked in a small voice.

Carl laughed. "For breaking and entering? No. But you'll both need to come downtown and give a statement."

"You okay, Sassy?" I asked.

"I feel a little shaky."

"Let me take Sassy home for a minute," I said to Carl. "Can we see you later?"

"Sure."

I put Sassy in the passenger seat of my car. We didn't talk much on the way to her condo. By now it was way past ten and I could tell Sassy was dead tired.

"Why don't you rest? Then we'll go to police station."

As soon as we unlocked the condo, Sassy went into her bedroom and shut the door while I searched the fridge. I poured myself a healthy dollop of white wine and sat down on the sofa.

What was going to happen to Orchid now? Did she have any family who should be called? Probably the school principal had her emergency contacts. Suddenly I remembered Jamie.

I called my neighbor and we agreed Jamie should stay overnight. I closed my eyes. The next thing I knew my cell phone was ringing. Carl wanted to know where we were.

The police department was a busy place. It was a Friday night, and the normal activity of drunk and disorderlies, accidental shootings, and security alarms made Orchid's medical emergency seem routine.

Carl met us in the lobby. "This is Detective Romero," Carl said. "He's going to take your statements."

"Sassy first, so she can go home right away," I said.

"Thanks, Tracy." She and the detective disappeared down a hallway to the interview rooms.

I followed Carl to the snack room. "Want something from the vending machine?" Carl asked.

I shook my head. "I just want to go home."

Carl put his arms around me as a patrolman came in and poured himself a cup of coffee. We didn't speak until the cop left.

"What's going to happen to Orchid?" I asked.

"It doesn't look good."

"You mean she's—"

"No, no. She'll pull through. They pumped her stomach and she's sleeping now."

"Then what's the bad news?"

"The pill bottles we found beside Orchid's bed belonged to owners of the burgled homes. All three are teachers at Jamie's school."

"So there is no doubt—Orchid is the pill thief."

"Her car contained a pry-bar and papers with the names and addresses of the entire staff at Sunshine Elementary. There was another address list too. Sassy's name was on it, Shelley Prothero's and ours."

"The book club."

"Looks like it." Carl's face looked grim.

"What else?" I asked.

"There were clippings from the newspaper for realtor open houses."

"What does that mean?"

"Orchid may have stolen pills from the medicine cabinets of those homes too."

I let out my breath. "Orchid was in a really bad way. Did you read her suicide note?"

Carl nodded. "She needs professional help. But she's going to be charged. You've got to steel yourself for that."

"Charged with what?"

"Felonies. Burglary, possession of a controlled substances, possession of drug paraphernalia. She's going to jail. When she gets out of the hospital, Tracy, she's going to jail."

Case 6

Officer Down

● ● ● ● ● ● ●

The funeral procession wound its way up a narrow dirt road surrounded by sagebrush hills. Carl and I followed the police cars; a parade of personal vehicles followed us. The hearse stopped next to a newly dug grave. We parked wherever we could find a spot and got out. The sun beat down; there was no shade. Sagebrush quivered all around.

Carl grasped my hand. Officers in uniform, the chief, the mayor, city councilors, city staffers, their wives and husbands, all crowded around the grave. Four pall bearers brought the casket, an American flag draped over it. The half-sized casket squeezed my heart.

There was a drumbeat. Men removed their hats. The police chaplain spoke.

"From the beginning of time after Cain killed his brother Abel there has been a need for law enforcement officers to protect the weak and bring evildoers to justice." The chaplain clutched his Bible, but didn't refer to notes. "This work is necessary in a sinful world and it is dangerous."

I squeezed Carl's hand. There are desperate people out there. I'm reminded of that every time Carl puts on his Kevlar vest.

"Today, we honor the sacrifice of a beloved member of our police force, who succumbed to gunshot wounds sustained in the line of duty. Lord

God, we are grateful for the life of K9 Barney who died protecting Officer Joseph Torgesen."

All eyes swiveled to Officer Torgesen. There was a bandage on his forehead.

"Help us never forget him," continued the chaplain. "Help us celebrate the life of K9 Barney and honor his sacrifice. Comfort the friends and colleagues of this fallen hero and give them your strength."

I glanced over at the array of city councilors. Martha Farquhar was wiping her eyes. Could the town's most vocal pet cemetery opponent be weeping over a dog?

"In commemorating the death of this hero, help us remember that death is not the end. Death is simply the transition to the glorious life to come. Dogs do go to heaven! We should look forward to the life to come with joy and thanksgiving. Amen."

We all said amen.

"And now," said the chaplain, "any officer who wishes to speak may step forward."

Officer Martinez moved up and saluted the coffin. "K9 Barney. You did a great job. Our condolences to your partner for his loss. Run free at the Rainbow Bridge and Godspeed. Not gone, just gone ahead. You pave the way for all of us."

Officer Young laid a wreath beside the casket. "It was a pleasure to train with you, K9 Barney," she said. "I remember watching you search for narcotics, doing what you did best."

Officer Witte moved forward. "Barney, you protected your two-legged partner and many of our officers during your time. Now it's your turn to run free and play with all the other dogs over the Rainbow Bridge. One day you and your partner will be reunited." He turned toward Officer Torgesen. "Stay strong."

Tears glistened on Officer Torgesen's face.

Carl released my hand and stepped forward. He took a paper out of his uniform pocket and unfolded it in the wind. "You are all familiar with the Rainbow Bridge poem," he said, "but I'll take this occasion to remind you of the poem's vision." He cleared his throat. "Just this side of heaven is a place called the Rainbow Bridge. When an animal dies who has been especially close to a human, that pet crosses the Rainbow Bridge. On the other side, there is plenty of food, water, and sunshine. All the animals who were ill and old are restored to health and vigor. Those who were hurt or maimed are made whole and strong again. All the animals run and play together over meadows and green hills. They are happy and content except for one thing: they each miss someone very special to them who was left behind."

As a bugler played taps, Officer Torgesen placed his hat over his heart and lifted his chin to the sky as if his tears would defy gravity and roll back into his eyes. The casket was lowered and flowers were tossed on top. Officer Torgesen tipped the first shovelful of dry, gritty earth over the coffin.

We headed toward our cars. After passing through the entrance gate, I looked back and saw the inscription on the arch. *Rainbow Gate*, the name of our community's new pet cemetery.

"I'm here!" The front door slammed. Cholly Chockworth swept into my salon. "Now Life can Begin!"

"There's nobody here but me," I said from the chair behind my computer.

"Now *your* life can begin." Cholly leaned over the desk and planted a kiss on my cheek. "Where shall we sit, my dear? Have you got coffee? I'm just dying for caffeine. Don't serve me, I can serve myself. Where is it? No, no, don't get up. I see it. I see it."

Cholly charged over to the coffee pot and poured himself a mug, draped himself on the sofa, and opened a notebook. He took a gulp.

"Delicious. You don't fool around do you? Only the best coffee beans at The Citrus Salon."

"I'm glad you approve." I sat in an upholstered chair opposite Cholly with my Notebook.

"I have an idea for something new this year," Cholly said. "A fashion show! I've already talked to the Blue Boutique and lined up Ms. Cowgirl and her First Attendant as models. What do you think?"

What could I think? It had all been arranged. "Brilliant!" I said.

"We need a new caterer. Last year the food was dull. Eileen at *Done to Your Taste Catering* is just the person we want. Did you know she catered the fundraising breakfast for Michelle Obama? You will love her!"

I ticked catering off my list of things to worry about. Cholly had this well in hand.

"Roxy Rafael is coming, but she will do facials instead of makeup, and Annabelle will do massages, of course."

Of course.

Cholly looked up as the front door opened. "Oh, ho! Who's *this*?"

A tall male figure in an Izod shirt and jeans stood in the entrance. The sun's rays outlined his powerful biceps and long legs.

"Delicious," Cholly muttered under his breath.

"Officer Torgesen," I rose from my chair and met him at the door. "What brings you here?"

"A gift certificate for Pamper Night," he said. "It's what every woman wants, isn't it?"

He had to have seen my display ad in the paper with the headline "What Every Woman Wants."

"Massages, facials, pedicures and Tarot card readings," I said.

"And a fashion show!" said Cholly. He stuck out his hand. "Hi. I'm Cholly Chockworth."

Officer Torgesen put his large, strong hand around Cholly's manicured palm. "Joe."

"Cholly heads up my event every year," I said. "He knows what every woman wants."

"I'll bet he does," said Officer Torgesen, his eyes twinkling.

"I think they want *you*," Cholly said.

"Me?"

"Women want to buy clothes for their men. You'd be a great model for our fashion show."

"We're showing *men's* fashions this year?" I asked Cholly.

"Absolutely," he said.

I'll bet you just thought of that.

"Would you do it?" Cholly asked Torgesen.

"Sure."

I was surprised at the answer, so soon after the tragic death of K9 Barney.

"Officer Torgesen doesn't have time to do this sort of thing," I said, thinking to let him off the hook.

"April wants me to get back into the swing of things." He touched his forehead where his bandage used to be. I was glad to see it had been replaced with a Band-Aid. "It's a form of grief management."

"Who's April?" asked Cholly.

"My sister. The gift certificate is for her."

"That wouldn't be the April who spent the night in the beer cooler at the Maverik gas station, would it?" I asked.

He nodded. "I helped her through that awful time and now she's helping me through mine."

I saw the question in Cholly's eyes. "Officer Torgesen's K9 partner was buried last month," I said to Cholly.

Cholly's face fell. Everyone in town had heard about K9 Barney. "I'm sorry for your loss," Cholly said.

"Thanks."

"Look," I said, going to my desk. "The gift certificate is on the house. You can pay for any extras like a massage or a pedicure."

"You don't need to do that."

"Yes, she does," said Cholly. "You're going to be a model, remember?"

Joe laughed. "Okay. I'd like April to have a massage *and* a pedicure."

"No Tarot card reading?" asked Cholly.

"*And* a Tarot card reading." Joe pulled out his wallet. "You're a very persuasive guy."

Cholly beamed.

I ran Joe's credit card while the two men talked about the fashion show. I heard them laughing. Cholly is such a charmer.

I handed Joe his gift certificate and emailed his receipt. Joe took his leave.

"Just my luck," said Cholly, when Joe closed the door.

"What's the matter?"

"He's straight."

My calendar said Mrs. Betsy Goodrich was due at three for a color and style. Today the hostess of the recent book club session looked long and lanky in a tailored blouse and slacks. Her face with its swept-back hair, patrician nose, and arched eyebrows reminded me of Katherine Graham, the heroic publisher of the *Washington Post*.

In my salon living room I offered her the array of goodies that usually put a new client at ease. But she selected ice water. Everything about her seemed sucked-in as if she were waiting for something distasteful to happen.

I suspected she was worried I would ruin her hair, so I tackled the problem right away. "What brings you to see me instead of your usual hairdresser?"

"My husband and I are going out to dinner tonight with the Chairman of the Board and his wife. They're flying in unexpectedly from Aspen and I don't have time to go to the big valley."

I nodded as if executives in Lear jets landed at our tiny municipal airport and visited me every day. "So you must look your best."

Her bones relaxed a nanosecond, then resumed their original position. "My hair needs work."

I evaluated the sculptured helmet curving around her face; frosted highlights glinting in the afternoon sun; not one hair out of place. "What would you like done?"

"My roots are showing," she said with a sharpness that informed me the problem was obvious.

"Yes, I see that." I let my voice became authoritative, hoping to inspire confidence. "I'll contact your hairdresser in the city for the formula so we have a match. You'll look perfect for the evening." I left her browsing my new box of Godiva chocolate-topped cookies while I telephoned.

We repaired to the workroom where I painted her roots. There was only a quarter inch of gray so I had to be precise. When I was done she rested on a recliner, although resting could hardly be the name for it. I got the feeling she believed vigilance would ward off any botched job.

When her hairstyle re-emerged, coiffed and true-to-color, she bestowed me with a radiant smile. "I meant to thank you for saving Orchid's life."

"I was just in the right place at the right time."

"Not to hear Sassy Morgan tell the story."

I pictured all the women at book club gathered round to learn the details from someone intimately involved in the day we burgled Orchid's cottage and found she'd overdosed.

"How did you know she was suicidal?" Mrs. Goodrich asked.

"I didn't. It was a feeling and I acted on it."

"Even I didn't recognize the symptoms," she said. "And I've seen a lot of it. Orchid is the fourth person I've helped."

"What do you mean?"

"I posted bail for her and she's living with me, waiting for her trial date."

"That's wonderful." I said, a little awestruck. Bail had been set at $94,000 and I had envisioned Orchid incarcerated for the millennium.

"I've engaged an excellent defense attorney to take her case. We're gathering character references who will testify on her behalf. Teachers from her school; in fact, the very teachers whose houses she robbed. They have forgiven her and so should the judge. Opioid addiction is an epidemic, not a crime. She will beat it."

"But how?"

"The Resort. They have an excellent success rate. She'll get the best of care."

"But how can she afford—" I stopped. Clearly Mrs. Goodrich was going to foot all the bills. "Mrs. Goodrich, you're a saint."

"No, Tracy, I'm a sinner. A redemptive sinner. I'm paying for my past. My children lost their childhood and I was a nightmare for my husband. But he stood by me and we won through. Now I pay it forward with young women like Orchid who deserve another chance."

A few days later I waited with Jamie at the bus stop. When I came through the back door, I was grabbed by familiar hands, carried to the living room sofa, and ravished. Being swept off my feet felt like the sexiest thing in the world.

Afterwards, we went upstairs and I watched Carl get dressed. He has the most gorgeous pecs I've seen on any male, even the models in *Gentleman's*

Quarterly. He pulled his T-shirt over his head and shrugged on his bullet proof vest.

I have a love-hate relationship with that vest. It reminds me he's in danger every day, but Kevlar is the only thing that separates a cop from a fatal gunshot wound and I'm grateful for its existence. A woman chemist at DuPont invented the stuff.

"What are you doing today?" I asked.

"Parking tickets and traffic stops."

He often says that to ease the endless worrying of a cop's wife. The answer sounds harmless, but I once watched a YouTube video of a routine traffic stop. As soon as the officer reached the car window, the driver pumped four rounds into him. Three bullets hit the Kevlar, but one entered the cop's abdomen just below the vest. The officer writhed and groaned on the asphalt. I had to turn it off.

"That's all you're doing today?"

"That, and helping little old ladies cross the street." Carl's teeth flashed white as he laughed at me. "Stop worrying. I'm only going up to Wolf Lake. Someone stole a log cabin up there."

"What?"

"Some out-of-towners went to their vacation property yesterday. All that remained of their log cabin was a cement block foundation with weeds in it. Looked like it'd been taken some time ago."

"How could somebody steal a cabin?"

"It was a ten-by-twenty prefabbed storage shed with log siding on it. Torgesen and I are driving up there this morning to interview the neighbors."

"Torgesen?"

"Joe's my partner now."

I told him about Joe's visit to the salon.

Carl laughed. "I'm glad I'm off the hook for that one! Mr. Stud Muffin! Wait 'til I tell the guys. He won't hear the end of it."

"Don't tell anyone! He might not do it and Cholly will be crushed."

"Cholly have the hots for him?"

I rolled my eyes.

"How am I going to keep this to myself?"

"It's an ongoing investigation, sweetheart," I said. "You know you can't reveal any details."

Carl chuckled.

When I arrived at the salon at 11:15, my masseuse, Annabelle Davina, had already opened up.

"The feet connect the body to the Earth," she was saying to Mrs. Argosy. "They support every muscle—the heart, the lungs, and the brain. Your feet are incredibly strong. Stand on your tiptoes for a moment."

Mrs. Argosy levitated like a ballerina.

"You see?" said Annabelle. "Our feet are our means of standing up in the world and facing every person and problem that comes our way. When the feet are well-cared for, we achieve true happiness and serenity."

"All right," said Mrs. Argosy, "add a pedicure."

Annabelle processed Mrs. Argosy's credit card and handed her a Pamper Night ticket. "I'm so glad you're coming," she said.

I ushered Mrs. Argosy to the front door. "You deserve to be pampered after that awful experience with the meth addict in your rental," I said.

"It's all right, Tracy. We have some good tenants now."

I returned to the desk and scrolled through the day's transactions.

"People have been stopping by since nine o'clock," Annabelle said. "I've sold thirty tickets already."

The front door opened and my noontime appointment walked in. I looked at the clock. It was eleven thirty.

"Tracy!" boomed Hawk Reynolds.

"Hey, Hawk."

"How's my favorite head shaper?"

"Got my chain saw ready."

"Who's this beautiful lady?" he asked.

"I'm Annabelle. Annabelle Davina."

Hawk whistled. "A mighty pretty name for a mighty pretty lady. You got a boyfriend?"

"No."

"You lookin' for one?"

"No."

"Gosh darn," he said.

Annabelle disappeared into the massage room.

Hawk had that effect on women.

I took Hawk into my back workroom and draped his burly body with a steel-grey cape. Reaching deep into the cabinet, I pulled out my pair of electric hedge clippers, turned them on, and poised them over his ear.

Hawk guffawed. He got a kick out of this gag every time. He loves to run heavy equipment, set semi-trucks upright, suck up oil spills, and use the Jaws of Life. If something big has to be moved, he's your go-to man.

I took out my iPad. "Let me show you some new hair designs." We went to Pinterest and I clicked through scalps with shaved hair art in stripes, circles, swirls, dots and dashes. There was even a picture of Bart Simpson.

Hawk shook his head. "You never know what people are thinkin'," he said. "Ain't they just ridiculous?"

I glanced at the tattoo on his arm—a death's head figure carrying a sickle. "Ridiculous," I murmured.

He pushed the iPad away. "I want the usual—Telly Savalas."

"Telly Savalas?" I said. "He's so seventies!"

"Patrick Stewart, then."

"So eighties."

"Bruce Willis!"

"Nineties!"

His eyes were popping out now. "Hawk Reynolds!"

"Twenty-first century!"

He guffawed.

"Gotcha!" I said.

I took out my barber's clippers and shaved his head. The buzz of the clippers overrode the sound of my spa music. As hair dropped down on the steel grey cape, his tattoo of a hawk on the wing re-emerged on his scalp.

I turned the shaver off. "Hawk?"

"Yeah."

"If you had to move a ten by twenty pre-fab storage shed, how would you do it?"

"I'd just winch it up on my slideback and drive away."

"That easy?"

"Piece a cake. You and Carl have a shed you want moved?"

I told him about the stolen log cabin. "Have you had any jobs like that? Anyone ask you to move a cabin up at Wolf Lake?"

Hawk gave it some thought. "Nope."

"You've pretty much got the corner on the towing market around here, right?"

"Yup."

"So nobody else is going to get the job?"

"Nope."

I got out my hair dryer and blew little hairs off his neck.

"Tracy," he said when I turned the dryer off.

"Yes?"

"Remember what happened last spring?"

"What?"

"When one of my slidebacks went missing for a night?"

This was ringing a bell.

"We operate twenty-four seven," Hawk said, "and dispatch thought Jake had the truck and Jake thought Larry had the truck and Larry thought Alfie had the truck. The next day the slideback was in the lot. I asked the guys who had it but no one owned up, remember? That tow truck went for a ride overnight and no one confessed."

"How many miles were driven?"

"A hunnert and sixty-eight."

"Interesting." I didn't wonder that Hawk remembered the exact mileage. He knew everything about his business. "Would you mind talking to Carl about it?"

"Sure thing."

"Okay." I removed the cape. "How do you like it?"

Hawk stood up, looked himself in the mirror, and gave me a thumbs up. "Yul Brynner," he said.

"So sixties!"

Carl praised me for solving the riddle of how the log cabin left home. Then we talked about where it could have gone. If Hawk's tow truck was indeed the getaway vehicle, the odometer mileage was low, so the cabin must still be in the county.

The cabin owners were circulating "Reward Offered" flyers all over town. So far no one had come forward. I was so busy planning my event that the whole thing took a back seat until Pamper Night.

The Citrus Salon was stuffed with women gorging themselves on First Lady Fare. My plate was piled high with seared Ahi tuna, crostini swabbed with wasabi-ginger, and maple-bourbon glazed pork on sweet potato chips.

Margaret Pyle brought me a glass of wine.

"How do you like the new caterer?" I asked.

"If she's good enough for Michelle Obama, she's good enough for me!" Margaret said, popping a cucumber round topped with smoked trout into her mouth.

"Not so loud," I whispered. "Half these people voted Republican."

"Well, aren't they silly!"

Shelley Prothero emerged from the massage room wrapped in one of my snow-white Turkish robes. "Tracy, I want you to meet my good friend Dita Steed."

I shook the hand of a deeply tanned young woman, who was also wearing a robe.

"That massage was perfect for my sore muscles," she said.

"Dita is Outlands Coordinator for the High Mountain Desert Wilderness Alliance," said Shelley. "She's staying at my house for a few days."

"What do you do for the Alliance?"

"I hike the remote areas analyzing land use. We protect the wilderness from oil and gas drillers, illegal road making, ATV damage—stuff like that. Right now I'm looking at the county land that borders the national forest."

"It's pretty wild up there, isn't it?"

"Used to be. There's a lot of building up there now, I'm sorry to say."

I told her about the log cabin. "Have you seen a little building like that?"

"No, but I'll keep a lookout."

We sipped our wine during one of those little lulls that happen during conversations with strangers. I was just about to go replenish the hors d'oeuvre table when she said, "We had a squatter case in the southern part of the state last year."

"What happened?"

"A guy took over a cabin on private property. He had a four-year supply of freeze-dried food and an arsenal that put the Marines to shame."

"Sounds dangerous."

"They had a tough time getting him out of there. He was one of those survivalists—wants the government to give all federal land away to private owners and no gun control."

"Just another wingnut," Margaret said.

"He should move to Virgin where it's against the law NOT to own a gun," I said. Virgin is a town down south in our state with a population of about 600.

"When they passed mandatory gun ownership," Dita said, "they also passed an ordinance banning the United Nations."

"As if the UN wants to cozy up to them," said Margaret. "The UN has better things to do."

"The UN's just a symbol," Dita said. "This is about people who are fearful. They feel threatened by forces they can't control. They think nuclear war is imminent."

"Did you know that town also approved an underground condo complex?" asked Margaret.

"No!" I said.

"They never built it, but the architect called for blast-proof doors and nuclear decontamination chambers." We all laughed. Margaret sipped her wine. "So where else do these gun loving survivalists hide out?"

"All over the state," Dita said.

"I guess you know all the kooks," I said. "Does this log cabin thief sound like anyone you've met?"

"I'd have to think about it," Dita said.

Cholly tapped his wine glass. "Time for the fashion show!" His voice was filled with glee. "Take a seat, everyone!"

The room settled down.

"We begin with the lovely Ms. Cowgirl," Cholly said, as Su Tsu emerged from the door of my back workroom. "She's wearing the ever popular teddy with silk bikini. Note the short lace hemline, meant to tantalize your man.

And those high-heeled slippers will show off your calves *and* your pedicure. Thank you, Su."

"Quite the runway walk," I whispered.

"Shoulders back, hips pushed forward," Margaret said.

Ms. Cowgirl disappeared behind the curtain and Tina White Horse took her place.

"Next we see Ms. Cowgirl's First Attendant in a stunning brocade corset. There's a matching G-string, ladies. Pay particular attention to the Velcro front lace closure. Your man will become a bodice ripper! Let's give Tina a hand."

"I would look like a blimp in that," whispered Shelley. "But she looks fabulous."

"Now, here we have Joe Torgesen wearing an attractive number that's easy on your bank account. This fashion statement makes dollars and cents. Really ladies, you can't go wrong buying these for your man."

Joe had emerged from behind the curtain, wearing nothing but tight, contoured, black briefs.

"What a hunk!" Margaret said.

Shelley was fanning herself. Annabelle was holding her breath.

Joe threaded his way through the audience, his briefs at eye level, so everyone could inspect the goods. The salon became steamy. One girl shouted, "Take it off!"

The room erupted.

I could see that Joe was enjoying himself.

Later that evening, as Cholly and I locked up, I gave credit where credit was due. "You certainly did a great job with that fashion show. It was a stroke of genius to feature men's fashions. I think we made a thousand dollars on those briefs alone."

"It's all about knowing what women want," Cholly said.

A vision of the Man of the Evening flashed through my mind. "That Joe Torgesen has an adorable cleft in his chin," I said.

Cholly looked surprised. "Not many of us were looking at his face."

A few days later Carl told me the County Code Enforcement department got a call from a property owner complaining that his stream was gone.

"Let me get this straight," I said to Carl. "You've now got a missing cabin *and* a missing stream?"

"Yeah." Carl laughed. "The property owner says his stream has dried up, which means somebody's diverting water up the mountain. He wants code enforcement to find out who."

"So why do they need you?"

"Because there's a 'No Trespassing' sign on the upstream property the likes of which they've never seen."

"What's wrong with it?"

"Reads like a legal brief."

"You mean it doesn't just say 'No Trespassing - Keep Out'?"

"It references the Second Amendment."

"The right to possess firearms?" I said. "You're not serious."

"True story."

"What kind of landowner posts a thing like that?"

"Someone who's hiding something."

"So he'll shoot first and ask questions later?"

Carl shrugged and tapped on his tablet. "The wording's on a gun rights site." Within seconds the sign was there, front and center, on the screen.

Warning Private Property
NO TRESPASSING
This includes any and all government agents.

Those so trespassing are subject to civil and criminal penalties per USC Title 18 Sections 241 & 242 and all other applicable Federal and state civil or criminal "Trespass" statutes.

VIOLATORS WILL BE TREATED AS INTRUDERS.

A government official agent or any other person entering this property without the express consent of the owner(s) and without proper warrant, as prescribed by the 4th and 14th Amendment of the Constitution, will be considered an intruder, and an attempt to extort, injure, threaten, harass, intimidate or otherwise jeopardize the life and property of the owner of this property. Violations can trigger fines of up to $10,000 and prison sentences of up to 10 years or both, pursuant to trespass law as above listed. The 2nd Amendment is applicable and use of necessary force may be applied at the sole discretion of the owners(s).

Property owner(s) address may be obtained from the County Assessor's office.

"This sounds like the nutcase I heard about the other day," I said. "He had more guns than the military and he was holed up in a vacation cabin turned into a survival bunker."

"The world is a disturbing place," Carl said. "Nine-eleven, Hurricane Katrina, Ebola, ISIS. People look at these things and dream up some frightening scenarios. That's why they stock these arsenals—they're trying to protect their homes and their families."

"But I want to protect *my* home and *my* family," I said. "If you set foot on that property, you could be shot."

Carl gathered me in his arms. "Don't worry. Most of these signs are just bluster and bravado. Code enforcement requested our support so they look more official."

"When are you going there?"

"As soon as the judge grants a warrant."

Water diversion is a big deal in the west. A landowner who dams or alters the flow of water traveling to his downhill neighbor is violating all sorts of regulations. Any judge will issue a warrant and my husband could be under fire. I dreaded the words Officer Down and hoped to God I'd never hear them.

I spent the next morning at the salon wandering around, forgetting what I was looking for, making mistakes on the computer, and listening for the phone to ring. I hoped I wasn't giving my customers the worst haircuts they'd ever had. When Carl came through the front door at noon, I felt my body relax.

"Thought I'd drop by for lunch," Carl said.

"I've got salad, lemon dressing, no bread," I said.

"On second thought, I'll go to the deli."

"Very funny," I said, "but please don't keep me waiting. What happened?"

"The guy had a long range rifle. He could have hit us if he wanted to, but he didn't. He shot at the trees behind us as soon as we rounded a bend in the drive, but we saw enough to know that it's definitely the stolen cabin."

I buried my face in his shoulder, my nose snuffling against his name tag. Carl held me for a long time.

When he released me, he said, "The chief wants to assemble a SWAT team."

My mouth dropped open.

"I know. We're all trying to get the chief see reason, but he wants to make the six o'clock news."

"Well, he will and it won't be good news."

"The chief is incensed. Not only did this guy steal the cabin, but he also stole the property."

"What d'you mean?"

"The property owners are some family in New York. They haven't been out west for years."

"Then he's a squatter?" When Carl nodded, I shook my head in complete disbelief. "I still think there's a less lethal way to enforce water rights than a SWAT team."

"The Feds gave the department all this military equipment and the chief's been dying to use it." Carl's shoulders were hunched up around his ears and I read that as: *Whaddya gonna do? It's the chief.*

"You should call Dita Steed," I said. "She works for the Wilderness Alliance and knows every survivalist and squatter in the state. Maybe she can find someone who knows this guy."

"It's worth a shot," he said.

The Manchurian Grill & Esteemed Buffet is a favorite hangout of Margaret's, our forensic accountant friend who rescued Shelley Prothero from insurance fraud. Not only are the margaritas half-price at Happy Hour but Cin Wang, the restaurant owner, always comps her visit to the buffet table as a thank you for setting up the restaurant's computerized management system. Since I'd accompanied Margaret for a quick one after work, I got free eats too.

We sidled up to the buffet table where I was not bashful about loading my plate with pork skewers, green onion pancakes, and egg foo yung.

"Hey, Tracy, whatcha got there?" The voice startled me and I slopped a spoonful of sauce on the table. I turned around to see Leslie Welker, the police department's medical examiner.

"Spicy cashews and peanuts in garlic chili sauce," I said. "It's one of Cin Wang's specialties."

Leslie turned to a diminutive white-haired lady standing next to her in the buffet line and repeated my answer. She elevated her voice so the elderly lady could hear her over the noise in the restaurant. "Do you want some?"

"I think I'll pass, thank you," said the lady. "But I'll have the chicken wings."

Leslie plunked three chicken wings on the lady's plate and helped herself too.

"Try the green onion pancakes," I said. "They're delicious."

"Don't mind if I do," Leslie said. "Mrs. Stembridge?"

My ears perked up. Stembridge was name of the survivalist suspected of holding out in the stolen cabin. Dita had given Carl six names. Sheriff's departments around the state checked on five men and determined they could not be involved. The sixth was a 75-year-old retired engineer who had disappeared from his home the spring before. Carl said his wife was frantic to find him.

I surveyed the little old lady trailing after Leslie. She didn't look frantic to me.

"Why don't you join us, Leslie? Margaret always gets the best booth over by the window."

Leslie looked a little relieved. I figured she'd been assigned to shepherd Mrs. Stembridge around town on the eve of the big confrontation. The chief still insisted on a SWAT team but had yielded to the police mediator's idea that he and the man's wife should try to talk Mr. Stembridge out of the cabin before a paramilitary team stormed the place.

Leslie introduced us and we threaded our way through the tables to the spot where Margaret and her margarita were becoming reacquainted. In fact, Margaret had such a friendship going with her drink that she'd ordered another. It was just arriving and Margaret had to gulp the last swig of her first cocktail and relinquish the empty glass to the waiter before he could set the fresh one on the table.

Mrs. Stembridge did not comment on this procedure. Our state's liquor laws must have made perfect sense to her.

We slid onto the booth seats, Margaret and I on one side, Leslie and Mrs. Stembridge on the other. The waiter brought their drinks over—a ginger beer for Leslie and a Coke for the lady. I decided it would be kind to let Mrs. Stembridge eat a chicken wing before I peppered her with questions, but Margaret had no such scruples. She'd read the papers, just like everyone else in town.

"So your husband's the cabin thief," she said, pointing a beef satay skewer at Mrs. Stembridge. "How on earth did he think he'd get away with that?"

Mrs. Stembridge cringed in her strawberry-colored shirtwaist and I felt compelled to come to her defense. "Mr. Stembridge—if that's who really took the cabin—is a prepper," I said. "There are lots of people who believe in preparedness in case of disaster. He doesn't want to rely on the government to save him if the worst happens."

"So he steals someone else's cabin?" Margaret said.

"I'm sure he had a good reason," I said.

Mrs. Stembridge had finished her Chinese chicken wing and was wiping her fingers on a napkin. "It's all Stephen King's fault," she said.

We looked at Mrs. Stembridge as if she'd grown horns.

"Forty years ago my husband was unduly influenced by King's novel, *The Stand*. It's about a strain of influenza that escaped a government laboratory. He was convinced horrific bugs could be unleashed on the world and we could all die awful deaths."

"Sounds ghoulish," said Margaret.

"When our children were growing up, he stockpiled his survival gear in the barn. I canned our crops for years. My husband made sure our sons could cook, clean, and make their own clothes. He taught our daughters how to change the oil in our Jeep and fix a flat tire."

"Your family was preparing for Armageddon," Leslie said.

"That was the idea, and it didn't help that a film called *Armageddon* came out in 1998. So then he was afraid asteroids also would end life as we know it."

"This sounds like borderline paranoia," said Leslie. "Did he ever get professional help?"

"Of course not," said Mrs. Stembridge. "We're a bunch of individualists in this state. Our pioneer ethic calls for self-reliance. All was perfectly normal to him and to all our neighbors."

"So what happened?" Margaret said. "Why did he leave you and take someone else's cabin?"

"The children grew up. They moved away to find jobs. My husband retired from the water department and had a lot more time on his hands. That's when he discovered the internet."

"Websites?" I said.

Mrs. Stembridge sipped her Coke. "Forums online. The American Prepper. The Zombie Squad. Emery found friends as obsessed as he was. What are the best camouflage patterns? Where to get a manual meat grinder. How to get a zombie charger that brings a car battery back from the dead."

Margaret laughed. "I always wanted one of those."

"Well, I didn't. I was fed up. Emery was spending our retirement savings on gadgets and gizmos and guns."

There was a silence at the table. As the noise from the other diners welled up to fill the gap, Leslie stepped in. "Tell us about the guns," she said.

"We always owned guns," Mrs. Stembridge said. "Deer hunting rifles, handguns, shotguns. Emery taught all the kids to shoot. But when he started buying Tasers, assault weapons, and then bazookas, I put my foot down."

I stopped nibbling on my cashews and peanuts in chili sauce and looked around the table. Our eyes were as round as green onion pancakes. "What did you do?"

"Do you know how it feels to have a semi-truck roll into your driveway and unload a pallet of weapons right at your front door? I refused the delivery!"

We all relaxed.

"But the driver unloaded them anyway. When Emery came home, we had it out. I told him he'd gone too far. I wouldn't tolerate this collection of weapons and they had to go or I would."

"Good for you," Margaret said.

"So the next day the driver came back with the semi-truck and some helpers. They took all his survival gear. I couldn't believe the parade of stuff from the barn. Took 'em two days."

"And then they left?" I said.

"And then they left," she said. "Trouble was, Emery left too and I haven't seen him since." Mrs. Stembridge's lower lip trembled. "Stupid old coot."

Her eyes glistened, revealing the remorse she must be feeling. To have turned away a husband of fifty years in the heat of the moment and not had any opportunity to take back harsh words—this sweet lady must be full of recrimination.

And now she must be so afraid her husband would be killed by an armed team of trained combatants. She had agreed to be escorted by a crisis mediator past the bend in the road to the cabin. They would try to talk him out. Considering all the rocket launchers and the AR-15s, was she afraid she'd never see him alive? Was she scared she might be killed in the crossfire?

I dropped my eyes and found that my plate was empty. "Why don't we get more goodies?" I said.

"I'd like to use the ladies' room," Mrs. Stembridge said.

Leslie scooted out of the booth. "I'll come with you."

We watched Mrs. Stembridge make her way through the dining room.

"Quite a story," Margaret said. "I would have given him the what-for about thirty years ago."

"You make me laugh. How could she fight that passion? Most women aren't as tough as you."

Margaret sipped her margarita. "Where's the cabin located?

"You know the forest road up to the Flats? It's about seven miles up."

"Near the White Cliffs?"

"Opposite the White Cliffs."

"Well, isn't that interesting." Margaret licked the salt off her glass. I didn't trust the glint in her eyes.

"What?"

"You can see that whole area from the White Cliffs."

We had all hung out on top of the White Cliffs in high school—the cheerleaders, the football team, members of the marching band. The cliffs faced west and the view of the mountains and the national forest was spectacular, but Carl and I hadn't looked at the view very much. We'd spent lots of time in the backseat of his dad's Dodge RAM Megacab.

"What are you thinking?"

"We go up there tomorrow and watch what happens."

"Oh no."

"Aren't you worried? Isn't Carl part of the tactical force? If something happens, wouldn't you want to know right away instead of after the fact?"

Margaret had touched a nerve. I was terrified that Carl would be killed or injured. With that kind of firepower, anything could happen.

"OK," I said, expelling a deep breath. "I'll re-schedule my appointments in the morning. We'll meet at the base of the Cliff Road."

"Eight am?" Margaret said.

"Better make it 7:30. I think they're starting early."

Margaret's pink 1962 Thunderbird lay in wait at the bottom of the cliff road, her headlights on even though the sun had risen hours before. I jumped in the passenger's seat, cradling my backpack in my lap. She took off at a pace that slammed me into the door at the first switchback.

"For crying out loud," I said.

"The operation's going down."

That's when I noticed the police scanner. Static burst. Then silence. Then, "Talker, are you in position?"

"Roger."

"You got Bunny Rabbit?"

"Approaching the bend now."

We careened around the next switchback, tires squealing. I fumbled for the binoculars in my pack—10 x 42s my father had given me. Finally, we made it to the top.

Margaret flung open the driver's side door and turned up the radio. I strode to the cliff edge and scanned the forest. The SWAT team was easy to find. Four armored vehicles sat in a clearing near the bend on a narrow dirt track, which I assumed was the road to the cabin. Try as I might, I couldn't see the cabin itself. Too many trees.

When SWAT vehicles were first donated by the Feds, police families had been invited on a tour. The command post was a van with sophisticated communications equipment, weapons storage, and bench seating for a dozen SWAT officers.

A Lenco Bearcat, looking like a cross between a Jeep and a Brink's security vehicle, was poised on the edge of the dirt track, ready to pounce at the first sign of trouble. The similarity to a Brink's truck ended when you realized the accessories included gun ports, roof hatches, a turret, and battering ram. Bearcat stands for Ballistic Engineered Armored Response Counter Attack Truck. Part of me hoped Carl was inside because it was completely bullet and rocket proof. The other part of me hoped not—it was a lethal weapon designed for destruction.

The scanner squawked. "Command, this is Talker. Bunny Rabbit rounding bend with me now."

My binoculars focused on a scrap of strawberry-colored skirt emerging from the trees. Mrs. Stembridge appeared in my view wearing a bulky Kevlar vest that said SWAT. A man in a blue uniform and SWAT vest held her elbow; I assumed he was the crisis mediator.

Suddenly a black bird obscured my field of view; there was a gun shot, static, then: "Drone down. Hold your fire."

Not a bird. A drone with a camera. So now the SWAT team was flying blind.

I looked at Margaret, her own binoculars pinned to her face. "Mr. Stembridge is quite a marksman," she said.

"With the kind of scopes he has," I said, "that drone was a sitting duck."

"Do you think he knows his wife is there?"

"Hard to say."

We watched the mediator and Mrs. Stembridge approach the next stand of trees. They disappeared from view, but the scanner did its job. "Have visual on cabin. Static. Not within shouting range yet."

My binoculars swiveled back to the command post. Twelve suited figures had materialized in the clearing wearing helmets and carrying assault weapons.

"This is Talker. Stand by." Using a bullhorn, the mediator said, "Mr. Stembridge."

Another shot rang out.

"I have your wife here. Your wife, Elizabeth."

Another shot.

"Emery! It's me. It's really me."

Static.

"Emery, I'm sorry. Emery, I want you to come home."

Silence.

"Let's talk it over. Let's talk it over for two minutes. That's all."

Margaret and I looked at each other.

"Emery, I'm sorry for all those things I said. I miss you; I want you back."

There was another pause, then more static from the police scanner.

"Emery, may I come in?"

"Just you."

"I'm going in there, Officer. Alone. All right?"

There was silence after that. I pictured Mrs. Stembridge making her way to the 10 x 20 storage shed tricked up to look like a log cabin. What could be happening? A tearful reunion? A resentful condemnation?

Twenty minutes passed; then thirty. I watched Chief Fort Dukes in my binoculars. He paced, he stalked, he conferred, he harangued. This pantomime made me afraid he would blow up any minute and order the sweltering SWAT team around the bend on full assault.

But then the scanner erupted: "Coming out now."

They appeared in the sunlight holding hands, stooped, leaning, strawberry-skirt swaying against legs swathed in camouflage trousers. No weapons.

I breathed again.

The SWAT team swarmed the property, but no one else was found. The old man had blocked the stream to make a pond and built an underground bunker with food, water, fuel, and enough firepower to fend off an alien invasion. True to Mrs. Stembridge's description, there were AR-15s, surface-to-air missiles, long and short range rifles, hand guns and Tasers. There was enough cyanide for the mass suicide of twenty people. The police confiscated all of it and hired Hawk to return the cabin to its perch overlooking Wolf Lake. The food went to a homeless shelter.

A judge sentenced Mr. Stembridge to two years of probation, restitution of the stream, and eight hundred hours of volunteer service for Habitat for Humanity.

"You may be seventy-five," the judge said, "but if you can move a ten by twenty foot log cabin by yourself and create an eight hundred square foot bunker, you can build houses for the homeless."

When Carl hangs up his Kevlar vest every night, I send up my silent prayers.

Thank you, God, for no Officer Down.

And thank you, DuPont lady, for discovering Kevlar.

Case 7

Going Postal

• • • • • • •

One morning, I found Paddy Hamburger's latest inciteful headline on the front page of the newspaper along with the mail delivered through the mail slot. I dashed through the salon, dropping letters behind me, and sank down on the sofa to read.

Fairy Tale Snooper POs PO

A 28-year-old woman faces a federal criminal charge after she broke into the downtown post office early Sunday morning and "played dress-up" with the uniforms.

Matilda "Tinker" Bell was discovered shortly after a silent alarm alerted the police. Deputies and federal officials arrived on the scene and collared Bell who was wearing a letter carrier's uniform shirt and shorts.

Bell told deputies she entered the back workroom from the lobby by crawling through a cubby. She said the workroom looked "like a movie set," that she was "acting out a fairy tale," and did not intend to steal anything.

A spokesman for Changing Lives Enterprises, the home for individuals with intellectual disabilities where Bell is a resident, said attendants discovered her missing at four a.m. Sunday morning and notified the city police department.

"We are sure our resident had no intention of theft or mail fraud and was simply acting out her most cherished fantasies," said Mike Abel, director of the resident facility. "We will furnish legal representation to Ms. Bell as her case proceeds through the justice system."

I chuckled. Everyone knew Tinker Bell. She worked at the recycling center and helped all of us sort our plastic, cardboard, and aluminum. I could just imagine her playing dress-up. She probably admired every mail carrier she saw. No judge in his right mind was going to convict her.

I looked up from the newspaper and saw a trail of mail scattered all over the salon floor. That Paddy Hamburger—always sucking you in with an outrageous headline and making you lose your mind. I picked up the mail and put it on the counter in front of my hair cutting station. My cell rang.

"Citrus Salon."

"Tracy, this is Katherine Putnam. I need to see you right away."

I pictured Katherine with a major hair disaster. "Can you make a ten thirty?"

"Thank God," Katherine said.

"I take that as a yes. What do you need done?"

"I have a job interview at noon. You've got to tone down the red."

Katherine and I had been making her look like a rock star with a fiery red color guaranteed to stop traffic when she crossed the street. The trouble was the rest of Katherine looked as squat as a fire hydrant. I'd been wanting to darken that red for a long time.

"No problem," I sang and hung up the phone just as Shirley Jones arrived.

"Tracy!"

"Hey, Shirley."

"I've brought you some muffins."

I took the bag from Shirley's hands. It was warm. "They smell so good."

"Blueberry."

Shirley worked at the vintage diner across the street. She was wearing her 1960s waitress uniform with the pert little cap.

"Just a trim, please," she said.

I draped her in a buttercup yellow cape with a cream-colored terry at the neck and removed her hat. "Your hair looks so healthy," I said.

"I use your Milky Moisture Mask after every shampoo."

"It's doing wonders for you," I said. "Let's go to the sink."

As I washed her hair, she told me all about boyfriend number five. "Joe's a computer programmer," she said, shouting over the noise of my spray nozzle. "Did you know there are five hundred unfilled jobs for software engineers? They pay well too."

I turned the taps off and squeezed the water out of her hair. "Lucky him. How does he like the commute to the big city?"

"Hates it. He'll probably move closer to his job and we'll break up."

This was the story of Shirley's life. She no sooner got a new boyfriend than something went wrong.

"Why don't you take some courses at the community college and get a job like that?" I asked.

"I was never any good at math and any of the stuff you have to do to code."

I sympathized. I could manipulate Quickbooks, but spending any more time in front of the computer would drive me berserk.

We went into the workroom and I began to trim Shirley's hair when she pointed to the mail on the counter. "Have you had any mail go missing lately?"

"I don't think so."

"I have. I was waiting for a rebate check from Tire Planet and it never came. Neither did my new credit card. I've been to the post office to complain, but our local clerks don't want to hear about it. They sent me to the national website."

"Did you go there?"

"Yeah. That website is a jungle. It took me fifteen minutes to find the right page. I filled out the form with the details about my missing mail. For days afterwards I got emails *and* phone calls asking me to rate my satisfaction with the postal service, but no reply about my mail."

Shirley's voice was filled with indignation. I didn't blame her. How could you rate a service satisfactory before you got any satisfaction? But that was the United States postal service for you.

We finished up and said goodbye. I opened my Client Notebook. After crossing out the last boyfriend's name in Shirley's entry, I wrote: Joe, computer programmer; missing mail—PO'd.

The front door opened with a bang and Katherine Putnam breezed in looking like a burning torch. She took her place in my workroom where I whipped out a red cape and flung it over her stubby body, then wheeled my color mixing table over to the chair.

"More auburn, less red?" I said.

"Yeah, I want to look subdued and corporate."

"You're going big time, eh?"

"Computer coding job. They're hiring anybody who can breathe. I took coding in high school, and last time I checked, I'm still breathing."

"Did you know there are five hundred unfilled computer software jobs in the big city?" I said, as if I had researched this fact all by myself.

"Yup. And they pay decent bucks," said Katherine. "That's why I want to look the image. Nose to the grindstone; meek as a mouse; speak the corporate speak. I want to look just as competent as any computer jockey from Gujarat."

"I have some curry you can dab on your wrists, if you think that will help."

"I'm not going to go that far." She sniffed.

I hoped I hadn't insulted her. Or the good people in the Indian state of Gujarat.

I was painting Katherine's scalp with auburn formula when she pointed to my mail on the counter.

"Have you been getting all your mail, Tracy?"

"I think so."

"The post office is ridiculous these days," she said. "I ordered a credit card from Macy's and it never arrived."

"Is anything else missing?"

"Not that I know of. So much stuff comes in the mail—flyers, offers, checks for fifty thousand dollars."

"I get those too—checks made out to The Citrus Salon for $58,000.00, negotiable immediately if I just sign up for a business loan at 25 percent."

"Such a deal!"

"Like Publisher's Clearinghouse—you've won a million dollars!"

"Do they think we'll really fall for that?" she said.

"These offers go right in my circular file." I kicked my wastebasket for emphasis. "How are you doing on your money-back deal from Candy Fiber?"

Katherine got scalded on a lose-weight-fast offer from our local dietary supplement maven.

"I caught up with Candy in the locker room at the fitness center," Katherine said. "While she took a shower, I hid her clothes and told her I wouldn't give them back until she coughed up the dough."

I laughed. "So she's still naked, then?"

"I'm afraid so."

We giggled. I pictured Candy Fiber au naturel and it was not a bad sight. Unfortunately for Katherine, Candy would stop every motorist by crossing the street in any state.

I finished painting and settled a shower cap snugly over Katherine's head. "Would you like to read a mystery story while you're processing?" I asked. "I have *Death in the Capitol* and *Pay Tax or Die* for your reading pleasure."

These stories took only half an hour to read—a perfect way to kill time while hair color set.

Katherine took *Pay Tax or Die* into my comfort room where she climbed up on my big massage chair and turned on the automatic back kneader. I filled up the pedicure tub with warm spearmint water and took her some jasmine tea.

I heard nothing from Katherine for the next 30 minutes and assumed she was absorbed in the machinations of an armchair detective/accountant who solved white collar crimes for her FBI lover. Theirs was a steamy affair.

The timer on my cell phone dinged.

"Hold on, hold on," said Katherine. "They're making love in the judges' chambers at the Supreme Court." Katherine's face was flushed and she was squirming in her seat.

I backed away politely and fiddled with the control knobs on my sprayer. When the water was the perfect temperature, I took another peek. Katherine was sitting back looking slightly spent.

"Time to rinse you out," I said and she followed me to the sink.

After Katherine left, I consulted my Client Notebook, wrote the change in color formula next to her name and added, 'missing mail.' I noticed that Katherine's home address was on the same street as Shirley's.

After lunch, Mrs. Oscar, owner of a gas station on Main Street, bent my ear about out-of-town punks while I marceled her hair.

"They're just driving through," she said, "and they use my trash cans as their personal dumping spot. I've had to increase our refuse collection to twice a week because these people don't seem to have their own garbage cans."

"It isn't the occasional candy wrapper or McDonald's bag?"

"We're talking household goods. Paint thinner, acetone, drain cleaner, starter fluid. I pay for trash collection and I'm tired of these bulky items being thrown in my convenience bins."

It was not my place to tell Mrs. Oscar about the ways of the world. Our town's Main Street was a major highway that the town forefathers, in their lack of wisdom, refused to re-route thirty years ago when there was plenty of open land. Instead we have every Tom, Dick and Harry driving through Main Street on their way to Somewhere Else and leaving their trash behind.

"It's a shame we can't have a highway bypass," I said.

"Highway bypass? Don't talk to me about a highway bypass." Mrs. Oscar had turned on her *Intimidating Voice.* "I told Martha Farquhar we needed a highway bypass way back in the eighties. Do you think she listened to me? Neither did any of those other old geezers on the city council. No, ma'am."

Mrs. Oscar slammed her hand on the arm of my salon chair. I jumped so high my curling iron yanked her hair. "Ow!" she said.

"I'm sorry, Mrs. Oscar."

"It makes me so damn mad. We have all the traffic going through town now, including those tankers from the oil fields on the reservation, and no way to stop 'em."

"Aren't you making more money from all the commercial traffic?"

"Yes, we are," she said, sounding a bit mollified. "But there's a limit."

I was reminded of my father who could be penny wise and pound foolish. Mrs. Oscar made it sound like she wanted to stop all traffic on Main Street just to avoid the extra expense of trash collection. I was glad my salon was on the road to the wealthy part of town. No one went to Main Street—it was too congested.

A month later, Katherine returned for a color change.

"Did you get the job?" I asked.

"Yes," she said.

"Is it everything you want it to be?"

"Yes," she said.

"Then why do you want the red back?"

"Because everyone else has green, purple, shaved, or striped hair. I look too ordinary."

And you look great!

I was mixing the red color formula when she said, "My identity got stolen."

"Oh no!" I started painting her roots

"It's been such a hassle. I got a bill from Macy's for more than a thousand dollars. You remember—my Macy's card never arrived. Then more credit card bills came, but I never applied for them, and utility bills for an apartment in New Jersey. Someone got ahold of my personal information and I don't know how."

I channeled my inner Picasso as I painted her brown head.

"All my accounts are on hold," she said. "I can't apply for any kind of credit for seven months. And it's not my fault."

My mind wandered to Shirley Jones. I wondered how she was faring.

"These identity thieves—they steal your information and sell it," she said with such vehemence that her head shook and my color application threatened to look like a real Picasso.

"I'd like to think my identity is now the property of a young mother with three children who desperately need new clothes at Macy's. Or perhaps it could be a crippled grandmother who wouldn't have enough money to pay for her winter heat if it weren't for me. But I know that's not true."

"Who do you think has your identity?"

"This guy from Gujarat at work says there are people who sit at computers and troll all day with botnets for people's personal information—their account numbers, socials, passwords, names, addresses, dates of birth. It's like going into the forest and harvesting trees."

I pictured some kind of sweatshop with guys from coding central fiendishly felling.

"He's dreamy," she said.

"Who's dreamy?"

"The guy from Gujarat. His name's Deepak." There was a faraway look in Katherine's eyes. "He likes red hair."

I saw then there was more involved here than keeping up with the green-tinted. "Do I detect a little romance?"

"He's smart, and kind, and the same height as me," she said. "Did you know the state of Gujarat is called the Jewel of India and is where Mahatma Gandhi marched to the sea?"

"Can't say that I do."

"It has an industrial economy. The area is wealthy and has a very rich history."

Katherine's eyes were starry and I wondered if she had been practicing any memorable scenes from *Pay Taxes or Die* with the Man from Gujarat.

"Sounds like a nice place."

"Deepak wants to make his mark here and then go back to India to start an orphanage for laundry children."

"Laundry children?"

"There are laundries in Mumbai where men come and pick up your things, and they can't read but they never, ever mix up your laundry with anybody else's, and they put it out to dry on outdoor clotheslines, and it comes back completely white and perfectly pressed. Did you know that?"

I shook my head.

"But if they die, their children have no one to take care of them if their mothers are dead. Deepak wants to make a difference there."

Meanwhile, he's writing code in the big city to the west of us where anyone who breathes can get a job, provided they know something about something that I know nothing of.

Katherine looked in the mirror with the most gaga expression on her face. I could see she was smitten.

After Katherine left, I put the "Back in 30 Minutes" sign on my door and walked across the street to the diner. Shirley was behind the counter looking glum.

"What's the matter?" I asked. "Boyfriend troubles?"

"I wish," she said. "My identity's been stolen."

That night, Carl and Joe were out on patrol when they stopped a car on Main Street with one of its tail-lights out. When he came home at five a.m., I woke up and he told me all about it.

"Before I could get to the driver's door, the guy took off," Carl said. "We gave chase all the way to the interstate. The guy exited at the worst place for him and the best place for us."

"Summit Park, I'll bet." The streets in Summit Park are windy and narrow. They dead end or loop around.

"Eventually, he realized he was cooked, so he stopped and ran into the forest."

"On foot? I'll bet you didn't chase him."

"Why bother? He had no place to go. We searched his car and found other people's checks totaling eight thousand dollars, a certificate of title, two money grams for five hundred dollars each, lots of unopened mail that were clearly credit card offers, and blank checks allowing the signer to pay for stuff by credit card."

"This all came out of people's mail boxes?"

"Yup. There was a burglary tool used to fish out mail from apartment mailboxes. And a bottle of sticky liquid they use to get mail to stick to the tool."

"What kind of sticky liquid?"

"The same kind that covers rat traps."

"Eeuuw."

"In fact, there were several rat traps in the car. And there was also a glass pipe and a plastic wrapper with crystal meth in it."

"So this guy is a cooker?"

"Or a user."

"Is he a local?

"Not likely or he would never have taken that exit off the highway."

"Has he been found?"

"The K9s tracked him to a hollow on the side of a mountain. He actually looked glad to see us. He was wet and freezing."

I laughed. "You do good work, honey. I hope he goes to prison."

We nuzzled and things accelerated from there. Before long, we made the sex scenes in *Pay Taxes or Die* look G-rated.

"Tracy! Are you here?"

I almost hid in my drape closet, I was so sure I didn't want to be here. Candy Fiber was speeding through the salon.

"Tracy, I need you!"

What for? An order for two hundred bottles of dietary supplements? A flat of vitamin elixirs? A gallon of rejuvenating potion?

Candy Fiber had added emollient wrinkle remover to her ever-growing list of miracle cures, and I wanted none of it.

"My identity has been stolen and I want Carl to fix it!"

I imagined a brigade of Candy Fibers, cloned and marching all over identity-theft land. I needed to sit down.

"My mail's been stolen from my mailbox," she said, "and I want justice!"

Then why aren't you at the police station? I wanted to say that. But of course, I didn't. "Tell me what happened."

"This has been going on for weeks. First, I was missing some checks, then some credit cards, and now my tax return. Gone—right out of my mailbox."

"Where do you live?"

She told me—right down the street from Katherine and Shirley.

"I think it's that mental retard who broke into the post office!"

I cringed. Surely, she couldn't mean Tinker Bell.

"The Changing Lives residence is on my corner," she said.

She *did* think it was Tinker Bell.

"I want Carl to ransack that place from top to bottom."

"Now, Candy, there's no evidence that says anyone at Changing Lives is–"

"Don't whitewash it. That little retard. Oh, I see you're offended. I need to be politically correct. That *intellectually-challenged* retard is stealing my mail."

"What makes you think so?" I asked.

"Because I've gotten bills from credit cards that I didn't apply for and checks have been cashed that never got to me."

"And you think she's done this?"

"Of course."

"I thought you said she was intellectually disabled. How'd she get the smarts all of a sudden to cash checks and submit credit card applications?"

Candy had no answer for that.

"I can see you're thinking twice now," I said, and told her about the meth head in the woods. Now she looked roundly chastened—an old-fashioned phrase that meant she was eating shit.

"Candy," I said. "Let's go see Carl."

I put the "Back in 30 Minutes" sign on the door and we took Candy's little MG down to the station.

Candy made an impact as soon as she arrived. Not only is she 36" 24" 36" but she was dispensing cigars from a box she keeps in the trunk of her little MG. She told her story to Chief Fort Dukes who, after he lit his stogie up, ordered Carl and Joe to conduct a stakeout of Candy's street.

For the next ten nights I hardly saw my beautiful man. Carl and Joe ate doughnuts, pizza, and Chinese takeout while they watched all the mailboxes on the streets of Candy's neighborhood. Yet one month later the incidence of identity theft in our town was still increasing and the police were no closer to a solution than when they started.

"Hello?" said a tentative voice from the front of my salon.

"Good morning," I said.

A woman with limp brown hair, dull brown eyes, and a pilled brown sweater entered. My computer said her name was Mary Owens. I picked up my Client Notebook and invited her to sit on my sofa.

"I'm so glad to meet you," I said. "What can I do for you?"

Mary said she would like a wash, a deep conditioning treatment, and a trim. I noted: "Limp hair, dingy color, sallow complexion, face sores" in my book. We chatted for a moment. "And your address?" I asked, poised over the page with my pen.

"You don't need my address," she said. "I don't want any junk mail."

"I know what you mean," I said. "Junk mail is so annoying. I don't send my clients junk mail and I never sell their personal information."

She still declined to give me her address or telephone number.

I led her to my workroom where I draped her in olive green. The color choice felt a little drab and I questioned myself. *Why choose a color that made her look sicker?* I took her to the sink. That's when I smelled the odor of cat pee. I sprayed her hair, shampooed with a Caribbean floral product, and hoped the fragrance of frangipani would do the trick. It didn't.

She still smelled like cat pee. It was coming from her clothes. Face sores, tired hair, pasty face, ammonia odor. And why won't she give her address? Could she be cooking meth?

I applied a deep conditioner, rinsed, towel dried her hair, and led her back to my styling chair, then began to clip away.

"Such a lot of roadwork we're having right now," I said.

"Yes," she agreed. The sound of my scissors filled the silence.

"Is there as much going on in your neighborhood as there is in mine?"

"What do you mean?"

"They're tearing up the street in front of my house," I said. "The information superhighway—Google Fiber."

"We haven't got it yet."

So she doesn't live in the condos, the apartments, Blue Cliffs, or any neighborhood within two miles of downtown.

I pressed on. "My son Jamie says he's enjoying school. He goes to Sunshine Elementary. Do your kids go there too?"

"No, Four Corners."

"I always thought that was a good school too."

"He likes it okay," she said.

Four Corners Elementary, one son, no high speed internet—that narrows it down.

I shaped her head as I continued to shape her conversation. "We're working so hard on our home this year. New siding and now the chimney's falling down. I almost think it's better to rent than to buy, don't you?"

"I've never owned a home."

A renter.

"But you like cats, don't you? I like them too. You're lucky your landlord allows cats."

"We don't have any cats."

Then why that smell? "You're done," I said. "Would you like to see the back?"

She picked up the mirror, looked briefly at the back of her head, and nodded.

"Blow dry?"

"Sure."

The cat smell blew around the salon. I couldn't wait to get her out the door.

"What do I owe you?" she asked, when I turned the blow dryer off.

"Thirty-five."

She took two twenties out of her purse. Then she shuffled out the front door.

I put the bills to my nose.

Cat pee.

I washed them in the sink, but they still smelled.

It was time to talk to Carl.

Carl and I met in our cars behind the Dairy Queen in the driver's-window-to-driver's window position you see cop cars assume with their tail pipes steaming. I always wondered what cops talk about, all cozied up like that, until Carl told me they just shoot the shit. That made me feel better about listening to gossip all day.

"I think I've found a meth lab," I said.

Carl's jaw hit the top of his collar, but he was ready to listen. Ever since I saved Orchid's life, he's paid attention. "What makes you say that?"

"I learned a thing or two about meth cooking from a client who owns a duplex. She rented her place to a meth addict, although she didn't know it at the time. She told me meth labs use toxic chemicals like ammonia. It makes the place smell like a litter box."

"Let me get this straight," Carl said. "You visited someone's house and it smells like a litter box so you think it's a meth lab."

"No, no. Someone visited *me* who smells like a litter box. Cooking meth gives off noxious gasses. She reeked of it."

"You think this woman is living in a house with a meth lab? I'd rather live in a nuclear reactor."

"She looks awful, Carl. Skin practically green, hair lifeless, face gaunt, open sores. She smells like cat pee but has no cats!"

"This is a little sketchy, Tracy."

"But it all fits," I said. "The missing mail, the identity theft. She needs cash to buy supplies. She's desperate because she's hooked just like that meth head you caught chasing his car in Summit Park."

"I don't know, darling. This could be another one of your wild ones."

"She has a kid, Carl," I said, my face screwed up with concern. "He goes to Four Corners Elementary. Think of the kid."

Carl rubbed his hands, then looked at me through the car window with a solemn expression. "The Four Corners neighborhood, huh?"

"Yeah, how big could that be? Just a few roads. We could cruise it right now."

"Nah uh," he said. "I'm on duty—that's not my beat."

"What's happening on Main Street? Nothing. What's happening in Four Corners? Plenty. Let's go."

He sighed. "We'll take your car. I'll meet you in the Gauntlet."

I followed him to a stretch of road everyone calls the Gauntlet. It's a straightaway leading out of town where motorists always accelerate over the speed limit. More drunk drivers had been caught here than any other piece of highway in our state. If you "Run the Gauntlet" after having a couple, watch out—even slowpokes get pulled over.

Carl parked his car with its nose pointed out, looking ready to pounce. I pulled up and he hopped in.

Four Corners is the most rural part of our county. The roads snake their way over sagebrush hills. Herds of cattle, dairy cows, sheep, and horses dot the landscape. Houses are few and far between and they're down long dirt driveways and can't be seen from the street.

After we passed the sign for the Rainbow Cemetery, we topped a little rise and saw a farmhouse in the distance. It was a beautiful spread with an orchard, a cornfield, and a big barn. Holsteins nuzzled the green grass by the river.

"That's Cody Manson's place," Carl said. "He's a polygamist."

Just as he said this, three women emerged from the barn wearing aprons followed by a herd of small children.

"Why aren't those kids in school?" I asked.

"Home schooled," Carl said.

We traveled further and turned onto a road where the homes were only half a mile apart. Mailboxes and trash cans punctuated the shoulder.

"This is a lot harder than I thought it would be," I said.

"Did you think the cooker's home was going to jump out and bite you?"

I laughed.

"People have a unique way of life out here," Carl said. "They raise big families and take care of their own. No one pokes into the lives of their neighbors and they go to church on Sundays. One thing we have in our favor, though, is trash collection."

I looked at him.

"Watch out!" he shouted.

A chicken was crossing the road. I swerved to avoid it and Carl gripped his armrest. "Tracy, let's trade places."

I pulled over and he took the wheel. Carl's mouth was a turned-down line.

"What's this about trash collection?" I asked, when he appeared to be calmer.

"Technically, anything you put in the trash on the street is considered abandoned. Anyone can root through your trash and it's not considered stealing."

I pondered this fact. Every homeless person in the big valley must know this. That's how they get food to eat and clothing to wear.

"In a meth lab situation, we'll contact the refuse company and arrange for them to collect all the suspect's trash with one of their trucks. Then we'll examine the trash in the back parking lot at the police station."

"What will you be looking for?"

"The ingredients for making meth—Sudafed bubble packs, caustic household items, paint thinner, acetone, drain cleaner."

A light bulb went on. "Mrs. Oscar was complaining the other day that all she seems to get in her trash bins lately is empty containers of stuff like that. And people are leaving batteries with the lithium removed at the recycling center."

Carl thought about this for a minute. "The recycling center just installed a surveillance camera, didn't they?"

"Yeah, but it's not hooked up to anything—it's a dummy."

"Too bad."

"But Mrs. Oscar has a surveillance system," I said. "I'll bet she stores all her videos in the Cloud."

"If we could get footage of your client leaving trash at Mrs. Oscar's gas station, that would be hard evidence."

"Then you think this is a real case?"

"Possibly."

"I've got a nose for crime," I said.

He winked. "You smelled cat piss."

"Well, what about that? An ammonia smell is a real clue, wouldn't you say? If she smells like that, the kid does too. Someone at school must have noticed it."

Carl nodded.

"Get the youth officer on it?"

"I'll get the youth officer on it," Carl said.

"And the trash officer?'"

"And the trash officer—that would be me."

"And the narcotics unit?"

"And the narcotics unit."

"Surely the chief will give you the detective position if you find a meth lab."

"Don't count on it."

I heard the disgust in his voice. The chief hadn't made a decision about the detective job. When he assigned the cat in the suitcase to Carl, the chief thought there was nothing to it, but that suitcase contained one of the biggest human interest crimes in the history of the department. Paddy Hamburger's stories made mincemeat out of the chief and praised Carl.

That's what's behind it—jealousy. Hell hath no fury like a police chief scorned.

"You've got to tread lightly with this one, don't you?" I said.

Carl sighed. "Yeah. Gotta make the chief look good."

"How can we do that?"

"Sic Mrs. Oscar on him," he said to me. "Then he'll ask me to look into the trash disposal problem and I'll turn everything I find out over to him."

"Gotcha," I said.

We ran the Gauntlet again and pulled up to Carl's patrol car. He got out and I slipped into the driver's seat. I drove straight to Mrs. Oscar's gas station where, as predicted, she had plenty to say.

The next day the chief asked Carl and Joe to get the "gas lady" off his back and find out who was dumping trash in her— he used a descriptive word.

When Carl arrived at the gas station, Mrs. Oscar called him a "dear boy" and gave him a huge box of empty household cleaning containers and an equally huge box of VHS tapes.

I raised my eyebrows.

"She needs a new surveillance system," Carl said.

The police department had no way to view VHS tapes, so Carl rooted through our attic and brought down the VHS player he had in grade school.

I made popcorn.

We spent the evening in bed watching Mrs. Oscar's videos. The tapes were dark and grainy. At times they were full of static. Shapes shifted across the screen looking like ghosts pumping God knows what into heavenly transports of shimmering metal. Humanoid shapes threw things into dimly lit holes.

"This is hella boring," I said in my best Valley Girl imitation.

Carl pulled a videocassette out of his old college knapsack. "Put this in."

It was Deep Throat. The rest of our evening was much more interesting.

For his part of the investigation, Joe sidestepped the youth officer and talked to Tina White Horse.

"She knows every teacher at Four Corners Elementary," Torgesen said, during my weekly dinner for nutrition-depleted police force bachelors.

"She's very attractive," I said.

He shrugged.

Joe Torgesen, you did not overlook that fact.

"Was she any help?" Carl asked.

"She gave me the name of a little boy at Four Corners Elementary who smells like a litter box. And I have his address."

"*Dude,*" said Carl.

Torgesen laughed.

Jamie chimed in. "A *cat* litter box? Pew!"

"Does anybody in your school smell like cat pee?" I asked.

"No," Jamie said, "but I know somebody who smells like a guinea pig."

"Who?" Carl asked.

"Mrs. Woodhouse, the science teacher. Her whole room smells like a guinea pig. She has one in a cage. Sometimes I get to feed it."

"What does it eat?"

"Carrots and celery."

After dinner, Carl and Joe disappeared into Carl's office while I helped Jamie with his homework. He was learning to multiply two 2-digit numbers together with a technique called "partial products."

Why couldn't he just learn math the way I did?

The partial products technique required tens and ones and multiplication and addition laid out in an "area chart" and the patience of Job.

"Let me show you how I learned," I said, picking up a pencil and stacking the two-digit numbers on top of each other. "Nine times six is sixty-three and carry the six," I said. "You see? This is much easier, Jamie."

Jamie did it his way. After a few minutes, he said, "Mommy, why did we get different answers?"

I eyeballed his area chart with its perfect math. Then I studied my math.

Oops. "I made a little mistake," I said, erasing the six and the three so vigorously I put a hole in the paper. "Of course, nine times six is fifty-four." *So much for 20th century math.*

After Jamie was tucked in, I went back to the kitchen where I sprayed a blackened pot with oven cleaner.

Carl and Joe joined me. "Are you cooking meth in here?"

"Very funny," I said to Carl, trying not to breathe the fumes.

"Why don't you join us in the den," he said.

I wiped my hands on a dish cloth, and headed for the desk where Joe and Carl were hunched over the computer.

"We're running the little boy's father through the system," Carl said. "No record, not even a speeding ticket."

"His mother's clean too," Joe said. "They have a webpage designing service which they run out of their home. It's under the husband's name— Mary Owens is the mother's maiden name."

I settled on the sofa. "Are they really married?"

"Couldn't find a record," Carl said.

Joe shrugged his shoulders. "Just a regular middle class family with student loans, credit card debt, and no home ownership."

"Where are they from?"

"Arkansas," said Carl. "There's no indication of why they came here."

"I'll do some more digging on Monday when Carl starts riding the garbage truck," Joe said.

"What fun," I said.

Over the next two weeks, Carl accompanied the trash men on their route through Four Corners and sifted through the neighborhood garbage in the back of the police station. He came across plenty of empty household cleaner containers, but nothing in huge concentrations and nothing from the suspects' address.

The narcotics division put the house on 24-hour surveillance, but the area was so deserted the stakeout was obvious. In fact, my wan, listless, sore-infested customer—Mary Owens—called the police about "the strange car outside her house."

So much for undercover work.

The case limped along until Carl came home one evening with a little job for me.

"I won't do it!"

"It's just a phone call," he said. "All you have to do is pretend you're Hazel Bigby."

"No one can impersonate Hazel Bigby. She whines like a mosquito."

Hazel Bigby ran the Good Landlord Program for the mayor. She nagged at landlords until they spent hours at her endless training program.

"Look, I told you I went to her," Carl reminded me. "I explained the problem—Mary Owens's landlord probably hasn't inspected his property in years. She still wouldn't make the call."

"But why me? Why don't you do it?"

"You're really good at making things up," he said.

Is that a compliment?

"And you're really good at thinking on your feet."

Do I hear a hairdresser joke somewhere in there?

He put his arm around my waist and nuzzled my neck. "Please do this for me," he said, his lips drawing closer to mine. I felt my legs melt.

"Do what?" Jamie bounded into the kitchen.

"Nothing, Jamie," I said, breaking away. "What do you need—a bedtime snack?"

"Ice cream."

"There's no more ice cream. How about toast with jam?"

"No."

"Carrots and celery like the guinea pig?"

"No."

"Captain Crunch?"

"Okay."

After I fixed him a bowl of cereal, we heard his footsteps racing up the stairs. I pictured the splashes of milk I would need to clean up later.

Carl handed me my cell phone and a pad with a name and number on it.

I shook my head.

"Tracy," he said. "Nine times out of ten the landlord discovers the meth lab. There's some kind of repair work or a routine inspection. Then he calls the police. Here we've got a property in a rural area where there are no neighbors to smell bad things, no deliverymen to get suspicious, and an absentee landlord who probably hasn't set foot in our state for fifteen years."

He sounded so logical I wanted to call him Judge Judy.

"We can't stake out the property unless we put a deer hide in the woods," he said. "I've followed them several times, but they never go to Mrs. Oscar's gas station. They're probably stacking their trash in the house and that's dangerous. Miss Hair Stylist Detective has a cat piss theory and that's all we have to go on, so what am I supposed to do?"

I looked at his face. He was the same handsome high school jock I fell in love with fifteen years earlier, but desperation made him look older. I suspected he was thinking of the detective's job and how much he wanted the promotion.

"How about if I just say I'm calling from the mayor's office and not give a name?" I said. "That way I won't need to sound like a mosquito."

"Good idea."

I took a deep breath and punched in the number. "Hello," I said when someone answered, "Is this Mr. Braithwaite? Karsten Braithwaite?"

"Who's this?"

I just love it when people are on the offensive right from the start.

"I'm calling from the mayor's office about your rental property at 27000 East 36700 South. Isn't that the address?"

"What business is it of yours?"

"We have no record that you've taken the training for our Good Landlord Program."

"I took that twice."

"We have no record of your certificate."

"I got the certificate. Why don't you people keep good records?"

"Well, I'm sorry to bother you, but we are calling all property owners. When was the last time you inspected the property?"

Silence on the line.

"When was the last time you inspected your property, sir?"

"The last time I was in town."

"When was that, sir?"

"Five years ago." He was starting to sound a bit sheepish now.

"Well, sir, quarterly property inspection is recommended, as I'm sure you know from the Good Landlord training. Our police department is especially concerned because rentals are used by meth cookers, especially rentals in remote rural areas like yours, sir."

"What?"

"Yes, there was a meth house in the next town over. The rental had to be condemned, sir. You don't want to fool around with meth."

"No."

"I notice you live in Hawaii, sir. Do you have a property management company locally?"

"Not yet."

A chink in the armor.

"There's a list of certified property management companies on our website. You want to be sure someone stops by. There are some bad renters out there."

"Thank you."

"Just doing my job, sir. The mayor believes in public service."

"I know the mayor."

"Be sure to tell him you like the service, sir. Have a nice evening, sir."

I pushed the end-call button.

"Nice work," said Carl. "Did he sound stirred up?"

"Yes."

"Then you did good. If your suspicions prove right, dispatch should get a call soon."

Three days later, the chief took a phone call in the squad room.

"Karsten Braithwaite called the chief personally," Carl said. "He answered the phone right at my work station. I could tell who he was talking to because you know what he said?"

I shook my head.

"'What Good Landlord program?' The chief didn't even know the mayor runs a Good Landlord program."

Go figure.

"Braithwaite hired a property management company and the guy didn't even get past the doorsill, the smell was so overwhelming. The chief ordered us to Four Corners right away.

"We raided the place in hazmat suits. The basement looked like a science fair project on steroids. Beakers, Bunsen burners, graduated cylinders, hot plates, rice steamers. And the crap they use to make this stuff—it's a wonder the house didn't explode."

"Like what?"

"Cans of alcohol, toluene, paint thinner. Gallons of kerosene. And anhydrous ammonia—that the source of the cat urine smell."

"What about the little boy?"

"He's safe now with Children and Family Services. A doctor's going to examine him tomorrow. Who knows what physical problems he has."

"And his mother?"

"In custody at the station with the father. She looked relieved."

I recalled Mary Owens with her mousy thin hair, facial sores, and sickly manner. She was probably tired of the cooker's life and ready for a clean cot in jail.

"I found out why there were no empty containers in their trash bins."

"Why not?"

"It was all stored on the property behind the house. A huge pile."

That night the chief was on the six o'clock news. "How did you bust the biggest meth lab ever found in your county, Chief?" asked the reporter, poking a microphone under his chin. I admired his makeup job—I had lightened the Chief's raccoon eyes with soft guinea pig tones.

The camera cut to Mrs. Oscar, standing in front of her convenience bin and frowning at a can of paint thinner and a large bottle of nail polish remover.

"We knew something was wrong," the chief said on voiceover, "when the waste products used to cook meth turned up in trash bins at our local gas station. The rest was good detective work."

"I understand you uncovered an identity theft ring as well?" said the reporter, keeping firm possession of the microphone as the chief made a move for it.

"Meth heads were stealing stuff right out of people's mailboxes. Our citizens have been robbed and we're going to give them their identities back." The chief looked straight at the camera as he said this, and I imagined he was talking directly to Candy Fiber, whose cigars seemed to have fascinated him as much as Monica Lewinsky's.

"If you have any advice to give our citizens, what would you say?"

"Join our Good Landlord Program," the chief said as if he'd known about it for years. "That's how to make sure your rental property doesn't get condemned."

The camera cut to the newsroom. "In other news," the anchorman said, "the United States post office has lost its suit against a 28-year-old woman accused of mail theft."

An artist's sketch of the courtroom appeared on the screen. "In dismissing the action against Matilda 'Tinker' Bell," the Ninth Circuit Court judge said, 'You'd think the government is in never-never land the way they've accused a disabled citizen of mail fraud. I'm beginning to believe the most *able* citizens are the ones *out* of a postal service uniform.'"

The reporter reappeared in a shot of Tinker throwing plastic into a recycle bin. "Tinker Bell is a model citizen who devotes hours of her time protecting our environment and educating citizens about recycling. Her foray into the postal office, where she dressed up as one of the letter carriers, was her means of expressing her belief that postal employees are true heroes."

The camera shifted to a poster that read, 'Neither snow nor rain nor heat nor gloom of night stays these couriers from the swift completion of their appointed rounds.'

The reporter continued, "Tinker Bell reveres the postal service. She created this poster with the help of some high school students."

The scene changed to the reporter with Tinker wearing a letter carrier's hat. "Now I'm a hero, too," she said.

"Back to you, Chet."

Case 8
'Til Death Do Us Part

● ● ● ● ● ● ● ● ● ● ● ●

"**A**lmighty Father, we thank you for bringing us together tonight. We love this City with all our hearts."

"Are we in church?" I whispered to Carl.

"The challenges that face our community demand the loyalty of every Citizen. We ask our Heavenly Father Above to grant us the Wisdom to recognize our Godly Mission and meet all threats. Keep our community on the right path and our people free. Amen."

I leaned over to Carl again. "Whatever happened to separation of Church and State?"

My husband shifted in his chair. Martha Farquhar shot me a "behave" face from her seat behind the enormous city council bench.

The mayor continued. "In his mighty struggle, Edward Everett Hale, a man of the cloth, gave us these words:

"I am only one, but still I am one;
I cannot do everything, but I can do something;
And because I cannot do everything,
I will not refuse to do something that I can do.

"Chief Fort Dukes does not refuse. He gives his heart and soul to make this community better. He is a citizen who steps up and does his part, and that is why our city council has voted—unanimously—to bestow on him the prestigious *Lawman of the Year* Award."

There was a round of applause. The chief shook hands with the mayor and all five city councilors. He faced council chambers and began his acceptance speech. It was a long one. The audience fidgeted—punch and cookies were waiting. I found myself wondering if there was a *Law-Woman of the Year* Award, when suddenly the chief stopped speaking. Martha Farquhar had come out from behind the bench and was escorting the chief out of council chambers to the refreshment table. I never thought I'd be grateful to Martha for anything, but she was outdoing herself that night.

We filled our little plates with cookies and jello cubes. I overheard Margaret Pyle talking to the squeaky-clean catering waitress. "Are these jello shots?" she asked, although she knew perfectly well they weren't.

The girl cast her eyes down, managed a polite smile, and slid away.

Margaret cornered the mayor. "Herbert!" she said. "What are you going to do if a gay couple wants you to marry them?"

The mayor glanced around. Perhaps he was hoping Martha Farquhar would rescue him; more likely, he feared that Paddy Hamburger was lurking somewhere.

"The legislature has spoken," he said, referring to yesterday's landmark decision to legalize gay marriage in our conservative state. "We must recognize the legitimate rights of all people."

Margaret flashed him a cheeky grin. "That's not what you said last week."

The mayor had vowed he would never perform a gay wedding. There was quite a crowd around him now, and they all knew where he stood.

"What if I were to fall in love with a woman next time?" Margaret pressed on, her voluptuous body getting closer. "After all, my first five husbands were duds."

The mayor poked a finger under his collar as if the room were too hot. "Margaret," he said finally, "if you bring me a woman, I'll be happy to marry you."

"Can I quote you on that, Mayor?" said Paddy Hamburger, materializing from somewhere, a camera in his hand.

"If you get that quote exactly right, Paddy, you can put it in the paper."

Everybody laughed. The mayor had just admitted he'd like to marry Margaret. She ran her hand down the sheath of her dress.

I left this august body and searched for Carl. He was talking to Joe Torgesen and Tina White Horse who were holding hands.

When did this happen? I suspected there was more going on in my workroom during the fashion show than simple undressing.

"Tracy!"

"Tina!"

We hugged.

"Tina's been named director of the after-school program," he said "It's in every elementary school now."

"Congratulations!"

Joe turned to Carl. "Tina says there's some trouble at the high school. I thought maybe you and I could give a talk."

"What about?

"Bullying."

Carl raised an eyebrow. "A Come to Jesus talk or a Stick Up for Yourself talk?"

"Both," said Tina. "We've got kids who are being bullied and kids who are doing the bullying. They could all use some perspective from law enforcement."

Cell phone calendars were checked and a date was set.

I finished the last of my cookie and put the cardboard plate and the plastic cup in a recycling bin. A few years ago, you wouldn't have found a recycling bin in City Hall; now it was standard at every event.

Change happens. Maybe someday the mayor would perform marriages for gay couples. You could bet he'd be doing that a lot sooner than he'd be marrying Margaret.

I was sorting through a shipment of hair care products when Cholly Chockworth entered my salon with a young man in tow. "We're here!" called Cholly. "Now life can begin!"

"Life is entirely too dreary," I said, rising from the tumble of packaging and dusting off my hands. I took in the handsome face next to Cholly's. "Who's this?"

"My fiancé."

"Oh ho!" I gazed into his warm hazel eyes and liked him immediately. He grasped my hand with a solid shake, then put his arm around Cholly and grinned.

"This is Soren." Cholly was absolutely glowing. There were more stars in his eyes than the firmament of heaven.

I cleared the mass of boxes and bottles out of the way. "Please have a seat."

Cholly and Soren sat on the sofa; I sat in an upholstered chair.

"When's the big day?" I asked.

"In June. We're going to have the ceremony at Brinksman's Pass and the reception at The Finery." Cholly giggled. "We want you to do everyone's hair and Roxy to do the makeup."

"Do you want massages?"

"No, I've hired Chip and Dale to do a strip-tease—just a little bachelor send-off. But Soren wants champagne and pedicures."

All this time, Soren hadn't said a word but nodded at appropriate moments.

"Sounds marvelous," I said. "Will it be a double ring ceremony?"

"Of course." Cholly looked into Soren's eyes and squeezed his hand.

"Where are you from, Soren?" I asked.

"He's from that dear valley in the ski town west of us," answered Cholly. "That's why we've chosen Brinksman's Pass for the ceremony."

Soren nodded.

"And how did you two meet?"

They looked at each other and laughed. "Soren and I went fishing on the same website and we got caught!" Cholly said.

Their joy was infectious. I was giggling too. "This calls for a celebration!" I went to my refrigerator and pulled out a magnum.

"That's huge!" Cholly said.

"Margaret's coming."

"Yoo hoo!"

I let Margaret descend on Cholly and his fiancé while I went in search of champagne coupes.

"Don't you ever let Soren talk?" Margaret was saying when I returned. "I asked *him* a question, not you."

Cholly looked abashed. Leave it to Margaret to flatten effervescence in a bottle.

Soren spoke up. "We haven't found anyone to officiate yet." He had a nice voice, straight as an arrow, and it matched his good looks.

"The mayor certainly won't," said Margaret, "but I know someone who will. Her name's Gay Lynn. She's not gay but two of her children are. She loves to marry gay couples."

I handed the magnum to Cholly and he popped the cork. Champagne foamed out the neck and spilled onto my bamboo floor. Cholly poured everyone a glass and we toasted the happy couple.

By closing time, I was blasted. Cholly left with Soren as his designated driver. Margaret staggered back to the hardware store on foot and I called Carl for a ride home.

"It's been absolutely awful, Tracy." Shelley Prothero sat in my workshop chair. "We woke up to see figures in masks and hoodies hurling toilet paper rolls all over our trees. They got back in their cars, gunned their motors, and ran over our mailbox. By the time the police arrived, they were long gone."

"Who's they?"

"Kids." Shelley's forehead had more trenches running through it than our mountain watershed. "We think they're Kayla's classmates."

"Why would they pick your house?"

"Kayla wrote an article for the school newspaper."

"So?"

"The topic was why gay kids should be supported."

"Oh." I looked at Shelley in the mirror. The weight of the world was again on her shoulders, just as it was when she was terrified of medical bankruptcy.

"Kayla's being harassed at school," Shelley continued. "Kids bump into her in the hall—one sent her backwards into a locker—and no one will sit with her at lunch. She doesn't eat at school anymore."

"What did the police say?"

"The chief said to get their license plates if it happens again." She frowned. "But he seemed more concerned about the vandals than us. He told us not to confront the kids."

"But they're trespassing on your property."

"We're still liable and their parents could sue if anything bad happens to them."

I mulled this over. More and more it appeared that victims had no rights.

"I know where you can get a wicked no trespassing sign," I said, recalling the elderly survivalist's message that struck the fear of God and the second amendment into all trespassers. "You can turn your property into an armed camp."

"Don't be absurd. We don't own guns and we don't want any."

I sorted through my mental 'Contacts' file. "I have a friend who's a hunter. He has a camera with an infra-red light and a motion detector. If they come around again, you would have a movie of the kids and maybe even a view of their license plates."

"That might work."

"I'll call him tonight." I resumed cutting Shelley's hair. The watershed creases on her forehead were shallower now. We spoke of other things.

"How's that?" I asked after ten minutes.

She surveyed herself in the mirror. "Oh, Tracy, you do take care of me!"

Gay Lynn was a vivacious forty-something with a wide smile made wider by coral lipstick and a bouncy blonde hairdo.

"You're the detective hairdresser," she said, as soon as she came in my door. "Have I got a story for you!"

I started to say something, but she jumped right in. "I live across the street from the high school. My husband and I decided to fly a rainbow flag on top of our hill out back, as a symbol of gay pride, you know. We fly it to support our kids. The next morning we woke up and the rainbow flag was gone. We figured it wasn't attached right, so we put another one up and it disappeared, too."

Gay Lynn made herself at home on my sofa without taking a breath.

"The next day I was sitting in my hot tub and darned if I didn't see a little bastard on top of our hill chinning up the pole and taking down the new flag. My husband was so mad he got in his truck and headed for the other side of the hill where he spotted the kid just coming down. It was our next door neighbor's son. Later that day, we confronted the parents, and d'you know what they said?"

She paused. I had my cue. "What?"

"'Our son is complying with the laws of God.'"

I sat back from the edge of my chair.

"I was born in the Mormon Church and I know how people think," Gay Lynn continued, "but my kids are who they are. If you believe in God, they're the way God made them and if you don't, then that's the way it is. Who is anyone to say they can't be part of society and society can't be a part of them?"

I opened my mouth to say that society in our conservative state can be hard on non-conformists but Gay Lynn plowed on. "We called the police early on, of course, but they can't do anything unless they catch the little bastards red-handed, so we wrote a Letter to the Editor, asking people for their support. The next week, a box of 100 rainbow flags arrived at our door. Now I can give a rainbow flag to anyone who wants to fly one."

I remembered Paddy Hamburger writing about this story. "You went to the high school principal, I think."

"We did. We wanted to give a talk about gay rights at an all-school assembly."

"But he said no, didn't he?"

"He's a devout Mormon," she said. "He thought we should go fly a kite."

"So what happened?"

"We kept flying the flags, the kids kept taking them down, and we kept putting them up, and then they got tired of it. Homecoming Weekend arrived and we decided to fly the football team's flag. Now when we fly either flag, no one takes it down."

"Sounds like you've got it licked."

"You just have to stick to your guns and open up people's heads," Gay Lynn said.

There was a nanosecond of silence and I thought it was my turn to talk. "Let's discuss your hair," I said.

I jotted down what she wanted in my Client Notebook—pecan highlights in her brown-blonde hair, a layered cut, and a Portuguese Pump-Up treatment to restore hair body.

Three and half hours later she looked smashing.

"I've got a gorgeous husband," she said, "and I like to look gorgeous for him."

"Well, you do."

"You'll meet him at Cholly and Soren's wedding," she said.

"I'm looking forward to it."

"I can't believe they had to move the reception. The Finery won't cater a gay wedding."

"But that's against the law. The Finery can't pick and choose what weddings they're going to do."

"They say they're booked."

"It's discrimination."

"You're telling me? They want to deny services based on their employees' religious beliefs," Gay Lynn said. "They're taking a cue from our state legislators—the House passed a bill that makes it legal for county clerks to refuse to marry gay people as long as they refer them to someone who will."

"But that bill never made it to the state senate."

"I know, but it just demonstrates the shaky ground we're walking on. What's to prevent businesses from denying service to anyone based on their employees' religious beliefs? Blacks, Latinos, gays, Jews—"

"It's the proverbial slippery slope."

"You got that right."

I took Gay Lynn's credit card and we made an appointment in four weeks. She headed for the door.

"Let me know how they do on finding another venue for the wedding reception," I said.

"I'll keep you posted."

What a frisky lady. I should get her together with Shelley Prothero—in this corner, thoughtless teenagers—in that corner, Gay Lynn. Now that would be a match I'd like to see.

I was in the back yard grilling chicken and basting zucchini slices with olive oil. The guys were playing soccer. I feel guilty for owning a backyard with grass. In the high mountain desert, it's a luxury to water a lawn, but soccer, football, badminton, volleyball, and bocce ball all seem to require turf.

I turned off the grill and piled each plate; then called the boys to the picnic table. They tucked in.

"How was your presentation at the high school?" I asked Carl.

"Good."

"What'd you talk about?"

"Anti-bullying laws and school policies and how to report something you see. There's no such thing as ratting on anybody and there's no stigma about being a victim. Kids have got to know that it's the law—they're required to speak up."

"We always tell," said Jamie. "We tell the principal."

I knew what Jamie was talking about. The playground at his elementary school wasn't for the faint of heart. I visited Jamie's school one day during recess. Half the school was lined up outside the principal's office waiting to complain about the other half.

"Carter kicked me in the shins today," Jamie said.

"Why?"

"Because I wouldn't give him the ball."

"That's not bullying, Jamie," Carl said. "Bullying is when a big person gangs up on a little person and tries to scare them, hurt them, and make them cry. It usually happens over and over again and the little kid feels bad and can't defend himself."

"I kicked Carter back—it wasn't his turn."

"You were both wrong," I said. "Kicking and hitting isn't the way to solve conflicts."

"You work it out," Carl said. "You come up with ways to make things fair."

"I let Carter have the ball after I took a shot," Jamie said.

"And how did that work out?"

"Good."

That settled, I asked Carl if he was aware of Kayla Prothero's case.

"What case?"

"She's being harassed because of a stand she took on gay rights."

"The principal didn't mention it."

"And what about the incident at Shelley's house last weekend?"

"What incident?"

I told him about the TP-ing and the infra-red camera set up.

"What's TP-ing?" Jamie piped up.

"It's when—"I wished I'd kept my mouth shut. "It's when the bathroom floor is covered with toilet paper."

"But I thought you said it was in the trees," Jamie said.

"Mommy's just making a joke, Jamie. Some bad kids threw toilet paper in the trees on Kayla's property," Carl said. "It made a mess and it's against the law. It's called vandalism and people can go to jail for that."

"I'd kick them in the shins!" Jamie said. He loves his babysitter.

I didn't say anything, but I felt like kicking those kids in the shins myself.

"May I be excused?" Jamie asked.

"Take your plate to the sink," I said.

My eyes followed Jamie as he balanced his plate and fork and tried to open the screen door at the same time. I relaxed when he managed to get inside without dropping everything on the deck.

I turned my attention back to Carl. "Why didn't the principal mention Kayla's case? Surely, he needs to report it to law enforcement."

"Only if it's criminal activity, otherwise, we'd hear about bullying and teasing all day. From what you tell me, the harassment is against school policy, but it's not a criminal act."

"What about the vandalism?" I asked.

"I'd be interested in what the surveillance camera shows."

"It's the chief's case."

"Then I *definitely* want to see it."

We smiled at each other as Jamie returned to the table.

"Dessert is strawberry shortcake," I said.

"Awesome!"

I love pleasing my men. It's so easy.

I was trimming the rose bushes in front of my house on Monday when Russell Huntsman pulled up in his Chevy Silverado with the gun rack on the back of the cab and the deer rack on its hood. He slipped out the front door as if he were dismounting from a bull, legs jumping to the ground, right arm in the air.

"Hello, Little Lady," he said, "long time no see."

"You never come for a haircut," I said.

He rubbed on his crew cut. "Sadie barbers the hell out of this old pate." Sadie was his seventeen-year-old daughter.

"What are you going to do when Sadie goes to college?"

"She's attendin' beautician school, so nothin's gonna change."

"You watch out," I said. "She'll learn how to do more than buzzcuts and want to practice on her dad."

Russell winked. "How'd ya think I'd look with a Mohawk?"

I rolled my eyes.

Russell reached into his pocket and pulled out a thumb drive. "Lookee here what I have for you."

My eyes must have lit up because he laughed. "Mighty incriminating piece of footage. Bunch a hooligans at a car rally."

"Could you tell who they were?"

"Not really."

"Let's go inside."

We went to the den where I plugged the memory stick into my computer and tapped on the keys. Dark grainy footage showed up and it took me a few seconds to get my bearings. A raccoon meandered across Shelley's front lawn. I could make out the mailbox at the end of the driveway, two roads intersecting, and the tall pine tree at the corner of her lot. The time stamp said 10:30 when the raccoon left the lawn and the motion sensor turned the camera off.

At 11:17 a parade of three cars zipped past the mailbox, rounded the corner, and continued up the street. That wasn't the disturbing part. Hooded figures leaned out of the car windows; one figure thrust his torso up through a sunroof waving in the air. His mouth was open. I could imagine the noise even though there was no sound—Shelley had told me how loud the kids hooted and hollered.

At 11: 21 the same cars careened back again, this time from the opposite direction. I paused the video and examined the white faces ringed by the black hoods but the picture was too gray and fuzzy to make out distinct features. I let the footage roll until the cars disappeared from view.

At 11:27 the cars returned, this time to pull onto the lawn and train their headlights on the house, almost blinding the camera. Black shapes emerged, twelve in all, and began throwing toilet paper. At least I thought that must be what they were doing; their movements resembled goblins with St. Vitus' dance. Within minutes, the shadowy shapes returned to their cars and drove off.

Finally, at 11:47 the video showed a squad car arriving. Shelley's husband walked slowly down the path to greet the police, his shoulders hunched. He gestured to the pine tree, now draped in toilet paper.

"I couldn't recognize the officers or the kids," I said. "The picture's too fuzzy."

"It's the cheapest motion detector system on the market," Russell said. "All I want to know is what game is coming around the water source on my land."

"Let's go back to 11:22." I pressed the reverse button. "I thought I saw something we could use."

I slowed the video when the parade of cars reappeared from the right side of the screen as if backing up. When the street light illuminated the front license plate of the lead car, I stopped the picture. "There. Do you see?"

"Sure do."

I think Carl can do something with this," I said.

The next day at dinner, Carl said, "The chief identified the owner of the car. It belongs to the high school principal. We believe his teenage son was driving."

"No!" I said.

"Yup," said Carl.

"What did the chief do?"

"Nothing."

"Nothing!

"Nothing."

I ruminated on this for a while. It was not my place to call him out but I think I understood our chief. He was embarrassed. He didn't want to be the bearer of bad news to someone who's in his ward and he didn't want to bring a vandalism charge against the offspring of someone who's in his ward. Chief Fort Dukes is not a coward—he's a political animal. Delivering news like that would be bad for his reputation.

"What are you going to do?" I asked Carl.

"I'm giving another talk at the high school this week. The principal's kid will be in the audience and I'm going to single him out. I'll make sure he knows that I know what's going down and I'll stress the penalties for harassment, vandalism, and bullying."

"Do you think it'll do any good?"

"Mormons have been taught since they were children that homosexuality is wrong. Now they have to un-learn that idea and it's not going to happen overnight."

"Do you think the principal knows about his kid?"

"If he does, he's turning a blind eye."

"It's God's law," I murmured.

"What?"

"That's what the parents said to Gay Lynn when she told her neighbors their kid was stealing their rainbow flag—'Our son is complying with God's law.'"

"But vandalism and harassment are against man's law," Carl said, "and that's the only law I'm interested in."

About a month later Kayla Prothero returned to my salon.

"Kayla!" I hugged her. "What's this?"

Kayla was crying. "I can't ever go back to school!"

"Oh, no."

"It's too horrible." Kayla went off into a paroxysm of sobbing.

"Whoa, whoa, hold on now. Sit down and tell me what happened." I got Kayla a tissue.

She blew her nose. "There's this boy at school I really like, and we were chatting—you know, online—and I thought he really liked me, and he asked me out, but he didn't show, and I was all alone at the movie theater, waiting for him, and later he chatted and said his mother grounded him, so we made another date, and I went again and he didn't show again, and then he chatted that he was sorry, so I went to school and I thanked him in person for his apology and he said, 'What apology?' And I said 'For our date at the movie theater,' and he said 'What date at the movie theater?' And he said "I never made a date to go to the movies with you—you're a Lez.'"

She finally took a breath, then more words rushed out. "It was all over Facebook and I realized I'd been set up. It was never him chatting with me at all. It was someone who set up a fake account and pretended to be him, and the cars are still coming every weekend and the vandals broke a window and they trampled Mother's flowerbeds and they won't stop and I wish I never wrote that article and I hate all of them and I hate my life and I'm never going back to that school ever again!"

Her wail was horrible to hear. I gathered Kayla up in my arms and told her that she was a brave, mature woman, not like the nasty, petty kids who played mean tricks on her, and someday she would laugh over this when she was a lawyer fighting for the rights of all individuals, not just gay people, and that she should have an aromatherapy facial right this minute with coconut and avocado butter massaged into her face by good-looking teenage boys who were not available right now, but would I do?

She stopped crying. I gave her some chocolate and took her to the massage room where she lay down on my heated massage table, and I applied unguents and emollients, essential oils and warm compresses until she fell asleep to my mellow-chill-out magic mix.

Gay Lynn emerged from my comfort room. "I heard the whole thing." She and her pecan highlights were processing while her feet were soaking in a warm bath of lavender water.

"It's heart wrenching," I said.

"It's cyber bullying," Gay Lynn said.

"I know."

"How stable is Kayla?"

"She's got her feet on the ground a lot more than other kids I know."

"That's good," said Gay Lynn, "because there have been suicides. There was a case recently where a girl sent her boyfriend a nude picture of herself, and then they broke up. He put it out on Facebook. She couldn't stand the humiliation and she took her own life. And there was another one where the taunting and name-calling over the internet caused a gay teen to hang himself."

I stared at Gay Lynn in horror.

"It's one thing to be humiliated in front of a few people," she said, "and quite another to have a cyber-setup with instantaneous messaging and a public Facebook bashing. Do you think Kayla's strong enough to ride this out?"

I was about to give an opinion when Gay Lynn asked, "And what's with the weekend warrior stuff?"

I told Gay Lynn about the vandalism and the car harassment.

"How long has this been going on?"

"At least a month."

"This is nuts," she said. "They've got to cut this shit out."

"How're we gonna stop 'em?"

"I've got a friend with big guns," she said, "and this is what we'll do."

The next Saturday night at Shelley and Jack Prothero's house, I put my tossed salad on the kitchen counter as Gay Lynn uncovered a platter of barbecued ribs. The house was full of our friends.

Margaret was dressed in a long camo vest, camo leggings, and combat boots. Somehow she made this look hot.

Annabelle Davina was wearing a long brown skirt with a camo sleeveless T-shirt over her flat-chested nubs.

Carl and Joe wore their uniforms and I wore red. *Let them see me.*

Gay Lynn introduced us to her friend from the big valley—Mel Baird. He was forty-something with black hair, a black mustache, a black T-shirt, and black cargo pants. Mel only had eyes for Margaret.

We sat down to dinner.

"Who's this young man?" asked Jack's mother. She had come to the dinner table dressed in a housecoat and slippers.

"This is Mel Baird, Mother," said Shelley, raising her voice and speaking distinctly.

"What do you do, young man?" asked Jack's mother.

"I sell pre-owned cars at a car dealership in the city," Mel replied.

"Pre-owned?" she repeated. With sudden understanding she said, "You mean *used* cars."

"Yes, ma'am," Melvin said, "but nobody wants to buy a used car anymore, Mrs. Prothero."

Grandma Prothero turned to her son. "I thought you said he was a gun salesman."

"I said he owns big guns," said Jack. "He doesn't sell them."

Grandma Prothero turned to Mel. "You a hunter?"

"No, I like golf."

Grandma Prothero looked confused.

Margaret flashed Mel a smile. "I like golf, too," she said.

She might as well have said 'I like sex, too' for the reaction she got. Mel looked as if he'd like to go for a hole in one.

I cleared my throat and turned to Shelley's husband. "Jack, what are the plans for tonight?"

"Our visitors usually don't come around until midnight," he said, "so let's play Apples to Apples while we wait. I've put up blackout curtains so they'll think we've gone to bed. At midnight, we'll go outside and wait and then POW!"

"You ready for that, Mel?" I asked.

"You bet," he said.

"You ready, Kayla?"

Kayla looked a little troubled and Annabelle grasped her hand. "We're ready," she said.

In a few hours, Grandma Prothero had gone to bed, Kayla was dozing on the sofa, and Gay Lynn was trying to convince Margaret that Dick Cheney was sexy in the Apples to Apples game. Then the grandfather clock chimed midnight. We went outside. I heard a rumbling in the west.

If I hadn't see this with my own eyes, I wouldn't have believed it. Five cars pulled onto the grass, headlights pointed at the house. Black figures tumbled out. When they were deep inside the property, Mel blasted them.

Two huge dealership spotlights illuminated the figures, which froze in a kind of deathly tableau. Then they scrambled all over each other trying to get back in their cars. But as soon as Carl and Joe emerged from the light, they froze again.

One boy's mouth dropped open so wide I was afraid his jaw would unhinge. A red-haired teen dropped his toilet paper roll and reached for the sky. Another kid prostrated himself on the grass. Two more drivers extracted themselves from their cars, heads bowed, shoulders slumped.

Carl and Joe did their work.

I would not have liked to be their parents. Every parent dreads the phone call that wakes them and gives them news they never wanted to hear.

Luckily, the news was not about an accident.

No one was dying; no one was dead.

But a little bit of innocence was lost that night.

And would never be reclaimed.

The summer breeze at Brinksman's Pass was soft as doeskin. I gazed at the magnificent mountain backdrop and marveled at nature. Soren and Cholly came up the aisle flanked by all their friends. They stood under a metal arch decorated in floral finery. Gay Lynn was waiting for them with a smile that beamed brighter than the sun.

I held Carl's hand as she began the ceremony. Her words were surprisingly traditional. "Dearly Beloved, we are gathered here to witness the union . . ." I would have thought Cholly and Soren would go for something more 21st century.

The happy couple were dressed in white suits. The backs of their jackets were embroidered elaborately with their initials—SCC intertwined with vines. It was a testament to Cholly that Soren would take his name.

I mused on the evolution of society—how a hundred years ago we women wore long skirts, couldn't vote and didn't own property; black people had Jim Crow in the south and the same but not in name in the north; backroom abortions were treacherous, the Pill was unheard of; the Industrial Age caused labor strife; and the Information Age was unimagined. Yet these mountains looked exactly the same. This view would endure here forever, no matter what we humans managed to do on our planet.

Gay Lynn's voice overtook my thoughts. "Will you take this man to be your lawfully wedded husband, to have and to hold from this day forward, for better and for worse, for richer, for poorer, in sickness and in health, to love and to cherish, 'til death do you part?"

"We do."

"Then," Gay Lynn said, "I pronounce you husband and husband."

I squeezed Carl's hand.

He squeezed back.

Case 9
Big Brother

● ● ● ● ● ●

A peculiar scrabbling noise came from some-where in the den.

Was a potgut in the house again?

Potguts are little ground squirrels that live in tunnels underneath the desert soil. One died in the walls once and stank up the house for a week.

I rushed into the den where I found my son transfixed by his iPad. On screen, two huge white-headed birds shuffled around a large nest. He was watching the Florida Bald Eagle Cam.

"Their names are Romeo and Juliet," Jamie whispered, as if he might disturb them.

One parent grasped a small silver fish in its huge yellow claws, ripped the fish's head off, and passed strips of pink flesh to a little white eaglet. The baby telescoped its spindly neck and scarfed down his breakfast while his brother watched. I wondered why the other eaglet was waiting his turn so politely when I read the screen: They were born yesterday.

Jet noise disrupted the mood. We scrolled down the screen to Eagle Cam 2. This camera shot upward from the forest floor so we could see the flash of metal wings behind the nest. All those people were flying to Miami and they had no idea there was an eagle's nest below them or that we were watching their airplane from our little city out west.

Technology is amazing.

I was stirring milk into my coffee at the salon coffee station when the door opened. "Good morning, Sassy. Have you had your coffee yet?"

"Is it ready now?"

"You bet." I poured Sassy Morgan a mug of Steep & Deep. "Full body wave treatment today?"

"Yes, but I must be out in 90 minutes—I've got to open the store."

My Client Notebook reminded me that Sassy had taken a job at the Main Street Boutique. "I'll have you out at quarter of eleven—plenty of time."

Sassy submitted to my expert hands. Within thirty minutes her hair was permed and rolled. The entire time, she checked her cell phone.

"You seem anxious, Sassy."

"Can't be late."

"Relax," I told her. "Would you like to soak your feet in a warm bath with gardenia oil or lie on a warm massage table with a cool lemon eye compress while you're processing?"

"I'm too wired."

"What's the matter?"

"It's my bosses in Florida. They know what time I open the store, what I'm doing, and everything I say."

"How?"

"They've installed cameras with microphones and they're watching me from their house."

My nose wrinkled. "That's creepy."

"If I don't sell, sell, sell I hear about it."

"What d'you mean?"

"They want me to push product, but most people want to browse. They'll say, 'Just looking,' and I'll say, 'If you see anything you like, please let me know.' But my employers want me to hover over them and talk about any item that catches their attention."

"I hate that kind of salesperson," I said with a snort. "They're annoying and then they disappear when you need them."

"I got a dressing down the other day like you would not believe. The store owners analyzed my every move. I felt like two cents afterwards."

Sassy is a beautiful girl, but her mouth had twisted upside down, her shoulders were slumped, and now that I'd finished her rollers, her head looked like a cluster of afterburners on a jet fighter.

"I know it's their shop," she said, "but I feel like a bug under a microscope. I've worked there for quite some time and I think I've done a good job—sales are up and we have repeat business—but all of a sudden I'm back at square one. I feel like a teenager being tracked by Mom and Dad."

"Have you told them this?"

"Not in so many words."

"Do the other salespeople feel this way?"

"They're newer—maybe they need supervision." She paused and looked at the cell phone as if time were getting away from her again. "There's been some shoplifting recently."

"Then that's why they installed the system—not to spy on you."

"Probably."

I poured us both another cup of Steep & Deep. "Perhaps things will settle down over time. People love new gadgets, but they lose interest after a while."

"I hope so."

"Hang in there and don't take it personally. Believe in your past performance."

I put the perm solution away and rinsed my mixing bowls.

"Tracy?"

"Yes."

"I think I'll take that cool lemon compress now."

I led Sassy to my massage room, put the chilled citrus cloth on her face, turned on "Musical Healing Chimes," and closed the door.

Sassy Morgan is a wonderful person. She'd been a good friend to Orchid Fisher ever since we discovered Orchid was addicted to prescription meds. Sassy's bosses were lucky to have her and they shouldn't have been micromanaging her with surveillance cameras.

Technology sucks.

It was late afternoon when Rabbi Josh walked through the front door. He removed his yarmulke. "What can you do with this?" he asked.

I surveyed his bald spot and snapped my fingers. "Keep your yarmulke on."

"You're a big help, Tracy."

"We aim to please at The Citrus Salon."

Rabbi Josh stopped by every month to purchase massages for his wife Sharon, who wrote screenplays for the wildly popular science fiction TV series "Vagabond Planet." Rumor had it that the Rabbi revealed clues about future episodes in all his sermons and this titillating notion packed the Temple every week.

"How's life, Josh?" I asked.

"I got a speeding ticket."

I laughed at the face he pulled. "Were you stopped by someone I know?"

"I wish."

"What happened?"

"Those damn traffic cams. A ticket arrived in the mail and I couldn't argue."

I smiled. Rabbi Josh was known for arguing. He did his thesis on religious polemics at Harvard Divinity School.

"How fast were you going?" I asked.

"Fifty in a thirty mile an hour zone."

"Rabbi!"

"I was late for a lecture and I was the lecturer." He observed my face. "It's not something I'm proud of."

"Cameras don't lie."

"They're expensive buggers. We just got a quote to replace the security system at the Temple—twenty-five thousand dollars."

"Jesus."

"He has nothing to do with it. Our insurer wants every entrance and exit covered, every function room, the Torah Ark, the entire exterior, and the parking lots. I asked them why they didn't want the bathrooms wired."

"What did they say?"

"Some things are best left to God."

I giggled.

"You know the trouble with being a rabbi?" he asked.

"No, what?"

"You think you're in charge of people's spiritual lives, but most of your time is spent as a building superintendent."

I handed Josh's credit card back to him and wrapped a pink bow around a set of Divine Davina Dalliance gift cards. "Sharon will enjoy these."

"Annabelle does wonders for her back," he said.

"And you do wonders for your congregation."

Rabbi Josh winked and went out the door.

Five minutes later, I realized I'd forgotten to ask the million dollar question: Why did the Temple need a new security system? I rushed out the front door, but all I saw was his car speeding up the street.

My next appointment was Tina White Horse. She'd become a good friend. We double-dated and I could see that Joe Torgesen was very much in love with her. I expected him to pop the question any day now.

Fragrant steam rose from Tina's footbath. I was shaking a bottle of Happy Tulip nail polish when she said, "Do you think our guys should be wearing body cams?"

I stared into the bubbling water. Another million dollar question. The answer was complicated and I was not sure I wanted to talk about it. "Tell me what you think."

"We don't have many black people in this community, but there are Native Americans like me, and Hispanics. We have the potential for racial profiling and racial incidents."

"I don't think our police force is like that," I said. "Our chief may be laughable but he believes in community policing. He's not like that martinet over in the next county."

Tina grimaced. She knew I was talking about a sheriff who acted like an army general and thought he was running a military unit.

I plucked Tina's shapely foot out of the warm water and perched it on the ledge in front of me. "Body cams can be invasive," I said. "There's no automatic technology to turn them off when innocent citizens are involved. What if I've been robbed? I call the police and consent to entry. They come in, cameras rolling. What happens to *that* footage?"

Tina smiled wickedly. "I've heard there's a lot of consensual entry going on at your house. We *all* want to see that footage."

I laughed and splashed water at her. "You should talk," I said, spreading cuticle softener on Tina's toes. After a while, I stopped smiling. "I've often thought a body cam would protect our guys, maybe even as much as Kevlar vests."

"I think so too," she said. "If anything happened, there would be a record of it. Questions could be answered."

I reached for Tina's right foot and applied my emery board. "It's hard being a cop these days," I said. "The media makes people believe police violence is pandemic and all cops are just a bunch of bigoted, authoritarian assholes."

"It's despicable—the racism, I mean."

"It does exist."

"It's about intergenerational post-traumatic stress," Tina said.

"What?" I stopped shaping Tina's toes.

"My tribe has PTSD. A hundred years ago we were forced to relocate to the only ugly place in this beautiful state. I don't think we've ever gotten over it. There's anxiety and depression among my people. We're poor. We drink. We do drugs. We've been told 'The only good Indian is a dead Indian,' and we've believed them. We are our own worst enemies because we beat down anyone who tries to climb out of the reservation and better their lives. There are some very smart people on the rez who never got anywhere. It's sad to see."

"How'd you get out?"

"I don't know that I have. I still think of myself as inferior and suspect people are prejudiced against me. Every day I try to ignore this feeling and I'm not always good at it."

Tina had revealed the way her world worked. It was a sobering picture and I didn't like it one bit. "Do you think there's a parallel with blacks in our country?" I asked.

"I can't speak for them, but slavery is humiliating. Its effects are wounding and they last for generations. For the oppressors as well as the oppressed."

"So it's always simmering under the surface?"

"People don't even know they're doing it. Think of those frat boys singing on the bus. They've been chanting the same song for years and nobody called them out on it. But along came someone with a cell phone and the video went viral."

A bunch of fraternity students from the University of Oklahoma were caught singing sick, racist lyrics to a little-kids' tune. Now when I hear 'If You're Happy and You Know It,' I no longer clap my hands.

Tina went on, "Our society has incarcerated more poor people and people of color than any other westernized country on the planet."

We fell silent. The scratching of my emery board was the only sound in the room. I wished every wrong could be righted, but life wasn't like that. At the moment, the only cure for the way we both felt was Happy Tulip nail polish.

I started applying color onto Tina's toes when she asked her original question. "Do you think our guys should be wearing body cams?"

"Yes," I said. "We need to know the truth."

Carl sat down at the dinner table and put his napkin in his lap. "Mrs. Oscar called me today on my cell phone," he said. "No, Jamie, don't reach across the table. Say, 'Please pass the juice, Dad.'"

"Please pass the juice, Dad."

Carl poured Jamie a glass and set the bottle on the table.

I covered my grin with my own napkin. My son was obedient and adorable, but he routinely forgot his manners.

"How'd she get your cell number?" I asked.

"She has her sources."

I marveled at the way this little old lady operated. *Whose ear did she twist this time?* "What did she want?"

"She's got a new security system."

"Praise the Lord," I said, remembering the useless VHS video footage of alien spacemen throwing things in her convenience bins.

"She wants me to fix her gas station security cameras. Every single one is on the fritz."

"That's a job for the security company."

"Stealth-Techt says it's vandalism."

"Don't tell me someone used them for target practice."

"They were disabled at five separate gas stations. The chief technician thinks it's a crank with a laser."

"A laser?"

"A security camera can be disabled with a pen laser—the kind lecturers use to illustrate PowerPoint presentations. The infra-red beam is pointed into the camera lens."

"If it's that easy, why doesn't every robber do it?"

"There's a little more to it than that. The state tech experts have the footage now. We're hoping there's an image of the laser shooter right before the picture goes blank. If there is and they can blow it up, we might be able to ID our guy."

"A *Laser Shooter*! That's awesome," said Jamie. "I'm building a robot with laser eyes. He just looks at people and they go blind. He's got a bionic eye that can see like a microscope and another eye that can explore the moon. He's off the clock."

Carl and I burst out laughing.

"And you're off the clock," said Carl. "Let's go play ball."

"Wait!" I said. "You didn't tell me if Mrs. Oscar's gas stations were robbed."

"Nope."

"Then why disable the security system?"

"That's what's so weird about this. There seems to be no motivation and the vandal had to drive all over town. If he was on a shooting spree, he could have taken out all the security cameras on Main Street but only the Oscars' gas stations got hit."

"Weird."

"Come on, sport," said Carl, hefting the football. My men went outside. The Law of Fast Forgetting was at work again—they didn't take their dishes to the sink.

A week later Rabbi Josh's wife, Sharon, arrived for a massage with Annabelle Davina. They disappeared into my massage room while I was doing computer work.

Accounting is the bane of my existence. My computer system is linked to my bank account, but there are glitches and inconsistencies that drive me crazy. I could print out reports, but then I have to comb the pages to find all the mistakes. It takes time that I don't have.

The phone rang.

"Citrus Salon."

"Tracy, this is Katherine Putnam."

"Katherine! How are you?"

She giggled. "I'm engaged!"

"To the Man from Gujarat?"

"Deepak."

"That's awesome, Katherine!"

"We wondered if you and Carl would like to come over Saturday night so you can meet him."

"What a nice invitation. What can we bring?"

"Wine is always good. Seven o'clock?"

"Seven."

"See you then."

I put down the phone and smiled. Our flaming red-haired Katherine had found true love with a tech guru from India. What were the odds of that?

Annabelle Davina emerged from the massage room, leaving Sharon inside. "I now know the season ending of 'Vagabond Planet.' It's a shocker."

"Do tell!"

"I would be reneging on the pact I've made with the screen writer," she said. "I can't violate her trust."

"That's not fair."

"You'll just have to watch it like everybody else."

A few years ago Sharon gave us the scoop on the grand finale of *The Sopranos*. We were prepared when the screen went black in the last minute of broadcast, but the whole country thought they'd lost their cable signal right at the climax. People were left panting, and the show's creators were laughing up their sleeves.

It was Climaxus Interruptus.

Sharon came out from the massage room and Annabelle handed her a glass of sparkling water. Her face glistened and she looked wrung out. She carries such tightness in her shoulders that Annabelle must pummel and knead to get all the tension out.

"Hi, Tracy," she said.

"Hi, Sharon."

Annabelle glided away as Sharon and I sank onto the sofa. Sharon flopped back like a prize fighter after the twelfth round. I didn't say anything.

After a while, she said. "How's everything with you?"

"Good," I said. "You?"

"Good now."

I let her rest some more.

"How's Jamie?" she asked.

"Wonderful. He's building a robot with laser eyes."

She laughed.

"He goes to Make-It Camp after school," I added. "They've got kids building all sorts of things."

"That's nice."

Silence.

"What else is new?" she asked.

I'd been waiting for this. I had found it best to tread lightly with Sharon after a massage. She's a very private person and hates probing questions.

"Carl's working on a case about security cameras," I told her. "Someone disabled them at all the Oscar gas stations."

"You're kidding."

"Their security experts think they were shot out by a laser. You ever heard of that?"

I waited.

"It's not possible," she said, half-rising from her prone position. "I had the researchers on my show check into it. No one has been able to perfect the technique, even the military. It's the stuff of science fiction."

"Which you thrive on."

"I'm not going to reveal my show's secrets. You and Annabelle know too much already." Sharon took a deep breath and nestled back into the sofa. "But I could be persuaded with chocolate."

I smiled. "Hershey's, Belgian, or Godiva?"

"Belgian."

I rose. "And herbal tea?"

"Yes, please."

"Peach berry Jasmine or Snow Geisha?"

"Snow Geisha."

When Sharon was sitting up and taking nourishment, I resumed my tap dance. "Chocolate good?"

"Divine."

"Tea okay?"

"Hai, arigato."

"Science fiction interesting?"

"You sly thing."

"Humor me."

"The problem is that the laser beam must be aimed into the camera at precisely the right place. To do that, a robber must look at the camera, which will then record his face. So, he has to disable the camera before he can disable the camera. It's counterintuitive."

"What about wearing a mask?"

"That's a solution, but if the guy's out in the open someone's bound to see him and other cameras can capture his image too. My plot calls for the perfect crime. Zap! I don't exist."

"Fascinating."

Sharon sipped her tea. She's a big woman, in her forties, with smooth auburn hair. Last year she won an Emmy. She and Josh went to Hollywood where they hobnobbed with the stars but couldn't wait to get back to the solitude of their ski chalet. I couldn't imagine what her life was like. All I knew was that she needed a massage twice a week and Annabelle was the only one who made her feel better.

"Josh is still investigating the security problem at the Temple," she went on. "Somehow all our security cameras were trashed at the same time and Stealth-Techt hasn't been able to tell us why. Our insurance company wants us to install a radical upgrade."

"Why?"

"Hate crimes."

"Hate crimes?"

"The incidence of hate crimes against Jews has risen significantly, about 17 percent. That's right behind hate crimes against black people, which have increased 21 percent. Surveillance cameras are the first line of defense."

John Lennon's song popped into my head. "We could live as one if there were no religion." But that's not the way the world worked and I couldn't tell him so because he was dead.

Annabelle flowed in. "How do you feel, Sharon?"

"Divine," she said, "but Tracy here is making me think too much about work."

Annabelle quoted Lao Tsu, one of her favorite ancient philosophers. "'Too many words cause exhaustion; better to abide in stillness.'" Her eyes were downcast and her presence was gentle. "Lao Tsu also reminds us that 'Peace is our original state.'"

"I keep trying to get back to my original state, over and over again," said Sharon, leaning back on the sofa.

"And I haven't helped," I said. "I'm sorry, Sharon."

"Don't worry, Tracy," Annabelle said. "Lao Tsu also says, 'Revere the unity of all-that-is, carry out your daily activities with compassion; if you do not limit your compassion, you yourself will not be limited.'"

If only people allowed the world to work that way.

On Saturday evening Carl and I drove to Katherine's house. She lived in a small cut-stone cottage dating from the late 1800s. Katherine led us to the kitchen where the Man from Gujarat was pouring glasses of red wine.

Deepak was five foot four inches tall and a bit pudgy. He had beautiful soft brown eyes, dazzling white teeth, and a ready laugh.

"We're going to have an Indian wedding right here in the U.S.A.," Katherine said, as Deepak handed me my wine glass. "The ceremony will be traditional Hindu. There will be an elephant and everything."

I imagined Katherine riding an elephant and the thought boggled my mind.

"My mother is ordering a silk wedding sari from India," said Deepak. "Katherine will look beautiful."

Indian saris make all women look feminine and elegant. I wish I could wear one every day. "Where will the ceremony take place?"

"In the big valley."

Carl helped himself to cheese and crackers. "I've heard Indian weddings last a long time."

"My whole family is coming from Gujarat," said Deepak. "We have booked two floors at the Little America hotel for a week."

The price tag for that investment staggered my mind. I had to sit down. I was looking around for a chair in Katherine's tiny kitchen when she said, "We want you to do the hair, Tracy. Will you?"

"I'm afraid I don't know anything about hairstyles for Indian weddings," I said.

"My sister-in-law will be arriving from Mumbai," said Deepak in his beautiful Indian accent. "She will take care of the Indian girls and you can get the American girls ready."

"Then I accept."

"This calls for a toast," Carl said, raising his glass.

We honored a couple whom I never could have guessed would get together. Katherine is a sweet girl but she's no looker. Local guys were always judging the outside of the package. Deepak was smart enough to value what's inside.

"So, Deepak," said Carl. "What do you do?"

"I'm an artificial intelligence programmer for a video game company."

Carl browsed through the carrots and celery. "What's that about?"

"I simulate the intelligence of enemies and opponents by developing the logic of time," he said.

I had no idea what he just said.

"Simulation substrata requires script sequencing and program pathology is contentious foraging."

Ditto, Deepak. "How did you get into that?" I asked.

"I started playing video games when I was very young. There's not a whole lot to do in Gujarat and the internet opened the world to me. I found it invigorating to play games with people in America and Europe and China. When I went to the Indian Institute of Technology in Delhi, I worked with the smartest people I ever met. They introduced me to artificial intelligence and I found my niche." Deepak swirled his wine glass. "What do you do, Carl?"

"I'm a policeman."

"Ah, yes, Katherine was telling me. You and Tracy solve crimes together."

"She's my eyes and ears." Carl put his arm around me.

"I heard about the identity theft case," Deepak said. "Botnets also steal personal information. They are insidious."

"I've never completely understood botnets," said Carl.

"When a computer is penetrated by malware, control of the computer goes to the creator of the botnet. Bots scan the environment and propagate themselves within the vulnerabilities. Generally, the more the replicated botnets, the more value-added to the botnet controller."

Katherine read my face and jumped in. "It's pretty simple, Tracy," she said. "If you're at a website and a pop-up window says 'Such and such a site wants you to allow access your location,' click no. If you say yes, you may let some bad guys into your computer and they'll get into all your stuff. These "bots," as they're called, could sneak around inside looking for your private information or they could just make annoying ads pop up every time you surf the 'net. It all depends on what the bad guys want. Either way your security has been compromised and you're defenseless."

Deepak kissed Katherine on the cheek. Her eyes shone like a starlet's.

"Asking for your location is just one example," said Deepak. "There are many more ways a botnet can breach your security. Most of the time you don't even know it. You just need to keep your anti-malware updated. The security companies are developing defensive logarithms all the time." He smiled and his brilliant white teeth gleamed in his brown face. "It's a constant battle between the bad guys and the good guys. Like my games."

"Carl's working on a security breach case right now." I turned to him. "Is it okay to tell them about it?"

"Sure, it's been in the papers. Two security systems in our area have been permanently disabled, we think by a guy with a pen laser. We have no idea how it's being done."

Deepak appeared to be absorbing this information. He sipped his wine, then topped a cracker with cheese. He took so long, I didn't think he was going to respond. Then he said, "Pen lasers do not disable cameras permanently. There's usually a bright red flash on the digital image, but when the laser is removed the camera is not harmed. It should keep recording."

"These cameras had to be tossed," Carl said.

"Interesting," he said, looking as captivated as if he were playing a video game with a crack opponent in China.

"In each instance, the camera recorded a picture of a figure whose entire body was obliterated by a glowing light," Carl explained. "Then the picture went completely black."

"*Very* interesting." Now Deepak looked as if he were playing with *two* gurus in China.

"The security company is baffled. The state police techs are too."

"*Extremely* interesting." He looked as if he were playing with a gang of four.

"You know something, don't you, Deepak?" Katherine nudged him.

His face split into a big wide grin and his brown eyes glinted. "Perhaps I do. You see, the technology community is very, shall we say, eccentric?"

Katherine poked him with a carrot stick.

"All right," he said, "we're weird. There's a guy here in our city who has been studying laser disabling technology for years. He was obsessed with Star Wars. Not the movie, but President Reagan's laser fighting in space. Do you remember that?"

Sure, I remember. I was in diapers then.

"And he was fascinated with the Gulf War Stingray," Deepak continued, "a weapon with laser beams that fired at anything glinting in the desert sun. He is 'rabid,' as you say here in America."

How about that—a rabid laser techie.

"What's his name?" asked Carl.

"I can't remember. I would have to make some enquiries for you."

"I'd appreciate it," Carl said.

"No problem."

We discussed other things—Hindu gods and Indian mothers and the rising real estate prices in the big valley. Katherine served chicken curry, Basmati rice, and cucumber raita with tangy yogurt sauce. *Delicious.* She was going to make a wonderful Indian wife.

Monday rolled around, my favorite day of the week. The salon was closed and I had reserved the afternoon for my special time with Jamie. We went to Gymboree, a gymnastics place on Main Street. It was equipped with trampolines, balance bars, rock climbing walls, and acres and acres of spongy surfaces to land on.

I could buy Jamie an hour of instruction or let him loose by himself. He decided on free play and I took off my shoes, too. By the time we finished our hour of constant movement, I was exhausted but Jamie wanted to keep going. I bought him an hour with a teenaged counselor who looked like she could take it, and waved bye-bye.

Main Street was a zoo. Traffic was stop-and-go as usual. The state highway dumps out onto Main Street and resumes again at the other end. I saw more oil tankers trailing "pups" than mama dogs have pups at the animal shelter.

I walked past the gas station and ogled the rooflines of Mrs. Oscar's convenience store. No cameras were perched on the building, under the eaves, or over the gas pumps, and I assumed her new security system hadn't been installed yet. I crossed the street, strolled up to my main competitor's salon, and peered inside the plate glass. Mrs. Alcott was sitting there reading *People* magazine.

No way!

I subscribed to *Architectural Digest* just for her! I remodeled my powder room so she wouldn't be offended every time she went! There she was, processing in front of a plate glass window where anybody could see her looking absolutely hideous. Then I remembered—locals avoided Main Street because of the traffic, so my competition was advertising deep discounts.

Mrs. Alcott wanted the discount, and she's supposedly wealthy. Isn't that just the way the world works?

Sassy's boutique was next. When I opened the front door, a loud buzzer made me jump. Sassy rushed to greet me, arms wide with a big hug. "What brings you here?"

"Just passing by," I said.

"I'm glad you did. What can I do for you?"

"Just looking," I glanced over my shoulder. "Who's watching us?"

She laughed. "We don't have to worry. Big Brother is no longer here."

"What a relief," I said.

"Someone disabled the security system." My eyebrows went up. "It happened yesterday. I was in the back getting a layaway dress. My customer said a man came in. There was a blinding flash of light, and then the light—the light, mind you—seemed to open the door, and go outside.

"Weird." I said.

"Totally."

"What did the man look like?"

"My customer couldn't describe him."

"Did you call the police?"

"The chief came himself."

"And?"

"He's mystified."

"Who's your security company?"

"Stealth-Techt."

I wanted to call Carl right away, but I'd left my cell phone in the car.

"Now I can look at my cell phone when I want to," Sassy said, "and go to the bathroom whenever I need to. It's liberating."

"I guess God gave you an early Christmas present."

"He's my guardian angel." Her hands arced in a large circle. "He's a big circle of light."

"What do you mean?"

"That's what my customer said. The light was a ball like the Good Witch of the South, only the bubble was opaque."

I could just imagine Paddy Hamburger's headline: *Woman Sees the Light—Cameras Go Dark*. Or maybe: *Man Turns into Ball of Light—Zaps Nosy Shop Owners*.

My urge to call Carl escalated to red alert.

"Sassy, I've got to pick up Jamie now."

"Okay, Tracy, good to see you."

"Ciao."

"Ciao."

Outside, I was on the run when I heard sirens. I saw police cruisers at the Oscar gas station, their light bars whirling. I dashed past an old truck parked near the gas pumps. Carl was standing in front of the convenience store holding his service revolver.

On the pavement in front of him was a body.

The next day at the salon Margaret Pyle held me as Annabelle applied a cold compress. Tina was wringing her hands. Shelley dished out a casserole as Sassy wiped hair off the counter. Kayla was home babysitting Jamie.

I was a mess.

Carl was suspected of the racially-motivated murder of a Native American. The chief put him on administrative leave pending determination. He hadn't been arrested, but Paddy Hamburger had written a story full of quotes from people accusing him of racial profiling. The tribe had filed a complaint with the Department of Justice. The FBI assigned an agent to the case.

Never mind there was a tire iron in the Ute Indian's hand. He was dead and the cameras weren't rolling.

Chief Fort Dukes spoke from two sides of his mouth. He was calming us *and* playing to public opinion. At a rally of Citizens Against Police Brutality, he said, "Justice will be done." Then he came to our house and put Carl on leave.

I closed the salon. I couldn't do anybody's hair. I couldn't talk to anybody—even my best girlfriends. All they could do was hold me and offer me plates of food. There was no tomorrow, only yesterday. I wanted to hide in my cape closet and never come out, but I had a husband and son to take care of. My only allegiance should be to them. Then why had I collapsed on my salon sofa and couldn't get up?

Why indeed?

The thought of doing anything illegal crushed me. I had always considered myself a righteous person, a person who would never consider breaking the rules. I would never want anyone to think badly of me—that I could do anything heinous or reprehensible.

"But you didn't do anything, Tracy," Margaret said. "You weren't even there."

I know that. You think I don't know that?

I felt guilty by association. To kill someone in cold blood, as Carl was accused of doing, was abhorrent to me. Of course, I knew my husband was not racist. Of course, I knew he was acting in self-defense.

I knew my man.

He was the most honest, ethical policeman in the world. He was more law-abiding than the Chief Justice of the Supreme Court. He had more integrity than the Pope. I knew he didn't do what they're saying he did.

So why was I so upset?

Why didn't I just pick myself off the sofa and hold my chin up and carry on, knowing the outcome would be favorable?

Because I knew the way the world worked.

People were saying cruel things. People were merciless. They would sacrifice a fine upstanding person on the pillory of public opinion at the first whiff of scandal. I was afraid for my beautiful husband and I was afraid that I couldn't do anything about it.

Someone was banging on the salon door. The noise became insistent. Margaret got up and arranged my head on a pillow. She went to the front door.

"Go away," she shouted.

"I just need a comment!" It was Paddy Hamburger.

"You're not welcome here!" I could see Margaret straighten up to her full height and search for a Venetian blind to cover the plate glass window. Of course, there wasn't one.

"One little quote."

"Tracy is not available for comment!"

Margaret returned to the sofa. "Do you want to talk to Paddy?"

I shook my head. Then I realized I had to. "All right," I said.

Margaret let him in.

He approached the sofa. I saw from his face that he was dismayed to find me this way. My eyes were swollen, my face was puffy, my complexion was red, and my hair was a shambles.

Margaret advanced on him—her six-foot frame towering over his five foot six—and he put his camera back in his satchel.

"I'm sorry, Tracy," he said, taking out his steno pad. "What would you like me to say?"

Paddy Hamburger was asking *me* what to write? Maybe he was human after all.

I told him that Carl had the highest regard for the Native American community and had helped their people find medical help and legal advice. I told him that Carl graduated from the best police academy in our state and believed the law was always to be upheld. I told him that Carl acted in self-defense—that the man was going to kill him with a tire iron. I asked him to put out a plea for witnesses, to beg anyone who saw anything to step forward and tell what they saw.

Paddy finished writing and closed his steno pad. "Keep the faith, Tracy," he said, and went out the door.

"You did well," Margaret said. "I think Paddy will quote you fair."

"Things look bleak now," said Shelley, "but you and Carl will pull through. Justice will prevail."

"The greatest prayer is patience," said Annabelle.

"The Native American community is with you," said Tina. "They know who Carl is. They know how that man was. He was sick."

Sassy came out of my workroom. "Tracy, do you have any Soft Scrub?" she asked.

Everybody laughed, even me.

Cleaning must go on and life must go on, whatever the circumstances.

Shelley's casserole found its way to our house but Carl didn't eat much of it. Neither did I.

Jamie chowed down. "This is good!" he said. "Chicken, rice and gravy. Your mom's a good cook, Kayla."

Kayla eyed us both. She'd been walking on egg shells all evening. "If you're finished, I'll take you upstairs and read you a story," she said to Jamie.

"Let's play Captain America. The bad guys know how to fight back, but I've gotten to Level Three. You can take a couple turns and help me get to Level Four."

"Take your plate to the sink," Kayla said.

Jamie obeyed. "What's for dessert?"

Kayla opened the freezer. "Popsicles."

After they disappeared upstairs, Carl and I sat for a long time. He picked up his fork and put it down again. I drank water.

"You know . . . " he said.

I didn't know. And I did know. I waited.

"You know, you work your whole career and you know this can happen. Every cop knows. The decisions you make every day could end up haunting you for the rest of your life. The guy came at me with a tire iron. I did what I'm trained to do. There was no thinking. There was no time. There was no right or wrong. There was just action." He fiddled with his fork again. "But there's always reaction. There's always politics and there's always two sides to every issue. There are multiple sides to this one and I'm caught in a net."

Carl's face was drawn. His eyes were slits. His mouth was a downward crescent. There were no dimples on his cheeks. I held him in my arms. He wept.

The chief and the district attorney were looking into the case. The deceased's name was Sam Eagle Feather. He was a thirty-five year old carpenter, the same age as Carl. Divorced, no children. For years he played on the rugby team with the local Tongans, and had even traveled to their island for a big tournament. But recently he'd missed work and lots of games. People who knew him said he'd injured himself on a coral reef in Tonga and contracted a bad infection. Multiple antibiotic regimes had not worked and the virus attacked his brain. Over time he become irrational and belligerent. That's why his marriage had broken up.

Carl told me the same story he told Internal Affairs. He parked his patrol car, went into the convenience store, and purchased a bottle of water. When he came out, he saw a man struggling to get the spare tire out of his pickup. The man swayed and fell.

When Carl approached the fallen man, he yelled, "Go away, Cop Man!" He staggered to his feet and grasped a tire iron. Carl avoided the first swing, but the man moved forward whipping the tire iron straight at Carl's head. He identified himself as a police officer and ordered him to freeze but the man kept coming, slicing at Carl's head over and over again. Carl fired his service revolver. The bullet hit Sam Eagle Feather square in the chest, killing him instantly.

"I'll never forget the look on his face," Carl said. "It was as if I were the cause of all his problems and he was finally going to get rid of them forever."

People were skeptical. Papers all over America had been running editorials about systematic racial discrimination and police violence. The atmosphere created by these cases had affected my husband's ability to defend his actions.

I reopened my store but cancellations poured in. No one bothered to call; they deleted their appointments online. I moved through my day like an automaton. I chucked every newspaper in the trash without reading it.

Carl stayed home alone. There was nothing for him to do while the district attorney and the chief sorted out the situation. I sent Jamie to school until I got a call from the principal's office. Kids taunted him at recess when he defended his father, and Jamie had done more than kick a kid in the shins.

I wanted my mother.

My parents live in the oldest trailer park in Palm Springs. It's homey, chummy, and fun. People say hi to each other. They tell jokes at the swimming pool. They play shuffleboard and backgammon. They have community barbecues. Mother has gotten younger ever since she moved there. My father is in seventh heaven. There are nine golf courses and he plays them all in regular foursomes.

We'd been in California for five days when the rhythm of our minds slowed down enough to match their pace. "Let's pick some oranges," I said to Jamie one morning. He grabbed a shopping bag and we went outside among the hummingbirds and the bougainvillea to the orange trees. Jamie picked up a long pole with a wire cradle on top and attempted to capture an orange. He teetered on his toes and missed.

I laughed. "Make it easy on yourself, try the lower branches!"

He dropped the basket down to the next branch, snagged an orange, and tossed it to the ground. When we had six oranges, we trooped back to the double-wide.

Jamie climbed on a stool and took the juicer out of the kitchen cupboard. He cut an orange in half and pressed it down. The motor did its work and pretty soon there was sweet, fresh ambrosia to savor. This was the most work we did all day. The rest of the time we rode bikes, sunbathed, and swam. My mother insisted on doing all the cooking; my father did the grocery shopping.

Life was good in never-never land. But lest we forget, the chief called to make sure we weren't on the lam, and Carl's attorney sent briefs that he read in private. We were going on the thirtieth day of our banishment when the phone rang.

"Hi, Tracy, this is Katherine Putnam."

My heart sank. *Was she calling to cancel my prep for her wedding?*

"I'm calling because Deepak wants to talk to you. Here he is."

"Tracy?" said Deepak. "How are you?"

"Just fine here in sunny California."

"I'm glad to hear that." His cheerful voice was pleasing to my ears, but I couldn't imagine what he wanted. "I would like to speak to Carl, but you should listen too, if you can push the speaker-phone button, please."

"Deepak, how are you?" Carl said into the little rectangular device on the kitchen counter.

"Fine," said Deepak. "You asked me to find the name of the man who is an expert on security camera disabling technology. Well, I have found him."

"Good," said Carl.

"He is the younger brother of the man who owns Stealth-Techt."

"No!" I said.

Carl said nothing.

"He is, shall we say, the black sheep of the family and he and his older brother are rivals. In fact, the younger brother has done everything possible to sabotage his older brother's business. Their enmity goes way back."

Deepak paused and I said, "Go on."

"The younger brother has developed the technology to create a light shield around a thief and an artificial intelligence laser. He can zap security cameras at one thousand meters and not be seen even when close-up."

Carl looked at me in disbelief.

"And he has used this technique to disable the security systems at three of Stealth-Techt's clients. I think you know which ones—the Main Street Boutique, the Jewish temple, and the Oscar gas stations. He is proving to his brother that he can do this because his brother said it couldn't be done."

"Wow," I said.

"You can assume the CEO of Stealth-Techt knew all the time who had disabled his clients' cameras, but he did not give his younger brother up to the authorities," said Deepak. "He believes it is a family matter."

"Unfortunately, it's not," Carl said.

"I know, Carl, that you are not in a position to arrest him where you are now," said Deepak, "and I wouldn't advise you to do so even if you could."

"Why not?" he asked.

"Because, you see, he has something that you need."

"And what is that?"

"Footage of the incident at the Oscar gas station."

Carl and I were speechless.

"Are you there?" Deepak asked.

"Yes, we're here," I said.

"This gentleman was walking by the Oscar gas station that day. He saw the Indian staggering around, just as you said. He always carries his cell phone and he stopped to take a video of the man even before you came out of the convenience store. He has what can be described as 'an eye for crime.' He recorded the whole thing."

I sucked in my breath.

"He is willing to come forward to the authorities in your city with this evidence. In exchange he asks that the investigation into the security camera incidents be dropped."

Carl and I looked at each other.

"I know this will be a hard decision for you. Katherine tells me what moral people you are, but if you can see your way to accepting this proposal, we think justice will be done."

Katherine came on the line. "Take the deal, Tracy. We want you back. We miss you!"

Tears sprang into my eyes.

Carl and I said thank you and told them we would call the next day with our answer. A hard night followed with more soul searching than we had experienced in our married life. Crimes against property had been committed. Carl had vowed he would never take a bribe on the job or condone any cop who did.

But Carl's career was at stake and my livelihood, too. We wanted to return to our home and restore our place in the fabric of our community. By dawn, we agreed. We would take the deal.

The next evening, after a long drive, we sat in Larry Brennan's office across the street from city hall. Larry was Carl's attorney. He had a barrel chest that made his suit jacket look like a box that fell off a UPS truck. His face was so red people thought he fell asleep in a tanning bed every week, but that was his Irish heritage. Jamie played with all five of Larry's kids, who looked like strawberry lollipops dressed up in clothes.

"This sounds more like Hollywood than real life," Larry said. "You sure you haven't been watching too much TV?"

Ordinarily, Carl and I would have laughed, but we were too worried.

"Laser techies, blazing light bubbles, two brothers who hate each other," Larry said. "Even Rabbi Josh's wife couldn't come up with a situation like this."

I looked down at my handkerchief. It was twisted into a little rope.

"Let's examine the facts," Larry went on, eyeing the notepad in front of him. "Number one. Your rogue techie is only charged with one count of criminal mischief for disabling the security cameras. Mrs. Oscar wants the district attorney to charge the guy with 'interfering with electronic communications fraud' but that's a third degree felony at best. It's nothing compared to a homicide."

My handkerchief untwisted slightly.

"Two. Immunity gets granted all the time. People come forward and ask for immunity in racketeering cases. It's routinely granted in order to nail the top guys."

You're comparing this to a RICO case? My handkerchief twisted back up.

"Three. Your record is squeaky clean. Your personnel file is impeccable—even laudatory. You have no pattern of racially motivated incidents, you've helped little old ladies cross the street, and your supervisor has given you a clean bill of health every year."

Thank you, Chief Fort Dukes.

"Four. Evidence shows the Native American was holding a tire iron. Friends said he'd been acting strangely ever since he went to Tonga with his rugby team last year. He had become ornery and failed to show up for practice and games. When he did, he was confrontational. Violent. He was injured in Tonga when he stepped on some coral. Cut himself. The illness has affected his personality."

My handkerchief did another somersault.

"Now let's look at the assumptions," continued our lawyer. "One. The district attorney wants to win this case against you, but the evidence is not open and shut."

I smoothed out the fabric.

"However, the case is high profile. It's made the national news. The tribe filed a formal complaint with the Justice Department. Section 1983 of the Civil Rights legislation is on everyone's lips. Our esteemed district attorney is beholden to public opinion. He can't drop the case without significant evidence."

I wanted to crawl in a hole.

"Two. From what you've told me, this Deepak is a smart and honest guy. He's seen the video and he believes it exonerates you. If we can convince the district attorney to give your laser techie immunity, which I think we can, I can introduce the video as evidence. So that's what we're going to do."

Yes!

"I'd like to meet this Deepak. After all, we only have his judgment. If he really believes the video proves your innocence, we'll go to bat for the laser techie who won't give up the tape without immunity. We can slap him with obstruction of justice, bribery and other offenses, but that action would be counterproductive if it makes him destroy the evidence."

You're damn right.

"We want this video to see the light of day. We want it to go viral. We want public opinion on your side."

Right on!

Carl nodded. "We'll arrange a meeting between you and Deepak this afternoon," he said.

I stopped sniveling now. There were tears on my hankie, but there was light at the end of the tunnel.

Some weeks later I was marcelling Mrs. Oscar's hair. The video had gone viral, just as our lawyer knew it would, and Mrs. Oscar couldn't talk about anything else.

"Your husband sure is nimble," she said. "He looks like Mohammed Ali dodging that tire iron!"

Float like a butterfly, sting like a bee.

"And that last swing," she cackled. "I thought for sure Carl's head would fly off!"

"I couldn't watch it," I told her.

"You're the only one who hasn't seen it then," she said. "It's had more than five million hits."

Sigh.

I was thrilled life was almost back to normal but I hadn't enjoyed the notoriety. People stopped me on in the supermarket and talked about my husband as if he were Jean-Claude Van Damme. Young twenty-somethings would squeal, "Your husband is *so* HOT."

That was a different worry.

I finished twirling my curling iron and spun Mrs. Oscar around. "How's that?" I asked.

Her response was interrupted by the owner of Live Signage Marketing. Sarah Binford shot into my workroom waving her arms as if she were flagging down vehicles in front of Wendy's Wooden Weejuns.

"Tracy, I'm being nibbled to death by ducks!"

"What do you mean?"

"Somehow my credit card is being charged fifty cents extra for this and twenty cents extra for that and I don't know who's doing it."

"Sounds like skimming to me!" crowed Mrs. Oscar.

I had no idea what skimming was, but I aimed to find out.

Don't Miss the Sequel:
Cutting for Fun & Profit

● ● ● ● ● ● ● ● ● ● ● ● ●

Tracy Lemon, owner of the Citrus Salon in a small western city, thinks she's married to the handsomest, sexiest policeman on the planet. But deep inside, husband Carl is still haunted by charges of police brutality after killing a Ute Indian in self-defense. Chief of Police Fort Dukes has passed him over for a detective position and hired Dwight Bassoon from the Los Angeles police force. When Carl is demoted to the traffic division, his feelings of remorse and despair trickle over into the couple's private life. Since Carl is barred from assisting Bassoon in any cases, Tracy and her friends must prove the innocence of Dixie Service, gas station cashier and mother of five, who is arrested for "skimming" credit card information. Meanwhile, the cousin of Tracy's 85-year-old client Mrs. Oscar returns from the Korean War after suffering from amnesia for 50 years. He cuts open an old safe and discovers a scandal that could cost Chief Fort Dukes his job. Margaret, Tracy's main partner in crime, is dating a luxury safari tour leader, and Linda Ironback, the oil field roustabout who's desperate to find a man, may just hold the key to making Detective Bassoon rush back where he came from.

About the Series

Cutting for Fun & Profit is the second in a series of *Citrus Salon* mysteries. In the first novel *Petty Crimes & Head Cases*, Tracy Lemon learns how to help her policeman husband solve crimes for the sole reason of furthering Carl's career. Nine cases explore today's pressing social issues—petty theft, prescription drug abuse, Medicare fraud, meth cooking, animal cruelty, gay rights, and police brutality. Told with subtle humor about a quirky cast of characters, *Petty Crimes & Head Cases* conveys the humanity in today's cops who have difficult bosses, tender family ties, and a deep sense of moral justice.

About the Author

At the turn of the millennium, Lola Beatlebrox changed her hair color. Since then she's logged more than 500 hours in the hairdresser's chair. The Citrus Salon mysteries were born from an infatuation with crime news stories that cause readers to marvel at the folly of mankind. Lola lives on a ranch near Park City, Utah, with her husband, three dogs and four llamas.